CHRISTMAS
for the
SHOP GIRLS

Jo worked on the production team of *The Archers* for ten years and then on the scriptwriting team for twenty. She's written several spin-off books about the programme and on TV wrote for *Crossroads*, *Family Affairs*, *Doctors* and *EastEnders*. *Christmas for the Shop Girls* is the fourth novel in the Shop Girls series.

Jo loves to hear from readers – find out more about the next book in the series on her Facebook page, Facebook.com/joannatoyewriter and do share a review on Goodreads or Amazon if you'd like to, as it really does help other readers.

Also by Joanna Toye

A Store at War
Wartime for the Shop Girls
Heartache for the Shop Girls

CHRISTMAS
for the
SHOP GIRLS

JOANNA TOYE

HarperCollins*Publishers*

HarperCollins*Publishers* Ltd
1 London Bridge Street,
London SE1 9GF

www.harpercollins.co.uk

First published by HarperCollins*Publishers* 2020

1

A catalogue record for this book is available from the British Library

ISBN: 978-0-00-829875-3

Typeset in Sabon by Palimpsest Book Production Ltd, Falkirk, Stirlingshire

Printed and bound in the UK by CPI Group (UK) Ltd, Croydon CR0 4YY

For Cressida, with love from Shosho xxx

Prologue

Christmas Eve, 1942

They'd been hanging the Christmas decorations, the balding tinsel and the frosted glass baubles, tatty now, but no chance of anything new after three years of war. Then Jim had his arms round her, smiling down, teasing her about what Father Christmas might bring, when suddenly there was noise – at first, far off, the nasal whine of the air raid siren, and then, overhead, more, a lot more. A great loud whoosh and a tearing squeal and then a massive booming, breathtaking thump.

Lily was torn away from Jim, sucked up and backwards and sideways, hurled against something hard and flung down again, rolling, bumping, like falling downstairs and hitting every step. Then finally coming to rest, her eyes and mouth full of dust, chunks of plaster all around, hemming her in, and everything gone dark and quiet, horribly quiet . . .

'Shh, Lily, shh, it's all right, it's all right.'

'What . . . what?'

'You were dreaming, love. You shouted out.'

Dazed, damp with sweat, Lily blinked. It wasn't dark and she wasn't enclosed. She was sitting up in bed, in her room. The landing light was on and her mother had her arms round her. Lily's heart was knocking at her ribs. She wondered if her mother could feel it too.

'Oh, Mum. I'm sorry. I woke you up.'

'You woke all of us up.'

Jim was standing in the doorway in his pyjamas, hair tousled, feet bare on the cold boards.

Lily closed her eyes. It had been a dream, just a dream, again. But the dreams were still as real as the night it had happened a few weeks ago, when she and Jim had been the last ones left in the store, finishing off the decorations to the Christmas grotto when the bomb had fallen in the street outside.

She raised her hand and touched the place where her collarbone had shattered. She was allowed to take her sling off at night and it felt strange; she was more used now to her arm being strapped across her

2

chest than to see it hanging free. She looked at Jim. He was supporting himself on the door frame.

Her mum, Dora, gave her a gentle squeeze.

'These dreams, love – it's the shock,' she said. 'And it's perfectly natural. But give it time and the . . . the bad memories, well, they might not go entirely, but they'll fade.'

Lily nodded.

Jim was smiling at Lily, the crooked smile she loved.

'I reckon this was all a ruse,' he said. 'You know what time it is, don't you? While we've been standing here, it's gone midnight. You just wanted your Christmas presents early! Typical!'

Chapter 1

April 1943

'Look at it!' said Lily. 'You'd think the bomb had dropped yesterday!' Ladies' Fashions, Model Gowns and Suits and Coats were in uproar.

Gladys darted her friend a look – only Lily could say that! Gladys wouldn't have dared, in case it brought that awful night flooding back. But Lily had been so strong, coming back to work when the memories must still have been so vivid and evidence of the destruction was still all around. Now, though, three months later, it looked as though the demolition squad was in again. The first floor was in chaos – and all because there was going to be a fashion show.

4

Harassed porters were assembling a catwalk under the supervision of the Model Gowns buyer: beside them the store's carpenters sawed and hammered. In the middle of it all, the buyers from the other two fashion departments were taking dresses and suits on and off a rail, evidently in dispute over what should make the final cut. Juniors scurried to and fro offering more garments for inspection, which were scrutinised and mostly rejected. If not, they scuttled off again to iron out the sort of creases visible only to a buyer's eye.

A potted palm wove its way uncertainly towards them and beneath it, Lily recognised Jim's suit trousers. Along with Peter Simmonds, the first-floor supervisor, Jim had been charged with getting the store back on its feet after the bomb and the fashion show was going to act as a sort of relaunch for Marlow's as well as highlighting the new spring and summer Utility styles. There was no doubt about it, Jim was on the way up. He was also – the thought still made her smile, inside and out – Lily's boyfriend of a few months' standing.

'Jim!' She hissed him over. 'How's it going?'

'Let me put this thing down.'

Lily helped him to rest the pot on a little plinth where a plaster baby was displaying a smocked romper suit and waving a rattle. Jim's tie was askew and his shirt untucked, not the sort of appearance Marlow's usually required of Mr J. Goodridge, second sales on Furniture and Household.

'If you really want to know,' Jim began, 'it's hell. Suits and Coats and Ladies' Fashions are at each other's throats over who gets to show more items and Model Gowns is sulking because she wanted her stuff to go out all in one block – a "tableau" she calls it – and not mixed in with the others.' He gave a despairing sigh. 'And they say never work with children or animals. I could add to that!'

'It'll be fine!' Lily tried to reassure him. 'It'll all come together at the last minute, you'll see.'

His eyes were deep-set and brown; his hair was sticking up where he'd pushed his hands through it in the way Lily loved and she had to stop herself from reaching up to smooth it down. Her boss on Childrenswear, Miss Frobisher, tall, blonde, and ever-elegant herself, was a stickler for smartness in appearance, but even on a day when the usual rules didn't apply, Lily didn't think she'd approve.

Jim pushed his fingers through his hair again, making it stick up even more.

'I don't see how. I knew we should have got more done last night – at least got the catwalk built!'

'Hah!' Lily retorted. 'You and I stayed late to finish off the Christmas grotto, didn't we, and look what happened!'

Gladys winced, but that was Lily for you, and the measure of Lily and Jim's relationship. They struck sparks off each other, but they both seemed to thrive on it. As if in proof, Jim was grinning and

Lily was smiling at him with a sort of 'Well? I'm right, aren't I?' expression. Even so, Gladys tactfully jumped in.

'Are the models here yet?'

Before the war, Marlow's had had its own models, but now they were in the WRNS or turning out shells in a factory somewhere. The models for today had been booked through an agency in London, and to Gladys were invested with an air of almost film-star glamour.

'That's another thing.' Jim looked at his watch. 'They should have been here three-quarters of an hour ago.'

'You know what the trains are like.'

'That's why I wanted them to come yesterday, but would You Know Who hear of it? Decided to scrimp on expenses.'

You Know Who was Cedric Marlow, the store's owner, notoriously careful with money.

'It doesn't really matter, does it?' Lily pointed out. 'There's nothing for them to prance up and down on yet.'

'Thanks for reminding me.'

In a further reminder, there was a monumental crash as a tower of gilt chairs tumbled from a trolley and hit the half-built catwalk.

'I'd better get over there.' Jim moved to pick up the palm, but before he could, Mr Simmonds approached. Tall and spare, he always moved at a lick, but this was speedy, even for him. He nodded to the girls and addressed Jim.

'They've had a telephone call upstairs – the models haven't left London yet. And I'm not sure they will.'

'What?'

'There's an unexploded bomb at Harrow-on-the Hill. No trains leaving in our direction at all. I think we'd better face it, they're not going to get here.' Mr Simmonds sounded remarkably calm, but then he was ex-Army, invalided out with a dodgy shoulder. 'We're going to have to regroup.'

'What does he mean, regroup?' asked Gladys.

Miss Frobisher had sent them both off to dinner early, saying she'd square it with Mr Bunting, Gladys's boss on Toys.

'Think of something else, I suppose,' shrugged Lily. 'I don't know.' Gladys looked worried. Lily persevered with her rissole but chewed cautiously: bits of bone weren't unknown. 'Maybe the salesgirls from Fashions could model them, they know the clothes.'

'They're all so old though!'

It was true: with all women between nineteen and forty-three conscripted into some kind of war work, Marlow's, like other shops and stores, was staffed by younger girls like themselves and, to put it politely, the middle-aged. 'Salesgirls' was a courtesy title: many of them had been brought back out of retirement.

'There's always the juniors.'

Gladys didn't look convinced.

'I can't see the juniors on Fashions swanking up and down a catwalk – they're like frightened rabbits! I'd be the same with their bosses.'

That was true as well: the fashion buyers were a fearsome bunch. Miss Wagstaff of Model Gowns was a tightly permed, tightly corseted martinet. Miss Drake (Dresses), petite and pretty, looked more approachable, though anyone who'd ever witnessed her beating down a wholesaler on price would have swiftly reassessed that opinion. Miss McIver of Suits and Coats was originally from Aberdeen and was a chip off the old block of that so-called granite city. All in all, Fashions was known to be the toughest department in which to work: Miss Frobisher had started there and survived, which was one of the reasons Lily admired her so much.

'Anyway, it's not our problem.' Gladys pushed her plate away and pulled her jam turnover towards her.

Lily was quiet. It was still a setback for Jim. His problems were her problems; she'd help him if she could. In fact, she often intervened when her help wasn't required – or desired.

'Gladys!' she exclaimed suddenly. 'It is! We've forgotten about Beryl!'

In her shop nearby, Beryl was getting ready to lock up. She picked up the card which had been propped in the window for the past fortnight.

Beryl's Brides will be showing one of our dresses as the <u>GRAND FINALE</u> to the Fashion Show to take place on the First Floor of Marlow's on Wednesday, 21st April.
  Entrance free but ticket required. Reserve early to secure your seat.
Enquire within or at the store for details.

Over the bottom corner she folded a slip of paper reading: *TODAY*.

Turning the sign to 'Closed' and stepping outside, she locked the shop. It wasn't much of a place – or hadn't been when she'd first seen it. But Beryl had always had an eye to the main chance and a way of talking herself into it.

Her little shop was one of Marlow's former ground-floor window spaces, blown in by the bomb. With no chance of replacing huge sheets of plate glass, opening up small units like Beryl's had seemed the best way forward. Cedric Marlow, always cautious, had taken some convincing, but persistence had paid off and within weeks Beryl had moved her bridal hire business from her front room to proper premises. She'd been talking for weeks about having one of her dresses in the show, all the more because Beryl's dresses were second-hand. 'As-new', she called it, but it meant the same. After her own wedding, she'd spotted an opening. With materials in short supply and clothes rationing biting, who could afford to splurge all their coupons on a dress you'd wear only once? And so her business had been born.

Having a Beryl's Brides gown as the finale to the fashion show was intended to give sales a boost, and Beryl was hanging every hope on it.

The dress she'd chosen for the catwalk was already upstairs in the store, and very classy it was too. Pre-war of course, Brussels lace, V-necked with a tiny stand collar and elbow-length sleeves. To go with it she'd chosen lacy gloves, a paste tiara and a short veil. Jim had promised he'd organise some kind of bouquet. It was going to be lovely.

Back in the staff canteen at Marlow's, the full horror had dawned on Gladys.

'You're right! Beryl's going to be devastated!'

Lily reached for her bowl; pudding might help her think. She was always hungry: everyone was always hungry.

'What *is* this jam?' she asked after a few mouthfuls. 'It's not carrot, for once. Is it marrow?'

But before Gladys could answer, Jim arrived at speed, practically screeching to a halt like something out of a cartoon.

'Lily! There you are! How big are you?'

'What?'

'How big?'

'You know how big,' Lily looked up at him, spoon poised. 'Five foot seven.'

'Not your height! Your – your – vital statistics!'

Gladys spluttered pastry all over the table. Lily stared at Jim.

'I beg your pardon!'

'Miss Drake thinks you're a thirty-six. Up top, anyway. Are you?'

Lily put down her spoon.

'Isn't this a bit of a private conversation to be having in a public place?'

'There's no time to be discreet. You're going to have to model!'

Chapter 2

As Jim dragged her away, Lily was still trying to take it in. Yes, she'd wanted to help him out but behind the scenes, not parading up and down in clothes she'd never usually wear and certainly could never afford!

'Why me?' she protested, struggling to keep up with Jim as he wove between the canteen tables. 'There's loads of other girls in the store who could do it!'

'I know,' he flung back over his shoulder. 'I've got two already, and they're delighted. Not like you, Miss Awkward!'

'Don't tell me,' groaned Lily. 'Gloria from Cosmetics. I bet she volunteered!'

'She did, actually, and Sally from China and Glass.'

'There you are then!' Lily was keeping pace with him now as they climbed the back stairs. 'You don't need me. There were only two models originally.'

'Yes, professionals! You lot'll take longer to get in and out of the clothes.'

Having scaled the back stairs two at a time, they'd reached the first floor and Jim was propelling her towards Ladies' Fashions, Lily still protesting.

'What about Brenda from Books?'

'Too shy.'

'Rachel from Travel Goods!'

'Can't see without her specs.'

'Magda! On Toiletries. She's beautiful.'

Jim stopped and turned to face her.

'So are you, Lily. Even when you're arguing, annoyingly.'

Well! He'd never said that before! It was nice to hear, and she didn't think he'd said it just to get round her. He wasn't like that. It could – should – have been a romantic moment, but there wasn't time for the violins to tune up and the bluebirds to start singing.

'Please,' pressed Jim. 'You will do it, won't you? For Marlow's? For me?'

It would be ungracious not to, especially after that compliment. Lily gave in.

'Oh, go on then,' she said. 'Flatterer! But I wish you'd asked me before I had my dinner. I've just had a rissole, a ton of potatoes and a huge jam turnover!'

* * *

The next couple of hours were like nothing she'd ever known. In all her time at the store, Lily had barely glimpsed behind the scenes on Ladies' Fashions. Now she was ushered through to the changing rooms like a proper customer to be handed one garment after another and told to try them on. She doubted the buyers would have been muttering quite so critically, though, if it had been a customer scrambling in and out of the clothes!

Eventually, like witches round a seething cauldron, the buyers went into a huddle over a pile of edge-to-edge jackets and a consensus emerged. Sally and Gloria, both nearly nineteen, would model what the buyers called the more sophisticated numbers: Lily was to model dresses and suits for a younger clientele. Sally and Gloria seemed flattered and Gloria simpered accordingly. Lily was pleased too and not surprised: she'd looked like lamb dressed as mutton in some of the clothes.

'And her hair!' she overheard one of the buyers lament.

Lily defensively touched her wayward blonde curls. None of this had been her idea!

Sally, a pale-skinned redhead, nudged her.

'Don't worry,' she said. 'They'll do our hair. I heard they're getting Monsieur Paul in.'

'And Elizabeth Arden's doing the make-up,' added Gloria.

'In person?' asked Lily, just to needle her. Gloria

15

was a pert brunette who wore a high hat, as the local saying had it. She'd already applied to the WAAF where she hoped – no, intended – to meet an officer – and not just any old Pilot Officer, but a Flying Officer at least, she'd been heard to say.

Outside of work, Lily liked to look nice if she could, but it wasn't easy on her wages, not to mention rationing. Most of her clothes were pass-ons or what she could find at jumble sales, altered to fit by her mum, Dora. She couldn't believe all this fuss over a few frocks!

By now it was now mid-afternoon and, to Lily's relief, she heard the words 'tea break'. Then, the girls were told, there'd be a proper rehearsal, during which, Miss Wagstaff informed them, they would learn to walk. There was evidently more to this modelling lark than met the eye.

When she emerged onto the sales floor for her break, a transformation had taken place. The catwalk was in place and violent purple felting was being nailed over it. At the top end, where the three girls would emerge, was a sort of slender pyramid, wrapped round with a gold lamé cloth. The gilt chairs had been laid out in rows and, on a little dais, a lectern had been set up with Jim's potted palm to one side. Here, because every fashion show needed a compère, Mr Simmonds would stand to announce the models one by one.

Lily looked around for Jim, but he was in conference

with a couple of brown-coated porters, of whom Les, Beryl's husband, was one. Suddenly Beryl herself, in dudgeon as high as it could be, accosted her.

'Lily! What the blinking hell's going on back there?'

'Oh, Beryl – haven't they told you?'

'I know the models aren't coming, but only 'cos Gladys told me! Wagstaff's told me nothing except to keep out the way till the Marlow's part of the show's been decided. A nice way to treat your grand finale!'

As she'd struggled in and out of various outfits, Lily had overheard the buyers discussing the problem of who would model the finale wedding dress now the London models wouldn't to be there to carry it off.

'I think it's Gloria who'll be your bride,' she said.

'I thought as much.' Beryl tossed her head. 'Always pushing herself forward, that one.'

Lily swallowed a smile: she'd thought much the same about Beryl when she'd first met her as another junior at Marlow's. But when Beryl had fallen pregnant it was Lily she'd turned to in a panic, and they'd become friends. Now Beryl and Les were married, happily, and the proud parents of little Bobby.

'You're being very good about it,' said Lily. 'You must be fed up it won't be a proper model swanning up and down.'

Beryl shrugged.

'I'd prefer someone with a bit of class to that jumped-up piece, but it's still a great chance for me,

17

all those mothers and daughters in the audience. I know Marlow's customers'd usually turn their noses up at a dress from a place like mine, but, well, it's like me with Gloria. What choice has any of us got? There's a war on, isn't there?'

Lily didn't need reminding of that when the rehearsal began: Miss Wagstaff would have given the average regimental sergeant major a run for his money.

'Glide, don't stride!' she hectored as Lily came down the catwalk. 'And eyes front! Keep your head still! You're in a fashion show, not a searchlight battery!'

Then she made Lily glide all over again with Mr Simmonds reading his lines: she was taking no prisoners there either.

'Kindly stick to the script!' she boomed. 'I know what's there, I wrote it myself! Number Thirteen – a versatile skirt suit in heather mix tweed by Harella, not Marella!'

'I'm sorry,' sputtered Mr Simmonds, 'but that's not what it says here.'

Lily had never seen him so cowed.

'I can't account for the typist's butterfingers!' Miss Wagstaff cut in. 'It's Harella, take my word for it! From the top, please. Back you go, Lily!'

By six, when the store closed briefly before the show started at seven, Lily was a mass of nerves. Worse was to come.

'You'd better start with this one,' Miss Drake

instructed the hairstylist, Monsieur Paul. 'She'll need the most attention!'

Thanks, thought Lily, sitting down at Monsieur Paul's gesture. He was small and whippet-thin, his skinny legs emerging from what looked like an artist's smock. He ran his fingers through Lily's hair, making it more unruly than ever. He pulled it this way and that, examined the roots, then the ends, and not so much shook his head as gave a little shudder. Was it her imagination or, as he covered her with a slithery pink cape, did he actually say under his breath *'Quelle horreur'*?

He began by yanking her head this way and that, smothering her hair in some pungent lotion and twirling it about with the end of a vicious-looking comb. Then he inserted rollers, blasted it with hot air, tugged the rollers out and doused the whole thing in hairspray. At the end he offered her a mirror, but before Lily could take it, Miss Drake reappeared and shooed her into another cubicle for 'make-up'.

Having her hair pulled had been bad enough, but it was nothing to the agony of having her eyebrows 'tidied', which Elizabeth Arden's top salesgirl, a lady of mature years, said was necessary to 'bring out those lovely eyes'. Having brought them out, she made Lily open them even wider while she applied mascara, then caked her face with powder – '"Dawn Blush" is the shade for you, dear. Remember that when you get your next pay packet!' After that, Lily hardly noticed the lipstick and rouge go on.

Thrilled with her work (and a possible sale – though she'd be lucky) the saleswoman stepped back and handed her a mirror.

'Quite a transformation!' she crowed.

Lily was speechless. She'd never used more than a slick of pale lipstick and the tiniest bit of boot-black on her eyelashes. Now she looked like a panda with a high fever. A panda in a blonde wig.

Giving up the chair to Sally, she staggered off, trying not to look at her reflection in the long fitting-room mirrors. She found that Miss Naylor, the Schoolwear buyer, had arrived to chaperone the models while the Fashion buyers took a break and changed into their finery for the evening.

Miss Naylor and Miss Wagstaff were friends, but Lily was wary of her. She and Miss Frobisher had had something of a set-to before Christmas; Miss Frobisher had won and Miss Naylor had not been best pleased.

She nodded coolly at Lily, whom she saw as a Frobisher ally, and then towards some sandwiches and lemon barley water on a trolley.

'Have something to eat,' she ordered. 'You'll need it.'

Lily nodded – you didn't say no to Miss Naylor lightly – but her stomach rolled at the thought. She poured herself a glass of lemon barley to show willing, and thankfully Miss Naylor spotted a couple of juniors giggling together and rushed off to deliver a lecture. Lily went in search of Gloria and found her in a quiet corner.

As a Cosmetics salesgirl, Gloria was considered competent to do her own make-up, so was already painted and preened. She was sipping from a hip flask which, she said, her boyfriend, Derek, had managed to smuggle in.

'Have a nip,' she said. 'Better than lemon barley! Calm your nerves.'

Lily shook her head.

'Not for me, thanks,' she said. 'But you're not nervous, surely?'

'Only that seeing me as the bride might give Derek ideas,' scoffed Gloria. 'As if I'm going to settle for a salesman off Shirts and Ties!'

In Number Three – 'a go-anywhere day dress in a pretty powder blue – note the contrast trim and neat self-belt – just 60/- and 11 coupons' (*'just!'*) – Lily peered out from behind the fitting room curtain. It was ten to seven.

She'd managed to blot off the worst of the make-up, making rather a mess of the cloakroom roller towel, but it couldn't be helped. The lipstick had worn off anyway, with all the nervous lip-licking, and she'd tried to loosen the concrete hairdo by waggling her fingers through it.

Out in front, the audience were arriving and the string quartet was tuning up. Beryl, wearing a sash with 'Beryl's Brides' on it, was handing out programmes. Gladys, who'd sneaked round earlier to tell Lily she'd begged to stay on and watch the show, was standing to one side with Miss Frobisher. Jim was beside a pillar, deep in conversation with Evelyn Brimble.

Might have known she'd be there, thought Lily: she was, after all, engaged to Mr Marlow's son, Robert. Presumably he was somewhere about too . . . yes, there he was, talking to a burly, florid man in a chalk-stripe suit with a carnation in his buttonhole. New money, as some of the older assistants at Marlow's, used to serving the district's gentry, would have sniffed.

As Lily wondered if she dared try to wave to Jim, Mr Simmonds came up to his little dais and took the microphone.

'Ladies and gentlemen, may I have your attention, please. On behalf of Mr Cedric Marlow and his staff, may I welcome you to this very special event for the store. We look forward to an evening of dazzling fashions, modelled for you tonight by some of our very own staff members, who have been practising all afternoon to give you a truly memorable evening. Without further ado, could I ask you to kindly take your seats so that the show can begin!'

There was a buzz of chatter as staff shepherded

the most important guests – including Robert, Evelyn and her parents, Sir Douglas and Lady Brimble, to seats in the front row beside Mr Marlow himself, who was smiling benignly.

Cedric Marlow was nearly seventy, very much of the old school of shopkeeping, and it showed. He was semi-retired now, leaving the floor supervisors in charge of day-to-day operations, but he liked to keep a guiding hand on the tiller (or stick his oar in, as Jim had been heard to mutter) – as with the London models' expenses. But the staff respected him; Mr Marlow had built up the store from the small draper's shop that his father had started, and Jim wasn't alone in giving him credit for that.

'That was decent of Simmonds, wasn't it?' Sally, in Number Two – 'a light woollen dress by Atrima – note the clever use of colour for the placket and mock pockets' – appeared behind her. 'He must have written that himself – Wagstaff would never have given us a mention!'

Lily was still hoping to catch Jim's eye. At that moment he looked up and gave her a huge grin and a thumbs-up.

'Good luck!' he mouthed.

At least he still recognised her. Perhaps the evening wouldn't be too bad after all.

Chapter 3

And it wasn't. To Lily's amazement, it went surprisingly smoothly. Any shyness she'd felt about cavorting around in her bra and knickers in front of the others had long gone and the juniors helped, holding dresses open so that Lily could step into them, untangling Gloria when she got her hair snagged on a button. And instead of criticising, the buyers were so keen that their own departments' offerings would shine that they were positively encouraging.

'Head up, shoulders back!' Miss McIver urged. 'You're doing really well!'

'Don't forget the bias-cut yoke when you hear Mr Simmonds mention it! Just point to it – and a nice smooth turn at the end like last time!' added Miss Drake.

The bridal finale was Number Seventy, and by the time the girls reached the high sixties, evening wear, Lily was almost enjoying herself. Then Gloria, coming off and ceding place to Sally, suddenly clutched at a curtain and went pale.

'I don't feel so good,' she said. 'Gone all light-headed.'

Miss Naylor was there like a shot with a velvet-buttoned stool.

'Sit down, head between your knees!' she commanded, shoving Gloria onto it.

Lily, half in and half out of a dress and with a junior holding Number Sixty-Nine ready, didn't like the look of it. None of them had touched the sandwiches, and what Gloria had been taking sips of all night wasn't lemon barley water, she knew. Despite her position facing the floor, Gloria remained a greenish white.

'I can't do it,' she moaned. 'I feel sick! And dizzy! You'll have to find someone else to do the bridal.'

'What's going on?' Miss Wagstaff bore down on them.

It was too much for Gloria. She clapped her hand over her mouth and pushed past her. Miss Wagstaff whirled around and went in pursuit.

'Gloria! Don't you dare get anything on my Hardy Amies!'

Miss McIver was gasping like a landed fish, but Miss Drake rounded on Lily.

'Right,' she said. 'We'll have to improvise. Lily – I need your help.'

The next five minutes passed in a blur. Sally had looked perplexed when frantic hand signals from Miss Drake had kept her twirling at the end of the catwalk three times, and then had been made to twirl again when she made it back to the fitting room end. The quartet's playing had become some-what manic, but Mr Simmonds had manfully burbled on about the dress Sally was showing being 'perfect for cocktail wear or, er, going on somewhere after-wards, um, Mr Hitler and his activities permitting,' which had even raised a laugh.

Now, the quartet starting scraping away at the Wedding March and Lily stepped onto the stage, just a few paces behind the bride. Miss Frobisher, the epitome, as always, of class and sophistication, preceded her in the Brussels lace, the tiara and the veil, with Lily in Number Sixty-Nine.

One of the juniors had rushed out to whisper to Miss Frobisher that she was needed urgently, and another to tell the musicians, but there'd been no way of warning Mr Simmonds about the change of model without alerting the audience. And as she and Miss Frobisher glided past, Lily couldn't help but notice his expression. Shock, of course, but also some-thing she couldn't quite put a name to, then a frantic scrabbling for his script.

His blurb about the wedding dress was the same, but Lily's delicate ice-blue dress, 'a charming little number with a sweetheart neckline, perfect for any young girl's debut' became, thanks to his quick thinking, 'and also, of course, suitable for any momentous occasion.'

If there was a slight hiatus, the audience didn't notice: they'd broken into spontaneous applause. As they made their way down the catwalk, Lily looked to left and right as much as she wanted – Miss Wagstaff could take a running jump. She could see several mothers and daughters squinting at their programmes – hopefully intending a visit to Beryl's Brides.

As Lily and Miss Frobisher executed a complex turn at the end of the catwalk, her boss gave Lily a conspiratorial smile. And as they swished past Mr Simmonds again, Lily was able to study his expression more closely. It was something like awe.

The show was over, the audience was gone, and, backstage, the buyers were supervising the re-hanging of the clothes. Gloria, pale and wan, had been poured into the arms of Derek from Shirts and Ties, and Sally was getting stuck into the curled-up sandwiches.

Lily had been walking on air when she'd stepped off stage, and her head was still buzzing with the applause.

'Well!' Miss Frobisher was back to normal, in her navy worsted suit. 'Not quite what I expected from the evening!'

Even so, she'd taken it all in her stride – or rather glide, which seemed to come naturally to her.

'I hope you didn't mind, Miss Frobisher.' Lily was also back in her own clothes. 'But when Gloria came over all funny—'

She couldn't say what she really thought, which was that she'd always thought Miss Frobisher would be perfect. She looked like a model anyway, tall and slim, with her honey blonde hair in its perfect French pleat, and she'd been a bride – it was only Marlow's tradition that stipulated that all female staff were addressed as 'Miss', married or not.

'I didn't mind in the least,' Miss Frobisher said now with a smile. 'I rather enjoyed it. And you did very well yourself, Lily. But you should get home. It's late.'

'And we've got work in the morning.'

'I didn't mean that. Take a couple of hours off tomorrow morning in lieu of tonight and come in for eleven. You can tell the timekeeper to check with me if he makes a fuss.'

'Thank you!'

Miss Frobisher was the best of bosses – firm but fair. She'd seen early on that Lily had potential, and she encouraged it – pushed her, even, sending her off to do sickness and holiday cover on other departments to widen her experience.

Lily said her goodnights and went out on to the sales floor, where the activity of the afternoon was happening in reverse, the purple felting being taken up and the catwalk dismantled. Jim, in shirtsleeves, was stacking chairs. Lily went over to him.

'Let me help.'

Jim stopped what he was doing and grinned.

'A bit beneath you, isn't it? Now you're a top model.'

Lily swiped at him and caught him on the arm.

'You're right. I'll help but I can't stay long. My mink-lined chauffeur-driven limousine's waiting.'

There was no limousine, just the usual walk through the blackout for the two of them to the street of terraced houses where Jim lodged with Lily and her mum. Lily wanted to hear how he felt the show had gone – it was important for him that it had gone well.

'Big thumbs-up,' said Jim. 'A lot of the audience were marking their programmes as you all tripped on and off, and Beryl was almost mobbed at the end.'

'Really? That's wonderful!'

'And she was thrilled it wasn't Gloria in her dress.'

'I bet she was! And did Mr Marlow congratulate you? Or Robert? Or Evelyn Brimble?'

'I didn't see them afterwards. Evelyn buttonholed me beforehand, though, full of her and Robert's wedding plans. Don't know why she thought I'd be interested, but that's one order Beryl won't be getting. Evelyn's got her dress already – well, it's being made by some posh place in London.'

Lily wrinkled her nose.

'No loss. I shouldn't think Beryl'd want to deal with that spoilt madam!'

A car passed them with dipped and slitted headlights, but in the brief moment of illumination, Lily looked at Jim and saw him grimace. Lily knew he felt that in marrying the pampered and demanding Evelyn, Robert Marlow might be getting his just desserts. They both did.

Jim's connection with the Marlows, father and son, was complex. Cedric Marlow had been married to Jim's mother's sister – a fairy-tale story of the shop girl who'd married the boss. Both women were dead now, Elsie Marlow soon after giving birth to Robert, and Jim's mother a few months ago, but all her life she'd been resentful of her sister's higher status and there'd been no contact between the two families. Jim's mum and his dad, a farmworker, had been very much the poor relations, the country cousins, but his father had been badly gassed in the Great War and the family had fallen on even leaner times. Jim had only come to work at the store after his mother had swallowed her pride and appealed to Cedric to give her boy a helping hand.

Jim and his cousin Robert were both only children, but they couldn't have been more different. Jim had started at the bottom, quite happily, and never mentioned, let alone traded on, the family connection – he'd got where he had by his own efforts. Robert had also been working at the store when Lily first started. Cedric had hoped that one day he'd take over the business, but Robert had repaid his trust with a delivery racket for favoured customers, Evelyn's father Sir Douglas included. When the mucky business had been uncovered, thanks to Jim and Lily, Robert had still managed to come out of it smelling of roses: Sir Douglas had offered him a job in his Birmingham stockbroking firm, and the next thing anyone knew, Robert and Evelyn Brimble were engaged.

That reminded Lily of the man she'd seen Robert talking to.

'Did you see Robert with a bloke who looked a bit – well, almost spivvy?'

'Chalk-stripe suit and a carnation?'

'Do you know him? Who is he?'

'Yes . . . well, no, but I've seen him somewhere, I can't think where. Maybe he was just out of context. Most men are, at a fashion show.'

'I suppose he came with his wife. Oh, well. None of our business.'

They were nearly home and Lily suddenly felt exhausted. The evening was still playing out in her head, but it was going all blurry, one outfit merging into another. She yawned, loudly.

Jim unhooked his arm from hers and put it round her shoulders.

'Missing your limousine? Or your glass coach? Come on, Cinders, not far to go.'

* * *

31

Thanks to Miss Frobisher, Lily had a lie-in next morning – she'd told her mum not to wake her – and by the time she came downstairs Dora was assembling her purse and string bag ready for the daily trip to the shops to see what, if anything, was on offer.

'I hope what was left of that make-up hasn't wiped itself all over your pillowslip!' was her mother's opening remark. 'Clean on Monday, that was!'

Dora Collins's mouth had practically fallen open the previous evening when she'd seen Lily all primped and made-up and heard how it had come about. But, good mother that she was, she'd seen that Lily was exhausted, and instead of pressing her for details, had spared some of her precious Pond's cream to get the worst of Lily's war paint off before shooing her into bed.

Now, over tea and toast, Lily relayed the whole story with relish, and Dora lapped it up. Small and trim, a thrifty housekeeper and a devoted mum, she lived for the children she'd brought up alone since their father had died.

'Honestly!' Dora exclaimed. 'If I'd have thought when you started at Marlow's you'd be getting up to that kind of caper – wait till you tell Sid and Reg!'

Lily's handsome, happy-go-lucky brother Sid was in London 'with the Admiralty' as Dora liked to say, though in reality it was a lowly clerking role after an injury in training had ruled him out of active service in the Navy. The elder one, Reg, on the other hand, was out in North Africa, a mechanic with the Eighth Army. He wasn't the best letter-writer, which could mean weeks of worry. Letters were rare, and uninformative when they came, which wasn't his fault – they were censored anyway. The family could only go on what they heard when they gathered every night round the crackly wireless. Reg, they assumed, was advancing steadily westwards with the so-called Desert Rats, set on driving Rommel and his Afrika Korps into the sea.

Her mum was right, thought Lily – it'd be a nice change to have something to tell her brothers apart from a bit of feather-pecking in the hens they kept in the back yard, or that Gladys's gran's latest (imaginary) ailment was a 'funny pain' in her big toe.

Dora suddenly noticed the hands of the mantelpiece clock.

'The butcher's making sausages!' she exclaimed. 'I'd better get a wriggle on!'

Lily stood up to take her plate and cup to the scullery.

'Me too,' she replied. 'Back to reality!'

Lily left her mum at the shops – the queue at the butcher's was already curling round the corner – and made it onto the sales floor just in time to let Miss Temple, the older 'salesgirl' on Childrenswear, go off to her morning break.

'Did you sleep well?' asked Miss Frobisher.

'Like a forest of logs!'

Miss Frobisher smiled and nodded towards a customer hovering by the boys' shirts. Lily knew what a nod from Miss Frobisher meant: enough of the small talk. She sped off to assist.

When the customer had gone – she'd come out with the wrong book of coupons – Jim sidled over, looking mysterious.

'I've had a message from upstairs,' he began. He didn't mean God, he meant the management floor, but it came to much the same thing. Lily's eyebrows asked the question, and he went on: 'No, not the old man – from Robert. He wants me to meet him. For lunch. Today.'

Lily's head poked forward in surprise.

'What about?'

Jim shrugged.

'I'll have to go to find out. One o'clock. At the White Lion, no less.'

Chapter 4

Lily had a lunch date herself as it happened, with Gladys and Beryl – not at the White Lion, but at Lyons. They usually favoured a small café called Peg's Pantry but they were treating themselves so they could chew over the fashion show in a bit more luxury with their cheese on toast. Lily and Gladys had to get passes out to leave the store at dinnertime, and Beryl had decided she could probably risk shutting up shop for half an hour without losing any business.

'It was a dream come true, Miss Frobisher in that frock,' she said as they settled themselves at a table. 'She carried it off beautiful. I wouldn't have had half the enquiries I've had if it had been Gloria.'

'It's done you some good, then?' asked Lily. Jim would be keen to know.

'I'll say! That dress alone's been booked out six times before the end of the summer! And quite a few of my others! I can never thank Jim enough for getting me in that show. And I'll tell you something else. If Peter Simmonds isn't sweet on Eileen Frobisher, then I'm a monkey's auntie.'

'No! Do you think so?' This was Gladys.

Lily smiled. Up on the catwalk, she'd easily picked out Gladys in the audience, eyes fixed, mouth slightly open, seeing nothing but her own wedding. Her fiancé, Bill, was in the Navy and his ship was on convoy duty – as far as they knew. But he was getting leave in the summer when his ship, the HMS *Jamaica*, was due for a refit, and he'd promised Gladys they'd be walking down the aisle.

'Course he is!' exclaimed Beryl. 'His hands were shaking so much fumbling for his script he nearly knocked the microphone off his lectern. Couldn't see what he was doing with his goo-goo eyes. Didn't you notice, Lily?'

'I did think he looked a bit odd.' Lily had graced his look with a bit more dignity than 'goo-goo eyes' but it had certainly been something more than shock at the departure from the expected running order.

'Ahhh, wouldn't that be perfect?' sighed Gladys. 'He's on his own, isn't he, a broken engagement in his past, they say, and, well, if what we think is right

– her husband's not in the picture any more – it'd be lovely for her little boy to have a daddy.'

Gladys wanted nothing more than happy endings for everyone. She'd even fantasised about a double wedding with Jim and Lily, who'd quickly put her right. She and Jim were very clear-sighted about their relationship, and their careers. They were far too young and they both wanted to go as far as they could at Marlow's before any of that sort of stuff got in the way.

The waitress approached, doing that clever waitress thing of balancing one of the plates on the heel of her hand. Lily looked at the thin skin of cheese and the thick slice of National Loaf – National Load, Jim called it, it was so heavy – and tried not to think of what lunch at the White Lion might be.

'There's no brown sauce.' Gladys looked around but the waitress had gone.

'You'll have to pinch some off another table. If there is any.' Beryl was already cutting into her food. ''Scuse me starting, but I've got to get back.'

Gladys went off on the hunt for sauce. Lily sawed at her toast. Now she could ask what she'd been dying to know.

'Did you see Robert Marlow there, Beryl? Did he see you?'

It would have been their first encounter since Jim and Lily had caught him trying it on with Beryl in her shop, expecting her to sleep with him in exchange for waiving her rent.

'He saw me all right!' sniffed Beryl. 'Looked away pronto, I can tell you, went and glued himself to Evelyn. As if I wanted to talk to him! I could have done, made things right awkward, but I didn't want a scene, did I?' She swallowed a large mouthful. 'Did you see her suit though? Got to be Chanel.'

'Chanel? French? Not very patriotic, is it?'

'It's a copy, more like. But a good copy.' Beryl sighed. 'I'd have had that off her back, no messing. But she's welcome to him.' She forked in another mouthful.

'And vice versa,' said Lily firmly. 'She's a proper little madam, as far as I can tell.'

'They deserve each other then, don't they?' said Beryl, with her usual practicality. 'At least they won't be ruining two other people's lives.'

Lily refrained from saying that Robert stood a pretty good chance of ruining his life anyway, given how he carried on. And he deserved that too.

Gladys came back disappointed.

'Not a bottle in the place, I even asked at the servery. Beryl, you're half finished! I want to hear all about who's booked out which dress! And if you've found one for me yet!'

'Sorry, Glad,' said Beryl. 'I'm on the lookout, but I haven't seen the right dress for you yet. But I will, and with the money I'm going to be raking in after last night, I shall make sure it's a stunner.'

Gladys beamed.

'And one for Lily too, don't forget.'

Beryl's stock also included bridesmaid's dresses and what she grandly termed 'occasion wear'.

'Yes, I'm not splashing my coupons on Number Sixty-Nine from Marlow's,' cautioned Lily. 'Even for you, Gladys.'

'I wouldn't expect you to!' said Gladys. 'But you did look nice in it.'

'"Nice"? We're not settling for nice!' exclaimed Beryl. 'Your wedding's going to knock Evelyn Brimble's into a cocked hat, Gladys, for all her six bridesmaids and her two pageboys and her fancy *trousseau*!'

Gladys beamed again as Beryl laid down her knife and fork, but Lily knew it was about more than making sure their friend had a day to remember. It was Beryl's way of showing Robert Marlow that she, and her shop, were doing just fine without any of his so-called 'help' with the rent.

Beryl glugged down her glass of water and laid some coins on the table for her share of the bill and the tip.

'I'll love you and leave you,' she said. 'Back to business!'

Lily smiled and Gladys waved her fork, both chomping their way through hefty chunks of cheese on toast. Lily often felt that you burned up more calories chewing the National Loaf than it gave you in energy.

'So,' she said, swallowing the doughy lump with

difficulty. 'Any word from Bill? I don't suppose you've had a letter?'

She knew what the answer would be: she'd have heard about it – at length – if there had been.

'Not a dicky bird,' Gladys replied. 'Five weeks now. And till they retrain seagulls as carrier pigeons, it could be another five.'

Lily made a sympathetic face.

'You're very brave about it, Gladys,' she said.

'We're all in the same boat, aren't we?' replied Gladys. 'That's what Bill says, anyway!'

Bless her, she even managed a smile.

The White Lion was their small town's smartest hotel. To be fair, it didn't have much competition, but it still tried hard, with a Union Jack fluttering outside and a uniformed bellboy to help you with your suitcases, if you had them. Jim didn't, so he went straight through to the dining room. Robert was already there. Inevitably, they'd given him the very best table in the centre of the room.

Jim wasn't used to this kind of setting. When he'd first confessed his connection with the Marlows, Lily had imagined him living in luxury with servants, starched tablecloths and silver cutlery himself, but he'd soon explained that his family were very much the poor relations. They lived in a simple cottage and did their own cooking and cleaning – and there was no family silver whatsoever.

Robert waved him over and stood up to shake hands.

'Great to see you, Jim. Have a seat.'

Jim's senses prickled: the last time he and Robert had had dealings, they hadn't been exactly friendly ones. He sat down without comment, but Robert blithely carried on.

'What'll you have? I'm on Scotch and a splash, but I suppose it's Adam's ale for you as you'll be going back to work?'

'Yes, water thanks.'

Robert poured him a glass from the carafe on the table.

'Let's order, then I'll tell you why you're here. I'm sure you're wondering.'

Jim picked up the menu. Never mind the Ministry of Food's motto of 'fair shares all round'. Meals out weren't included in the ration: if you could afford it, you could eat out every night without sacrificing a single coupon.

'If it helps, I'm having asparagus soup, then saddle of lamb, leeks *à la crème* and straw potatoes,' Robert advised.

'I'll have the same.'

Anything to get the whole thing over with.

Robert gave their order, along with a glass of Chablis for himself, and once his wine had arrived, he leant forward.

On the face of it he was attractive, handsome even,

broad-shouldered with smooth blond hair, blue eyes
and healthy pink cheeks, set off by a well-cut suit,
snowy white shirt, silk tie and matching pocket
square. It was his character that was so unattractive.

'I'll come straight out with it,' Robert began. 'When
I was here in Hinton over the winter, I indulged in
a bit of, shall we say, extracurricular activity.'

After the devastation of the bomb, Robert had
come back to Hinton for a couple of months to buoy
up his father and help get the store back in business.
He'd worked hard alongside Peter Simmonds and
Jim, who was increasingly Mr Simmonds's second
lieutenant, and Jim had been pleasantly surprised.
Until that evening when he and Lily had caught
Robert trying to force himself on Beryl.

'You mean Beryl,' said Jim coldly.

Surely there hadn't been more women on the side?
Among Marlow's staff perhaps? Surely Robert wasn't
going to tell him one of them was pregnant? If so,
what was Jim supposed to do about it? But Robert
shook his head.

'No, not that. Extracurricular in the sense of – oh,
look, I met this chap. The long and short of it is, he
proposed a deal. He's a haulier, and he'd had a nice
little number going with Burrell's over their fuel
supplies. Whatever their allocation, he delivered a
ton less, sold it off on the BM, and he and his Burrell's
contact split the proceeds. So—'

Horrified, Jim was there before him. Burrell's,

Hinton's other big store, had been all but wiped out in the pre-Christmas bomb.

'So with Burrell's out of action, he suggested the same to you. Don't tell me you agreed?'

Instead of a reply, Robert picked up his glass and took a swig.

'Why?' demanded Jim. 'That delivery racket you set up when you worked at the store before – it's obvious that was to get in with Sir Douglas as a way of getting in with Evelyn. But the black market! Something that risky! What were you thinking? What could possibly be in it for you?'

Robert shushed him as their soup arrived. When the waiter had flapped their napkins onto their laps and departed, he picked up his spoon.

'It's just a different way of doing business, isn't it?'

'Business? It's a crime. A serious crime.'

Robert drank his soup.

'Don't be so wet. No one got hurt.'

'No one? We've been shivering all winter at Marlow's, and now I know why! More important, what about the poor bloody miners working their you-know-whats off, and the men dying at sea to keep up supplies? And the blokes in the Forces that need coal far more than we do – apart from them, you've been robbing your own father! Why would you do that?'

Robert gave a tiny shrug. He had no answer and his nonchalance made Jim long to slap him.

'It's not as if you need the money!' he said instead. 'You of all people!'

'You don't understand, do you? Any of it.' Robert put down his spoon and dabbed his mouth with his napkin. 'It's not about the money, it's about the – the excitement. You don't know what my life's like, Jim.'

'Do tell me. It's a hard one, is it?'

'You've no idea. Back here I was living with Dad, with him going on every night about Marlow's, Marlow's, Marlow's, and in Birmingham – well! I'm living in a mansion flat under the beady eye of Evelyn and her parents. Every evening it's drinks, dinner, bridge, news at nine then a chaste kiss and night-night, Robert – no hanky-panky, I can tell you. On top of which, I'm working for Sir Douglas, God help me, so I've got him all day every day as well! This was my last chance for a flutter, to spread my wings!'

'A flutter?' Jim had picked up his spoon but he put it down again. 'Like you thought you'd have with Beryl? Cheating your own father! Risking prosecution? You know it'd kill him if anything happened to Marlow's' reputation! Too right I don't understand. But the thing I most don't understand is why the confession. Why tell me? And why now?'

Chapter 5

Robert had begun to sweat.

'Drink your soup,' he said.

Jim obeyed. He might as well. There was obviously more to come.

Robert lowered his voice.

'This haulier chap, he won't let me go, he wants it to carry on. Not with coal – going into summer there's not so much demand, so he wants to make it up with other things.'

'What things?'

'I don't know! Anything in the store! Soap, razor blades, stockings, batteries and spare parts for radios from the repair workshop . . . he was even going on about Thermos flasks!'

Down went Jim's spoon again. When they could get them, which was rare, Thermos flasks were sold on Small Household Goods – part of his own department.

'Robert, you can't!'

'I know I can't! I'm not even here any more, am I? I'm in Birmingham!'

'That wasn't what I meant – and I should hope that's not the only reason!'

'Of course not. It was—'

'If you say fun—'

'It was a one-off,' pleaded Robert. 'I want out.'

'So tell him.'

'Don't you think I've tried? He's putting the arm on me, coming on strong. Saying he'll make sure Dad finds out and worse – saying he'll tell Sir Douglas. The wedding's three months away, I can't have that! You've got to get him off my back, Jim.'

'Me? Why me? Why should I?'

Surely Robert wasn't trying to play the 'family loyalty' card? One look at him told Jim he was. Or at least Jim's loyalty to Cedric and the store – and in that, he was on to something, blast him. Jim took a moment to think.

'If I agreed to help – *if* – how am I supposed to do it?'

Robert clearly took this as a sign that Jim had caved in. He relaxed and the infuriating devil-may-care arrogance was back.

'I don't know,' he shrugged with a grin. 'Concrete boots?'

'Oh, for goodness' sake!'

'Well, OK, maybe not. But you're a bright bloke. Jim. You'll see a way through.'

'Yes, I do! It's simple. The bloke's a crook! Go to the police!'

Robert made a 'pipe down' gesture; the waiter was hovering. Jim quickly spooned up the rest of his soup and their plates were removed. Robert leant forward, annoyed now.

'I don't think you're taking this seriously.'

'*I'm* not taking it seriously?'

'I can't go to the police! I know what you'll say, tell them this fellow tried to blackmail me. You don't know him. He's a proper player round here. He keeps up a respectable front, but he's got contacts with some real shady characters. I won't live to see him prosecuted!'

'I don't see what else you can do,' Jim replied firmly.

The waiter reappeared and put their main course in front of them. It looked and smelt delicious. It was the best meal Jim had seen since the start of the war, possibly ever, and though they both started to eat, he couldn't enjoy any of it.

'Please, Jim,' Robert said simply. 'The simple fact is – I don't have anyone else to turn to.'

Jim chewed, tasting nothing. There was no reason why he should help. He could eat his lunch, walk away, let him get on with it. But Robert was such a hothead, he might do anything in desperation, something crazy like try to get this other bloke beaten up or worse, and whatever he did it was bound to end in disaster. Then what? Robert's, Cedric's and the store's reputation dragged through the mire? That wasn't going to help anybody.

'Look,' Jim said reluctantly. 'I'm not saying I'll help you. I don't know that I can. But tell me who this bloke is. It's not the one you were talking to last night, is it, at the fashion show? Flash Harry type?'

'Not Harry,' said Robert. 'Barry. Barry Bigley.'

Of course! Barry Bigley! Now he had a name, Jim could place the face. He'd seen him once or twice, in old trousers and a brown dust coat, getting in or out of his lorry in the delivery bay. His name had been painted on the lorry's side. And now something else was coming back to him.

'Barry Bigley,' he said slowly. 'He's got the scrap metal contract at Tatchell's.'

Tatchell's was one of Hinton's few factories, which had turned from making car parts to aircraft parts.

'So?'

'I worked there for a while.'

'Really? And?'

'I did a few night shifts, and I remember seeing Bigley's lorries arrive empty and leave piled with scrap. At least, I assumed it was scrap. But it was a damn funny time to be collecting it, don't you think, two o'clock in the morning?'

'You reckon it was a fiddle?'

'What if,' said Jim slowly, 'some of it wasn't scrap, but was good stuff underneath. From what you've said about Bigley . . . and the driver was very pally with the foreman, Deakin. I never liked him, nasty little man—'

'Deakin?' said Robert keenly. 'I'm sure Barry mentioned that name.'

'It's not exactly proof,' mused Jim. Despite himself, he was interested now. 'It's not even evidence. Just supposition.'

'But it's something else on Bigley! Possibly.' Robert took a gulp of wine. 'But what do we do with it? Maybe *you* could go to the police!'

'And maybe I couldn't!' Was there nothing Robert wouldn't have him do? 'I suppose though . . . if this is still going on . . . an anonymous tip-off . . . tell the police to watch Tatchell's, spot-check Bigley's lorries . . .'

'That's the one!' Robert seized on the suggestion.

'Look, it may not work. Even if the police catch Bigley or one of his drivers in the act, if Bigley's as slippery as you say, he might wriggle out of it. But with luck he'll at least take it as a warning, move his activities a bit further afield. And it might stop him bothering you.'

'That's brilliant, Jim. When can you do it?'

'What?'

'This anonymous phone call. I assume you mean a phone call.'

They were right back where they'd started!

'Hang on,' protested Jim. 'Why me? You're nothing to do with Tatchell's! There could be no comeback for you.'

'There won't be for you if it's anonymous!' Robert speared the last succulent morsel of meat on his plate and delivered it to his mouth. 'That was delicious. Look, do stay and have a pudding if you've got time, Jim – on me, of course.'

'What?'

How Robert could turn the conversation so lightly to the dessert trolley was beyond Jim. Robert took a final swig of his wine.

'I've got to shoot straight back to Birmingham. Evelyn's mother's giving one of her blasted soirées – I had to make an excuse for not going back with them this morning. And it'd look highly suspicious to make a trunk call from Birmingham about a firm in Hinton; they can trace them, you know.'

He was absolutely shameless.

'You never agreed, Jim?' Lily was disgusted.

'He wasn't going to let me go till I did, and it was nearly two o'clock, I had to get back! I had to get a special dispensation from Simmonds to go in the first place.'

The working day was over and they were walking home. There was no fashion show excitement tonight, but it was one of those suddenly sunny April evenings, clouds bouncing along merrily in a stiff breeze, sparrows and starlings chirping from the chimney pots. If it hadn't been for Robert Marlow, Lily might have felt all the joys of spring.

'Every time he shows his face in Hinton it means trouble,' she said bitterly. 'And you always seem to get dragged into it. *We* seem to get dragged into it.'

When his delivery racket had been discovered, Robert had tried to pin the blame on Jim.

'Yes, well, he's gone now,' replied Jim, 'back to Birmingham and his terrible life there – or so he'd have me believe.'

'Leaving you to clear up his mess!'

'Which is why I'm going to knock this whole wretched thing on the head. Now.'

As Jim spoke, he was opening the door of a telephone box and nudging her inside.

'You're going to call the police right this minute?'

Squashed in the kiosk, Lily eased her gas mask case around so it wasn't sticking in her ribs.

'May as well get it over with.' Jim dug in his pocket for change. 'Look me up the number, will you?'

Lily found the number for the local police station in the directory and read it out as Jim fed coins into the slot and dialled.

'You haven't put your hanky over the mouthpiece,' she chided as he waited for the connection. It was what they always did in the films. But Jim shushed her as the phone was picked up at the other end. He pressed the button and Lily, craning her neck to listen, heard a voice say, 'Hinton Police.'

Jim kept it short, said what he had to, mentioned Bigley, scrap metal and Tatchell's, then put the receiver down quickly.

'Come on,' he said, 'Let's get out of here.'

They bundled out of the box and scuttled off as if they were the criminals, Lily clutching Jim's arm when she saw a policeman at the crossroads. He nodded them kindly across and Lily gave him a ghastly grin back.

'What did the police say?' she demanded when they were out of hearing.

'I only spoke to the desk sergeant,' Jim replied. 'He said he'd pass it on.'

'Is that all?'

'What did you expect? A black Maria shooting off to Bigley's straight away?'

'Well, no, but . . . how do we find out if they investigate? We'll never know.'

'We'll have to keep an eye on the *Chronicle*.' It was Hinton's local newspaper. 'It'd be a big story for them if Bigley was exposed. Who knows what else he's been up to?'

'You might have uncovered a whole crime ring!'

'Yes, a real local hero! I can tell you one thing though. Next time Robert Marlow asks me to lunch, I'm not going. Not even for soup and saddle of lamb and leeks *à la crème.*'

Lily's eyes could have passed as soup plates themselves.

'You never ate that lot!'

'I did,' said Jim.

'And all to get you to make a phone call? I'd have done anything for that!'

'You've changed your tune! Shows how easily you can be bought!' retorted Jim.

They'd reached the park, their shortcut home, though it wasn't really a park any more, most of it ploughed up for 'Dig for Victory' allotments. Jim stopped and felt in his pocket.

'If it's any consolation,' he added, 'I didn't taste any of it. But I brought you these.'

He produced a grubby envelope and gave it to her. Inside were two very squashed peppermint creams.

'I sneaked them off another table on my way out – they'd left them, can you believe!'

'Jim! We've been going on about Robert and Barry Bigley being crooks, and you're thieving chocolates from the White Lion! You're no better than they are! I've got a good mind to go back to that phone box, and—'

She was only teasing, he knew. Jim grabbed her and pulled her towards him.

53

'Oh shut up and give me a kiss.'
'Ow! Careful! You're squashing my chocolates!'
But she gave in.

Chapter 6

When Lily met Gladys by the lockers in the bustle of the staff cloakroom next day, her friend was a different person, fresh-faced and cheerful.

'A letter,' she trilled excitedly. 'Waiting for me when I got in!'

Lily didn't need to ask who it was from. She could have dropped to her knees and sung Hallelujah right there on the cold stone floor.

Perfect! – exactly what Gladys needed. But there was more.

'He can't tell me the whys and wherefores . . .' Gladys bundled her handbag, jacket and gas mask into her locker. One of her precious photos of Bill was taped to the inside of the door. 'I don't know how he knows, but he's told me to definitely book the church! July the tenth!'

'Oh Gladys! That's wonderful! A date!' Lily clasped her hands. 'That's not long at all!'

'Not quite ten weeks!'

Of course, Gladys had worked it out.

'There'll be a lot to do.'

Neither of them had a dress yet; there was the church to organise, and a place for a reception, and the catering to sort, and the flowers, and then the extras Gladys would want – plenty to think about.

'Oh I know, and I can't wait to get started. I can leave the dress to Beryl, she knows what I want, I'm not worried about that, but the rest . . . you will help, won't you, Lily? And your mum, with the food? And make the cake, of course. I'll put by as much dried fruit as I can . . . and sugar . . . and thank goodness for your hens! We'll be stuck for icing sugar, but isn't everyone . . .'

'Gladys! Calm down!' Lily couldn't help smiling. 'We've got ten weeks, not ten days! Of course Mum'll help, she'd be offended not to! We'll all pull together.'

'Oh, thank you! I knew you would. We'll all do our best. It's only that . . .' Gladys tailed off, her eyes clouding.

'What?'

'Well . . . I just want it to be as nice as it can be. There'll be some things missing, we can't help that . . .'

Confetti, thought Lily. Icing for the cake. Bells at the church . . . Gladys had listed them before, many times.

'I know, but it's the war, isn't it?'

'Not just things. People, too.'

'Sid's got enough notice. Barring emergencies, he'll be able to get leave—' Lily began.

It couldn't be Reg Gladys was bothered about; she hardly knew him, but she had a very soft spot for Sid. Most women did.

'It's not Sid I was thinking of,' said Gladys quietly, and Lily could have bitten her tongue off.

Gladys wasn't originally from Hinton. She'd been born and brought up in Coventry, but her parents had been killed in the Blitz on the city and she lived with her gran, who was pretty much wrapped up in herself and her ailments and took advantage of Gladys's good nature. Her gran'd be at the wedding, of course, but no mum, and no dad to give Gladys away . . .

Lily put a hand on her friend's arm.

'I'm so sorry,' she said. 'I wish I could—'

She didn't finish; she didn't know what she could say.

'No, I know, it is what it is. I've got used to not having my mum and dad anyway, as time's gone on. But for Bill to have no family there either . . .'

Now there was even less to say.

Bill had been brought up in a children's home, left

there by his mother as a baby. That was all he knew. Of his father, he knew absolutely nothing.

'I know it's barmy,' Gladys went on, 'but sometimes I have this dream of . . . well, it's more a fairy tale really, thinking I could find her for him.'

There were no words. As Lily stood at a loss, Gladys rescued her.

'But I can't, so that's that.'

Lily seized the moment.

'That's right, Gladys. Onwards and upwards. Let's concentrate on what we can do.'

'Yes,' Gladys nodded. 'First things first. I'd better find some nice cards for the invitations. I've been having a look around . . .'

The cloakroom was emptying now as salesgirls scurried to their departments. Lily steered Gladys gently in their wake as she chattered on.

'There's not much about. What I'd like best is a plain card with a cherub in each corner blowing a trumpet and trailing a ribbon, so if you see anything like that on your travels . . .'

Lily smiled to herself. Dear Gladys. Ten weeks of this!

Unbeknown to Lily, someone else at Marlow's had had a letter – and not one they were anything like as pleased to receive.

Peter Simmonds picked up the envelope that was lying on his desk – hardly more than a shelf – in the cramped little space he called his office. Once again he squinted at the postmark, which was unhelpfully blurred. It might be Hinton but it could have been Tipton, a town nearby. It could even, at a stretch, have been London. Laying it down, he picked up the sheet of cheap paper that had been inside.

On it was a typed message in capital letters.

EILEEN FROBISHER IS A SLUT AND HER SON IS A BASTARD

SHE WAS NEVER MARRIED SHE DOESN'T BELONG AT MARLOW'S

Peter felt sick, sick to his stomach. What a thing to say about anyone – and about Eileen in particular! He didn't believe it for a moment, but who could dislike her – even hate her – so much that they'd think, let alone write, such a thing?

With the letter in his hand, he tried to think dispassionately.

Apart from the content, it was a puzzling note. It was correctly spelt – they'd even used the Marlow's apostrophe – but there was no punctuation. Did that mean it had been written in the white heat of fury? He came back to the first question he'd asked himself. Who could hate Eileen so much as to spew out such a disgusting stream of spite?

Ever since the bomb, he and Miss Frobisher had gradually got to know each other better. At the hospital, visiting Lily and Jim, they'd shared the guilt they felt about leaving two junior members of staff in the store to finish off the Christmas preparations after hours. Logically, they both knew that no one could have predicted that some Luftwaffe pilot would randomly offload a bomb on Hinton, but it didn't stop them feeling that way.

Over the weeks that followed, they'd occasionally coincided their morning or afternoon breaks – anything more frequent would have attracted attention and started the Marlow's rumour mill whirling. With both of them the souls of discretion, their friendship had remained unobtrusive. Eileen was married, after all – at least that was the story.

Peter had never asked about Eileen Frobisher's husband, and wouldn't have dreamt of doing so, but having walked her home a few times and even once been invited in, he noted that there were no photographs of her young son's father on display. He held to the theory which he'd long held and had shared with Jim – that Eileen and her husband were separated. That didn't necessarily make her a free agent though, and it gave him a problem, because since the fashion show, and the vision of loveliness she'd been in the finale, he'd been forced to acknowledge that what he felt for her was far more than you'd feel for a friend. He'd fallen for her. Hard.

He rubbed his hand over his forehead. What next?

There was nothing else for it. He picked up the internal telephone and asked for Mr Marlow.

'Oh, so you've had one now, have you?'

Sitting in Cedric Marlow's rather more spacious and better-appointed office, Peter was surprised.

'You mean you have as well, sir?'

'Goodness me, yes.' Cedric pushed the letter Peter had shown him back across the broad mahogany desk. 'And all about Miss Frobisher. Not couched in quite such strong language, but I've been getting one or two a week for the last . . . what would it be . . . three or four weeks, I suppose.'

'May I see them?'

'I don't have them. I threw them away.'

That was stupid, thought Peter, but he could hardly say so.

'That's a shame,' he remarked circumspectly. 'What did they say?'

'Oh, I really can't remember.' Cedric Marlow looked up to the ceiling as if the answer might be written there. '"Eileen Frobisher is no better than she should be" – that was one of them, I think. And the others in much the same vein.'

'But you chose not to do anything about them?'

'These things are best ignored, surely?' Cedric looked at him over his half-moon glasses. 'It's arrant nonsense, Miss Frobisher's a respectable married woman.'

'Well, yes, of course,' said Peter quickly. This wasn't the time or place for his own speculations about Eileen's situation. 'But things have moved on, haven't they? I've had a letter now, and from what you say, the language has become far more offensive.'

'Yes, that's true.' Mr Marlow had the grace to sound uncomfortable. 'But these things usually sort themselves out in time. The letter-writer gets bored when there's no reaction.'

'But that's not what's happening, is it? The letters keep coming and they're getting worse.' There was no reply from Cedric, so he pressed on. 'I'm not sure we can ignore it any longer, sir. It'll have to be investigated.'

A look of panic crossed Cedric Marlow's face.

'You don't mean . . . the police?' he stuttered. 'Oh, I don't think so. We can't have them sniffing around in the store! What would it look like?'

This was classic Cedric, or the Cedric of recent months.

Everyone knew the old man had been shattered by the bomb and the damage to his beloved store, but slowly, over the winter, he'd seemed to rally, thanks to the efforts of Robert, Jim, and Peter himself. Now he wondered. Had it all been too much? Not so long ago it would have been Cedric coming to him the moment the first letter had arrived, wanting it sorted out, and quickly. Was Cedric Marlow losing his touch? Even if he was, he was still the boss. Peter daren't go over his head.

'I can understand your reluctance,' he said slowly. 'But . . . well, look, sir, how about if we wait a short while and see if either of us receives any more of these . . . communications. And then maybe we can talk again.'

'I suppose so. Yes, yes, very well.'

With that, Cedric seemed to regard the matter closed. For now, thought Peter, for now. He stood up and replaced his chair at the precise angle to the desk which the old man required.

'Thank you, sir,' he said. 'Naturally you're concerned about the store's reputation. We all are. But I'd like to think that extends to the reputation of its staff. That's valuable too, don't you think?'

It was as far as he dared to go, and Cedric's tone told him he'd probably gone too far as it was.

'Thank you, Mr Simmonds,' he said. 'I'm sure you have more pressing matters to attend to on the shop floor.'

With an inclination of his head, Peter made for the door, closing it quietly behind him.

He'd done his best. But where Eileen was concerned, his best didn't feel nearly good enough.

Inevitably, the first person he saw when he emerged through the double doors on to the first floor was Eileen. She was walking with one of the regular customers, Mrs Jenkins, to the lift, and explaining that boys' bathing trunks were a particular problem to get hold of.

'Might you try knitting some yourself?' she was asking.

Mrs Jenkins laughed.

'Frankly, no! With my knitting they'd be round the poor boy's ankles before he went anywhere near the water!'

'Have you thought about joining our classes?' Miss Frobisher persisted. 'They're very popular.'

Knitting and sewing classes, for free, as long as the materials were bought in the store, had been one of Jim and Peter's initiatives to keep the customers coming, and he was pleased to hear Miss Frobisher recommending them.

He gave her a brief smile as they passed and she nodded in acknowledgement, then she was gone, in her black pencil skirt and silky blouse, her hair in its usual smooth roll. At the hospital, out of hours, she'd worn it loose on her shoulders. As they'd talked, she'd sometimes twisted a strand of it in her fingers, and he'd almost had to sit on his hands to stop himself from reaching out and touching it.

He stared after her, unable to believe what was in the letters. How had Eileen Frobisher stirred up such evil thoughts? Who could it be? Someone from her past? A spurned lover? A jealous rival? The errant husband?

Pull yourself together, he thought, as he saw Miss Wagstaff bearing down on him. Mind on the job!

'Miss Wagstaff,' he said. 'What can I do for you?'

She flourished a sheaf of paper.

'We have a meeting,' she said crisply. 'About weekly targets. At your request, if you remember.' She raised an eyebrow. 'If, that is, you're not too distracted?'

Lily lifted her spoon. Today's canteen pudding had been advertised as simply 'cake', which meant that, as usual, it would be mostly carrot. Never mind see in the dark, it was a wonder they didn't all glow in the dark, the amount of carrots they consumed.

Over their first course, she'd told Jim about Bill's letter, and the wedding date being set, but also Gladys's sorrow that neither she nor Bill would have any family there.

'So you see, Jim, we've got to make it up to her,' she urged now. 'We'll have to be the family they haven't got. And we've got to make this wedding absolutely perfect for them.' Jim had nearly finished his pudding; hollow legs, Dora said. He scraped the last crumbs from his bowl. 'Well?'

Jim laid down his spoon.

'I'll do my best, you know I will,' he said. 'But I can't get involved in all this girls' talk about – I dunno, veils and dresses and stockings and whatnot.'

'I'm not asking you to! But she's going to ask you

65

to give her away, I know she is, so just, well, act delighted.'

'I won't have to act anything! I'm very fond of Gladys. There's nothing I'd like more.'

'Thank you.' Lily beamed happily. 'And Sid's going to be best man as he was the one who introduced them, oh and she's going to ask you to lend your camera to Les, so he can take the photographs. And if you happen to see any cards that'd do for the invitations . . . ideally with a cherub at each corner blowing a—'

Jim reached over and rapped her knuckles with his spoon.

'Oy! Enough! What did I just say?'

Lily had the good grace to back down.

'OK, I'll let you off the invitations. But you'd better pace yourself, Jim. We've got ten weeks of this.'

Jim groaned.

'Ten weeks! It's not only Gladys who'll be counting the days!'

Chapter 7

Peter Simmonds was also counting the days – until he could tackle Mr Marlow again. He didn't have long to wait.

The following week, he received another letter. This time the postmark was clear – it had been posted locally, in Hinton, and its typed message was even more pointed.

WHY DON'T YOU WAKE UP AND LISTEN?

FROBISHER'S NOTHING BUT A—

It was the ugliest of ugly words and he could hardly bear to read it. Summoning every ounce of self-control, he folded the letter, replaced it in the envelope and locked it in his drawer. Then he strode purposefully on to the sales floor.

Enough was enough. It was time for action.

'What do you think, Miss Frobisher?' asked Lily. 'It looks as though the weather's set fair for the next few days.'

'If we can believe it!'

Lily had suggested changing the outfits on the Childrenswear mannequins and she and her boss were debating it when Peter Simmonds approached and indicated that he'd like a word.

Miss Frobisher moved slightly towards him.

'Very well, then, Miss Collins.' She addressed Lily over her shoulder. 'The boy first. Fawn drill shorts and a short-sleeved shirt. But a sleeveless pullover on top, please.'

'Yes, Miss Frobisher.'

Lily faded away to find something suitable, and Eileen turned to Peter with a smile.

'I was looking for you earlier about that delivery that hasn't materialised. Any news?'

'No, nothing,' he said, his mouth dry. 'And it's not about that. I wondered . . . if your neighbour would babysit . . . could you be free this evening?' He didn't want to talk to her about the letters in his tiny office, and he knew her elderly neighbour often looked after her son. 'There's something I'd like to talk to you about and I'd rather not do it in the store.'

'I see!' She sounded intrigued.

No, you don't, he thought sadly. If only he were taking her out on a date, as he'd often thought of suggesting but had never quite dared.

'I'll telephone at lunchtime and ask her,' Eileen offered. 'She's always saying it doesn't make any difference to her whether she sits in her flat or mine.'

'That's because she's using your electricity!'

'Now, now,' Miss Frobisher chided, 'she's very good. I'd like to put John to bed myself though, so perhaps . . . eight o'clock?'

'I'll call for you.'

'Fine. I'll see you later.'

Smiling to herself, she watched him go. A ribbed pullover in her hand, Lily watched her watching him. Well, well, she thought. Maybe there was something between those two after all . . .

Eileen dressed carefully for her evening out, even though she told herself it wouldn't be a date as such. Peter probably wanted to sound her out about some new idea that Mr Marlow was resisting – he'd done that before. Even so, he usually did so by walking her home, not by taking her out. She didn't get out much – well, at all really, and it was nice to have an excuse.

The evening was fine and warm, as Lily had predicted, and at eight it was still light, so she picked out a dress splashed with poppies and cornflowers, with red shoes and handbag. Like everyone else, she was restricted by coupons, but she'd always loved clothes from her time in the Fashion departments at Marlow's and then in London. Before the war, before John had been born, she'd spent every spare penny on good clothes and they were serving her well now that things were so hard to come by.

Peter was prompt – that was ex-Army for you – and she was amused to see that he'd dressed carefully too, in fawn slacks and an open-necked soft shirt. When they'd met off duty at the hospital, he'd worn his regimental blazer and tie. Recently, though, as they passed Gentlemen's Outfitting on the way to their breaks, Eileen had taken to casually pointing out certain items with a favourable comment, and she was pleased to see he'd taken the hint.

He suggested a pub nearby and with assurances to the babysitting neighbour that they wouldn't be late, they set off. Peter found them a table in the beer garden and went to fetch the shandy she'd asked for, and a beer for himself. They chinked glasses and made the usual disparaging comments about the weakness of the beer. Then he took a piece of paper from his pocket.

'I'll get straight to the point,' he said. 'I'm afraid I've received this.'

'A letter?'

'Poison pen.'

Eileen gasped, shocked. And she hadn't any idea, he thought miserably, that it was about her, or that he'd today had another, even more poisonous one.

'It's the first one to me, but Mr Marlow's been getting them over the past few weeks. I don't know why he didn't do anything about it, but I intend to. But I'll need your help. I'm afraid you'll have to read it.'

Baffled, never suspecting she might be the subject, Eileen took the letter and read the ugly words.

EILEEN FROBISHER IS A SLUT AND HER SON IS A BASTARD

SHE WAS NEVER MARRIED SHE DOESN'T BELONG AT MARLOW'S

She didn't say a word but folded it and laid it down again.

'It's nonsense of course—' he began, but she held up her hand, the one with the slim wedding band on her third finger.

'It's not nonsense, Peter,' she said. 'It's all true. Except perhaps for the last bit.'

'Eileen, please—'

'No, no.' She was perfectly calm. 'Let me tell you. I'd like to.'

'I was young,' she began, 'and I can't say exactly innocent – but still young and stupid and naïve. I moved to London, to a job as a junior buyer at Marshall and Snelgrove's. I loved it, everything about

71

it, the work, the store, the big city, my life. I was promoted to under-buyer, then buyer. There was travel, and in those days – well, we, the buyers, had the power. We weren't going cap in hand to manufacturers begging like we have to now. The reps used to court us, if you like. Meals out, the theatre, little gifts.'

She'd been talking directly to him, meeting his eyes. Now she looked away.

'He was one of them. Older, charming, very experienced, very good at his job. I fell for him. I was completely captivated.' She gave a tiny shrug, remembering. 'Reps! I know better now. Not all of them, but for quite a few a roving brief means a roving eye . . . he was married, of course. Once I found out, I should have ended it. I'm not proud of myself. I should have been stronger but . . .'

She looked down into her glass, then up at him again.

'I didn't mean to get pregnant; I wasn't trying to trap him, I swear, but when I told him about the baby – well, he'd always promised to leave his wife for me and, idiot that I was, I believed him.' She shook her head, impatient, regretful. 'Of course, that all changed – he got a sudden attack of conscience. It turned out he'd been married not once but twice and he already had children by both marriages. He hadn't mentioned that, funnily enough.' She compressed her lips: Peter could see she found it difficult to talk about, even after so many years. 'He couldn't break up another family, he said – very noble of him. He wanted me to get rid of the baby. I was devastated, and the next thing was, he'd left his job and disappeared – to make sure I had no way of contacting him, I suppose, or asking for money, or making trouble with his wife, or wives – not that I'd have dreamt of it. Or of getting rid of the baby. Ever.'

'Eileen,' Peter said again. 'I'm so sorry.'

'It was my own fault.'

'No, it wasn't!' He was surprised by how strongly he wanted to defend her. 'He took advantage.'

'You're very kind. Too kind. But it takes two to tango, and all that.'

He found he couldn't bear her taking the blame. He tried to move things on.

'How did you manage?'

'I managed,' she said, 'to hide the pregnancy for about five months, then I had to give in my notice and leave. My father was still here in Hinton, but I couldn't go to him, I knew that. I have an aunt in Lincoln, I went there. She wasn't exactly thrilled, but she found me a nursing home and I gave birth to John. The war was coming. I wasn't sure what to do. I didn't want to go back to London, there was no point, I had no one there, so I came back here. I hoped that my father would come round and offer me a home once John was actually here. He didn't. Far from it.' She sighed, then shrugged off the memory, saying crisply, 'It wasn't a good time. I rented a room, and then quite suddenly, just after the start of the war, my father died, and I took over what had been his flat.'

Peter let out a breath.

'You've had a very hard time.'

'Not at all,' she said, refusing to accept his sympathy. 'I'm not the first and I won't be the last. You've only got to look around you at the number of war babies. I've been very lucky, really. I have my son, a good job and somewhere to live. Plenty of women in my position have none of that.'

Peter dipped his head: she was putting a gloss on it, of course. She must have had some very dark times.

'Perhaps not. Even so . . .' He swilled his beer around in his glass, then put it down again. 'But there's one thing I don't understand. When you came back to Marlow's, why invent a husband? Why not simply say you were a widow?'

Eileen took a sip of her drink. Her hair was loose and she hooked it behind her ear. Her earrings were like little red buttons.

'Good question. It was stupid of me. I couldn't be called up because of John, but I needed to earn some money – I had somewhere to live but I needed an income. I knew Marlow's would have me back like a shot, and when I came for the interview, I was wearing the ring I'd bought myself, and it was assumed that I was married and my husband was in the Forces. And I – well, stupidly I went along with it. I knew I'd be addressed as Miss Frobisher at work anyway and Staff Office were so pressed they didn't even ask this fictional husband's name. Of course it would have been easier to say I'd been widowed, I made things far too complicated for myself! But it's a bit late now.'

Things might have seemed complicated to her, but for Peter everything suddenly seemed much simpler. If she was free . . . but he was getting distracted. They had to get back to the letter.

'And this?' He touched the folded sheet.

She lifted her shoulders and the poppies and cornflowers on her bodice rose and fell.

'Someone knows.'

'Well, yes, except they've put their own despicable interpretation on it!' Peter took a long swig of his own drink. He needed it. 'Do you have any idea who it could be?'

He expected a 'no', but she surprised him.

'Any idea? I have a very good idea.'

'Really? There's someone in the world who hates you that much?'

'Oh, yes,' she said. 'You might like to get us some more drinks. It's another long story.'

First thing next morning, at eight o'clock sharp, Peter Simmonds was tapping on Mr Marlow's door.

He'd slept better than he had for days, and not

just because he now had a plan of action. That was satisfying enough, but he knew the most refreshing rest had come because he was flattered – honoured even – by the confidences Eileen had entrusted him with, thrilled to know she was free of any ties, and excited to think he could get to know her better . . . and better. If his resolve to go into battle for her had been firm before, it was steely now. He knew he'd fight to his last breath for her if Cedric Marlow tried to resist.

But when he heard Peter's suspicions, Cedric was so stunned he simply nodded dumbly. He didn't ask how Peter had come to the conclusion he had, and Peter didn't name names, just in case Eileen had been wrong. He knew he needed proof.

'I need your permission, sir, to carry out a locker check. For every member of staff, from juniors right up to management. I'm hoping to find the evidence I need to confront them.'

'Someone in the store . . .' the old man repeated. 'You must do all you can, we have to root this out. Someone in the store . . . we can't have that!'

Downstairs, not knowing what was to come, the usual clatter and chatter prevailed in the cloakrooms, and no one was chattering more than Gladys.

'Look, Lily, look,' she squeaked excitedly, arriving beside her friend, hat askew and gas mask case flying.

Lily calmly closed her locker door, but before she

could turn her head, Gladys was thrusting something under her nose.

'I've got the cards!' she cried. 'Look!'

'Whoa, whoa . . . when did this happen?' gasped Lily. 'I thought we were still hunting for them!'

'You won't believe it,' Gladys said. 'Brenda from Books gave them to me. Her brother got married – oh, years ago, before the war, and she knew her sister-in-law had some left over and she was sure she'd saved them. So she asked her at the weekend and her sister-in-law found them and Brenda came round with them last night!'

'How lucky!' said Lily. 'And how kind.'

'I know,' said Gladys. 'And they're going to come to the church to see us married, and all, the pair of them. What do you think?'

She beamed, a smile as wide as the sea Bill sailed on. Lily obediently studied the card: Gladys would expect no less. There were no cherubs and no trumpets – well, you couldn't have everything – but Gladys had got her ribbons, trailed by silver bells in each corner.

'They're perfect,' she began, but was cut off by the sudden appearance in the doorway of Miss Garner from the Staff Office. She clapped her hands for silence.

'Thank you, ladies, girls, if I could have some quiet, please?'

Anyone still chattering was quickly shushed by

their neighbour: Miss Garner was another of the store's formidable females. Almost eighty pairs of eyes turned towards her expectantly.

'We need to carry out a locker check. Can you please open your lockers and stand beside them until it's completed. Thank you.'

Everyone turned away with a variety of grimaces, mutterings, and raised eyebrows.

Locker checks happened about once every six months, usually when there was a suspicion of staff shoplifting. Someone had once been found with an unglamorous stash of tooth powder; another time it had been a pair of suede gloves. A more lucrative haul had been several pouches of pipe tobacco.

'I'd like to assure you,' Miss Garner added as her minions began moving methodically along the rows, 'that the management lockers are being checked as well.'

There were more eyebrows raised.

'No stone unturned,' whispered the girl next to Lily. 'There must be something pretty nasty underneath.'

Chapter 8

'Would you care to explain, Miss Naylor?'

Jennifer Naylor, who'd been summoned from Schoolwear, folded her hands. Cedric Marlow was seated behind his desk, but it was Peter Simmonds, standing beside it, who was asking the question. The locker check had been more of a success than he'd dared hope.

'You can see what it is,' she said curtly. 'A letter.'

'Exactly. An envelope, typed, addressed to me, stamped, yet to be posted.'

'It's nothing to do with me. I don't know how it got there.'

'Really?' asked Peter. 'Let's look at the contents, shall we?'

He took out the letter, typed in the same capitals as before, on the same cheap paper.

EILEEN FROBISHER IS A BITCH AND A TART AND—

Then the same ugly word again. He produced the other two letters he'd received and their envelopes and laid them alongside. 'You see the connection I'm making?'

Miss Naylor looked at the letters and shrugged.

'I see what you're getting at, but it doesn't prove anything. I've told you, I haven't a clue how that letter got into my locker. Someone's got it in for me. Miss Frobisher herself, perhaps.'

'What?'

'For all you know, she's writing them herself and trying to pin the blame on me! She's never liked me.'

Peter had to stop himself from throttling her: the nerve of the woman!

He collected himself: he must try not to get too heated. He went on coldly:

'That's a bit far-fetched, isn't it?' Miss Naylor met his eyes directly, defiantly: maybe she was a little unhinged. 'I'm sorry, but if you continue to deny all knowledge when the facts point directly to you, I shall have to involve the police, who'll conduct a search of your home for the typewriter.' It was an empty threat: Cedric still shrank from getting the police involved, but Miss Naylor didn't know that. 'It's easy to identify one typewriter from another. Especially when the ribbon's worn and some of the letters' – he tapped the sheets with his finger – 'almost cut through the paper. The "O" for example, and the "B"—'

'I think, Miss Naylor,' Cedric intervened, 'that you may as well admit it.'

Mr Marlow didn't know anything of the personal circumstances that Eileen had confessed to Peter Simmonds, nor that she'd gone on to explain the long-standing hostility between herself and Jennifer Naylor. But Cedric had worked that out for himself.

Presented with the evidence, he remembered an animosity between Jennifer Naylor and Eileen Frobisher that went back years – back to when they'd both been juniors on Ladies' Fashions. Young Eileen had started at the store six months after Jennifer, but it was clear from the first that she had a feel for the clothes and a way with the customers that they liked. Jennifer, on the other hand, was perfectly efficient, but mechanical in her approach, and when she found the newcomer in favour . . .

Cedric remembered the Ladies' Fashions buyer coming to him and asking that Jennifer be transferred. When he'd asked why, she'd explained that there was a bad atmosphere in the department, and that it was Jennifer who was causing it. Such things happened from time to time, and Cedric had agreed, but he'd kept his eye on Jennifer Naylor over the years. Bad atmospheres seemed to follow her around, but a difficult personality, though unfortunate, wasn't a good enough reason to sack her. He'd discussed it with Miss Garner: their only hope had been that Miss Naylor would leave of her own accord. But she never did, and he'd even had to promote her through sheer length of service. She'd moved through several departments creating bad atmospheres before Cedric had settled on Schoolwear as the safest berth for her. It required no flair and not much charm; Marlow's was the only supplier of uniform for various schools in the area, so customers couldn't shop elsewhere even if they wanted to. It was only ever busy in certain months of the year, so Miss Naylor relied on 'floating' members of staff at busy times, and a full-time junior who Miss Garner watched over to make sure they weren't being too fiercely bullied.

Eileen Frobisher had left, inevitably, lured away to the bright lights of London, and since she'd come back, there'd been no chance for her and Jennifer to clash. Though he did remember coming across them before Christmas, before the bomb, in something of a stand-off – over the store's rocking horse, of all things. Cedric had tactfully had to intervene.

From across the desk, Jennifer Naylor looked sullenly at him. She was only in her thirties but her dark hair was already starting to lose its lustre. She was thin, too thin, neatly but plainly turned out in a charcoal grey suit and cream blouse, almost a school uniform in itself. He suddenly felt sorry for her. She must envy Eileen Frobisher, pure and simple, he thought, though he did wonder why her envy had boiled up now.

'The choice is quite straightforward,' he said. 'You realise I have to sack you. Or you could pre-empt me and resign, which would be slightly more dignified.'

'She fell on her sword,' Peter told Eileen. He'd called her into his little office, though he was regretting it: her nearness, her stockinged legs, the faint trace of her perfume, was making him rather hot under the collar. He pressed on, hoping to disguise it. 'Going quietly was the only thing she could do, really. I stood over her while she collected her things, made sure she handed in her name badge and pass, and she was seen off the premises. Cash Office will send on anything she's owed.'

'Oh Peter.' Eileen bit her lip. He wished she wouldn't do that; it was too tantalising. 'I feel dreadful for her.'

'What?' It was the last reaction he'd expected. 'She didn't have much conscience about you!'

'Maybe not, but—'

'We couldn't let it go on,' he insisted. 'From what you told me she'd had it in for you for years! Who knows where it might have ended?'

Eileen looked sceptical.

'What was she going to do, snap my pencils? Steal my hole punch?'

'Now you're being facetious,' he chided. 'And since you'd be lucky to replace them, it might have been a good tactic!'

She smiled indulgently.

'I know, but really, what were you imagining? Her running amok with a pair of pinking shears, taking me hostage or something?'

'It's not funny,' Peter insisted. 'I've seen it in the Army. It starts with a bit of ribbing, a bit of name-calling, an apple-pie bed, and the next thing is they're putting some poor bloke's head down the lavatory.'

That checked her and she conceded, 'I'm sorry. You're right. And I'm very lucky – that Mr Marlow didn't believe the letters in the first place – but even more so that you acted so quickly. Thank you.' She paused. 'But Jennifer Naylor's got nothing and no one, as far as I know. And what's she going to do for work?'

'Don't be silly,' he said crisply. 'There's plenty of war work, she should have been doing it already, a single woman of her age.'

'I believe she has asthma,' said Miss Frobisher. 'And she does a couple of stints a week at the hospital. Reading to patients.'

'What, Gothic horrors? Ghost stories? I should think that sets back their recovery!'

'Now who's being facetious? And mean!'

He held up his hands, a gesture of defeat.

'All right, I'm sorry. But truly, Eileen, she'll have no trouble finding work. She's perfectly able – I can't think of an industry that isn't crying out for women. Miss Garner will give her a reference that says she's efficient and punctual and all that. What it won't say is that she's a first-class, gold-plated—'

He stopped himself in time.

'And what about the vacancy here?'

'Ah,' said Peter Simmonds. 'I was coming to that.'

'Oh, there's a catch, is there?' She smiled her curving smile. 'Let me guess. You – or Mr Marlow – want me to combine the roles.'

'Yes, please – temporarily, at least. There'll be a slight increment in salary, naturally.'

'I should hope so!' She seemed to be considering something. 'Am I allowed a suggestion of my own?'

'Go ahead.'

'I can't be in two places at once. So move Lily Collins to Schoolwear. She's ready for more responsibility – she's getting bored on Childrenswear and there's no more I can teach her.'

Peter straightened his tie, no longer the regimental stripe, but a navy background with fawn trellis pattern. That meant, she knew, that he was thinking. She added:

'The summer stock on Schoolwear's already here and the stuff for the autumn term is ordered. All it needs is a competent salesgirl. You'd have to boost Lily up to second sales, of course.'

'Oh really? You don't want much!'

'I'm solving a big problem for you. You can't leave the junior on her own day-to-day and I know all the floating staff are already spoken for. I'll keep an eye on Lily. She'll fly, I promise.'

'Second sales, you say?'

'Yes. And I'm not asking for a replacement on my department – I'll manage with Miss Temple and Miss Thomas. So it won't add to the wages bill!'

Peter Simmonds gave in.

'All right. Don't say anything to Miss Collins yet. I'll have to put it to Mr Marlow.'

'Is that all?' It was a challenge, but at the same time a tease. 'I was hoping you'd recommend it.'

'Don't push your luck!'

But her tone was encouraging. It made him feel he might be able to push his.

'One thing I don't understand,' he said. 'Well, two. First, how do you think Jennifer Naylor found out?'

Eileen shook her head. Her hair was in a different style today, rolled back gently off her face, and up at the back. It suited her.

'That I don't know. I can only think that one of the reps she dealt with knows John's father and what went on between us. Perhaps something was said.'

Peter considered this.

'Perhaps . . . But the second thing is – why now? I mean, why did all that bile suddenly surface in the last few weeks?' Thoughtful, he answered his own question.

'Of course, maybe they're connected. Maybe she only recently found out.'

'Maybe.'

Eileen nodded agreement but she was smiling again, this time to herself.

She hadn't been overly impressed with Peter Simmonds when he'd got the job as first-floor supervisor. At first, he'd seemed to throw his ex-Army weight around – instructions, even suggestions, flung out so briskly that they seemed like orders. 'Bringing the barrack-square to Marlow's,' some of the other buyers, who'd had their eye on the supervisor role for themselves, had grumbled. But over the months, Eileen had come to realise that his brusqueness was only a front – covering a shyness, almost, probably because as a career soldier he wasn't used to being surrounded by so many women.

Now she knew him to be gentle and gentlemanly and, in his own way, sweetly obtuse. It wasn't just Lily and Beryl who'd registered the look on his face as she'd floated up and down the catwalk in the bridal gown. Eileen had seen it too – and so, she was sure, had Jennifer Naylor, watching from the wings. From her eyrie on Schoolwear, Jennifer had probably been watching them as they took their breaks together, too. Eileen didn't think she'd entertained hopes of Peter Simmonds for herself – or maybe she had? Either way, the thought that her old rival might be the object of his affections must have simply derailed her.

Peter was studying her, looking worried.

'You're thinking.'

'Yes, I was. Sorry.'

'No, I'm sorry if all this has upset you.'

'It hasn't,' she assured him. 'That is, it would have upset me far more if I hadn't had you to go into bat for me. I owe you a lot. And I'm so glad you know the truth.'

She met his eyes fully. They were nice eyes, grey, but warm.

'Me too.'

Their eyes held each other's for a moment, then she looked down, and up again.

'Erm . . . when I said going into bat . . .'

'Yes?'

'John's desperate to learn cricket. And I'm afraid I'm at a bit of a loss.'

Was she asking what he thought she was asking?

Some time ago, in a bid to keep up staff morale, Mr Marlow had asked for ideas and Peter had been quick to suggest sports teams. The girls played a few games of netball and rounders when they could muster some opposition, but it was the football and cricket teams that had really taken off. Peter was the cricket captain.

'Well . . . erm . . . If you'd like me to give him a few lessons . . .'

'Would you?' she said at once. 'He'd be thrilled.'

'I'd be delighted!'

'Thank you!' Her smile lit up the poky office like a searchlight. 'Well – are you busy on Sundays? In the afternoon? We could go to the park – there's still a couple of patches of grass. I could bring a picnic?'

He could hardly believe it.

'I'd like that very much.'

'Good! That's settled, then.'

He gave her a smile and Eileen looked modestly down at the band on her wedding finger. She'd leave it there for the moment. But in time, perhaps quite soon, she'd take it off and publicly admit the truth about John's father. And the freedom that would give her, to be herself, and maybe to start again, was absolutely exhilarating.

Chapter 9

Lily lay back and wriggled her toes. Beryl had let her have a go with her 'Monte Carlo Pink' nail varnish as a try-out for the wedding. 'Black Market Pink,' Jim had sniffed, but Lily had pointed out that he hadn't been above snaffling under-the-counter chocolates from the White Lion, so they were quits. And he'd had to agree her toenails did look pretty.

The weather had continued fine, and the younger salesgirls had taken to coming up to sunbathe on the store's flat roof. With stockings a rarity, naturally tanned legs beat gravy browning every time. They had to compete for space with the firewatchers' hut and the Fowl Club's hen coops, but Lily had found a spot near an air vent where she could stretch out in the sun. She sighed happily.

The locker check the other day hadn't thrown up anything suspicious in the ladies' staff cloakroom, or the gents', Jim had told her, and presumably the search of the management lockers had been for form's sake only, so the only possible cloud in the sky had sailed away.

She glanced over to where Jim was talking to one of the Fowl Club stalwarts about some new kind of feeder they were trying to invent. As well as the hens in the Collins's backyard, the store's Fowl Club had been Jim's idea. Coming from the countryside, he'd known where to get hold of the Buff Orpingtons and Light Sussex hens which he said were good layers, and how to construct a hen run. And a lot of the staff had seen the logic of swapping their weekly egg coupon for a ration of feed grain and the promise of at least two eggs a week each for taking a turn mucking out and feeding. There were thirty-six hens on the roof now, and over fifty members of the Fowl Club.

'Want a read of this?'

One of the girls whose dinner hour was over was holding out the *Chronicle*'s midday edition. Lily sat up to take it.

'Yes, please! Thanks.'

Before she could open it, Jim flopped down beside her and snatched it away, leafing rapidly through.

'Oy!'

Jim had always mocked Hinton's local paper, and it was a pretty dismal effort. A typical lead story was *Horse Puts Hoof Through Slatted Bridge* – painful for the horse and worrying for its owner, perhaps, but not really sensational enough to make you part with a penny for the paper. But lately, always hoping to see that Barry Bigley had been arrested and charged, Jim tried never to miss it.

'I don't believe it!'

'What?' Lily tried to look over his shoulder. 'Is it Bigley? They've caught him at last?'

Jim passed her the newspaper.

'He's caught all right – on camera!'

Lily looked at the paper, the photograph, and the caption.

Well-known local businessman Mr Barry Bigley shares a joke with Detective Chief Inspector Norman Gregson at the Hinton Golf Club Ball. The final sum raised for the Mayor's Spitfire Fund has yet to be ascertained, but it is believed that Mr Bigley made a sizeable personal dona-tion, which modesty prevents him from revealing.

'"Modesty prevents him . . . ?" "Shares a joke?" I think the joke's on us,' said Jim bitterly.

Lily lowered the paper, her face dark.

'You don't think . . . you do, don't you? The Spitfire Fund isn't the only donation Barry Bigley's been making.'

'I'd started to wonder,' Jim admitted, 'as there's been nothing in the paper. Robert said Bigley had all sorts of contacts. What's the betting he's got someone like DCI Gregson – and others in the police, maybe – taking nice backhanders.'

'You mean the desk sergeant you spoke to never passed the message on?'

'Who knows? Maybe he did, maybe he didn't. But if he did, Bigley's chum Gregson isn't going to do anything about it, is he?'

'So Bigley's going to get away with it? And he'll go on getting away with it? Oh, Jim!' Lily huffed in frustration. 'But if Bigley's still doing his black marketeering, why isn't he still leaning on Robert Marlow? Robert hasn't been on to you again, bleating for help, has he?'

'I imagine Bigley's police contacts warned him off, told him to cool things round here for a while. Bigley's a chancer. He won't mind, he'll see it as a challenge. He'll just start up some other racket a bit further afield.'

'And there's nothing else we can do?'

'I'm as fed up as you are,' said Jim wearily, 'but let's face it, I didn't want to get involved in the first place and you gave me hell when you found out I had. So – no. There's no more we can do.' Before she could start to argue, he went on, 'And I have heard from Robert, actually. This was waiting for me when I got to the department this morning.'

His jacket was hanging nearby. Reaching for it, he passed her an envelope, addressed in handwriting she didn't recognise. Curious, Lily opened it and took out a thick, formal card with raised copperplate printing.

Sir Douglas and Lady Brimble
request the pleasure of your company
at the marriage of their daughter
Evelyn Mary
to
Mr Robert Cedric Marlow
at St George's Church, Edgbaston,
Birmingham,
on Saturday, 10th July 1943
at 12 noon
and afterwards at
The Grand Hotel, Birmingham

There was an address to which you were supposed to RSVP, whatever that meant, but Lily didn't bother about any of that, because across the top was written in flourishing turquoise ink:

Mr J. Goodridge and Partner

She looked at Jim dumbfounded.

'No! You – we – are invited?'

'Well, I am his cousin,' said Jim importantly. 'And heaven knows Robert owes me a favour.'

'But . . .' Lily weighed the card in her hand, a world away from the flimsy, slightly yellowed card Gladys had shown her, and which her friend was so proud of. 'We're not going to go, are we? I mean, look at the date!'

'I know.' Jim frowned. 'Same day as Gladys and Bill's wedding. It's a tough one, isn't it?'

Lily gaped.

'Jim, you're not serious? You're not going to make me go! I can't let Gladys down – I'm her bridesmaid! I can't—'

Jim burst out laughing.

'Of course I'm not serious! Do you think I want to go to a posh wedding in Birmingham with all those stuffed shirts? I'd probably have to hire a frock coat and everything!'

'And a top hat!' cried Lily, laughing now she knew she was off the hook. 'Now I'm tempted!'

'Well, I'm not!' Jim took the invitation card from her and tucked it away. He unfolded his long legs and pulled her to her feet. 'It's nearly half past, we'd better get back.'

He brushed down the back of her dress while Lily wiggled her feet into her shoes. With a visible shudder, Mr Marlow had had to agree to bare legs for work – the stocking shortage again.

Lily stooped to pick up the paper; she'd pass it on to someone else. Jim held the low door to the stairs open for her and she ducked under the lintel. At the top of the narrow stairs, he gave her a quick kiss.

'I'll decline, then, pleading a previous engagement,' he said. 'And we won't lose out entirely. We can see how the other half lives when we go to the Brimbles' place for the fete.'

Dora had come back from her Red Cross Committee meeting only the other day with the news that Sir Douglas and Lady Brimble had generously offered their garden for the big summer fund-raiser.

'As long as Bigley isn't there,' countered Lily. 'Because if there's a shooting gallery, you might find me chasing him with a rifle!'

It wasn't good news about Barry Bigley, but the BBC's evening bulletin brought some more which pretty much wiped him and his criminal pursuits from Lily's mind.

The wireless had been on all evening – Victor Silvester and his orchestra – her mum's favourite – followed by a variety show. Lily had only been half-listening, lying on the rug flicking through Dora's *Woman's Weekly*, but she sat up with her arms round her knees when the recorded chimes of Big Ben signalled the start of the news.

The newsreader began in his usual measured tones:

'*Tunis has fallen. The Allies, including the British First and Eighth Armies, entered the city earlier today, and the German commander, General Erwin Rommel, and the Italian commander, General*

Giovanni Messe, have surrendered, resulting in some 275,000 prisoners of war.'

He paused before adding with an emotion which even he, the ultimate professional, could not conceal:

'The long struggle for North Africa is over, and it has ended in victory for the Allies.'

Like any news that you've been waiting for, when it came it was a total shock. Dora lost her place in the stitches she was counting; Jim, who was checking Beryl's cash books for her, stopped his totting up.

'I knew we'd do it!' cried Lily, jumping up and hugging Jim, then her mum. 'It's all down to Reg, it must be!'

Dora hugged her daughter back and held her tight, glad that Lily's shoulder hid the tears that were smarting her eyes.

Reg's letters had become even less frequent as the Eighth Army had pressed on, and when they arrived, were weeks out of date. All the last one had talked about was dust and flies and longing for a cold beer, though Reg had added that there'd been a concert party in a lull – in the advance, presumably. A Laurel and Hardy routine he'd done with one of his mates had apparently gone down a (sand)storm.

Dora was grateful for anything, but it wasn't the sort of letter she craved. She wanted to know what her boy was feeling, and how he really was. Had he received those thick socks she'd knitted? (The desert nights were cold, he'd told them.) Did he have enough to eat and drink? (He'd looked thinner, she thought, in the last snap he'd sent.) Did he think of them when he was lying under his truck with his hands over his head as the star shells burst above, and wonder if he'd ever see them again? Or was he too busy simply praying that he wouldn't be the one who copped it this time?

Dora eased Lily off, then stood up and switched off the wireless. Had Reg been in the thick of the fighting? What would come next? The best they could hope for was that somehow he might get a proper letter to them, perhaps with someone invalided home. He'd managed that once before, when he'd gone missing after El Alamein, and it had been such a relief to hear the full story. He'd had a lucky escape that time, but as long as he was out there the worry never went away.

Chapter 10

Mothers had to put their ongoing worries to one side, however, because next day, the whole country was over the moon about the news. As Lily and Jim walked to work, the newsboys were all shouting about it and shopkeepers were hanging tattered bunting. In its usual dignified way, Marlow's put a large portrait photograph of General Montgomery on an easel at the main entrance, with a laurel wreath hung over one corner – and Beryl got in on the act too. She arranged a blue garter, a pearl belt and a red carnation in her window – she didn't miss a trick. But the Allies' victory was especially sweet for her.

Les had been out in North Africa too, till he'd been invalided home with a tropical fever which meant he was medically unfit for the Army. It had taken time to build up his strength, but these days he was fully restored to the cheery, cheeky Les that Beryl had first flirted with, a fact which was proved when Beryl turned up at Lily's that evening with a wedding dress that needed altering.

Before her marriage, Dora had been a machinist at Hinton's corset factory – now making parachute webbing and camouflage nets – and Beryl had quickly snapped her up as her alterations hand. Dresses had to be taken up and down, in and out, according to the various brides' requirements, so she was kept pretty busy. Beryl paid her for the work, of course, so it was a useful boost to the housekeeping.

'This war'll be over by Christmas, you mark my words!' Beryl crowed as she helped to feed the underskirt through Dora's trusty Singer. 'Les is running a book on it! Has he had sixpence off you yet, Lily?'

'A book?' Lily was horrified. Betting was illegal, even at this level: Mr Marlow would have had a blue fit. 'And he's going round the store with it?'

Beryl was having none of it.

'It's only a bit of fun! Blimey, I bet us taking Tunis steamed up Hitler's specs good and proper! I wouldn't like to be in Rommel's jackboots now!'

Dora bent silently over her machine. 'Over by Christmas' was what they'd said about the First War, and look how that had gone on.

Lily watched the needle rise and fall. She could tell what her mother was thinking, and she hadn't missed her mum's blinking away tears at last night's news, either. She knew that winning a battle didn't mean winning the war.

'Almost as important,' she said, to change the subject, 'or more, if you're Gladys . . . you know she's got her invitation cards?'

'Came to tell me specially, didn't she?' was Beryl's reply. 'And informed me exactly how many days I've got left to find you both your dresses! By the way,' she went on, 'you've heard she's changed her mind about the flowers again?'

'What is it now?'

Anything would be an improvement on the apricot roses Gladys had been talking about. They'd have landed Lily in a dress the same colour, and the prospect of a day looking like an anaemic goldfish.

'Sweet peas,' said Beryl grimly.

'That's all right!' Lily was cheered. 'You've got a nice pale blue dress that'd fit me, haven't you? I'd rather not have sugar pink, if it's all the same to you.'

'You won't have to,' said Beryl tartly. 'She fancies you in mauve.'

Lily buried her face in her hands as Dora, with a faint smile, adjusted the slack thread take-up on the machine.

'Don't worry about it,' said Beryl. 'It'll be something else next week.'

When Beryl left to get Bobby to bed, Lily took over as machinist's assistant. As she watched her mother concentrate, she thought how much she loved her and with a pang, how little she ever thought about her, really thought about her, that is.

'Mum . . .' she began.

Dora didn't look up.

'Hm?'

'Don't mind me asking, but . . . this work you do for Beryl. Wedding dresses and that. Doesn't it make you sad?'

Dora lifted her foot from the treadle and looked at her daughter, puzzled.

'Sad? It's the happiest day of your life! Should be.'

'That's what I mean. Doesn't it make you think back? And, well, miss Dad?'

Dora sat back in her chair.

'Only I never ask . . .' Lily blundered on. 'And since I've been with Jim, I've begun to realise . . . well, what a difference it makes. If you ever met anyone, I wouldn't mind, you know, I'd be pleased. You deserve it – to be happy.'

Dora reached out and squeezed her daughter's hand.

'Oh, Lily, you are sweet. But I am happy, love, as long as you children are all safe and well. Yes, life'd be easier if your dad was still here, but I'm used to things how they are. And I've had my chance, haven't I?'

'But you deserve another!' Lily was surprised about

how strongly she felt. 'You're still young, Mum, why not? Why shouldn't you have a life of your own?'

'I do have a life,' smiled Dora. 'I get out, don't I? The WVS and the Red Cross, and my Knitting Circle and to-ing and fro-ing into town with Beryl's alterations?'

'I know you do, but . . .' Lily tailed off. She could hardly say that she meant her mother to have a love life. 'It's all women, isn't it?' she finished lamely.

'Oh I see,' laughed Dora. 'And there's men queuing up to meet a widow with three children, are there? I don't know where – I'm not exactly tripping over them!'

'Well, you never know.'

'I think I do! Now make us a cup of tea, there's a love. I've got to get on with this while there's still some daylight.'

That was typical of her mum, Lily thought, as Dora bent to her sewing again. Always putting duty and the family first. But now they were all grown up, she really should think of herself a bit more.

Left alone, Dora did start to think. She had met a man, actually, back in the autumn, and she had tripped over him, or rather she'd tripped on a broken paving stone. He'd saved her from falling. He'd been a major in the Canadian Army, stationed nearby until his regiment had been transferred down south.

Lily and Jim had no idea when Dora sat down

with the paper of an evening that, as well as any news from North Africa, she was scouring it for mention of the 1st Canadian Infantry and what they were doing, not that she'd ever discovered. Hugh – Hugh Anderson was his name – could be anywhere by now. He'd had a dog, Buddy, a golden cocker spaniel that had stayed behind in Hinton. She wondered how *he* was doing now.

The machine stalled and Dora tutted. The bobbin had run out of thread and she hadn't even noticed. She must pull herself together. She'd only ever met Hugh three times. He'd been charming and gentlemanly and nice to talk to, but now he'd gone from her life and even when he'd been in it, there could never have been anything between them. A man of his rank was well out of her reach.

She must concentrate – she had plenty of other things to think about. Getting this dress done, for one thing, and the Red Cross fete, which was fast approaching. The charity had been given a special allocation of sugar, fat, dried egg and flour, and Dora was baking for the tea tent and the cake stall. Yes, there was plenty to think about without Lily's notion – bless her – of romance!

On Sunday morning, Lily was still in the scullery getting her breakfast when there was a tap on the back door.

'Crikey, Gladys, I've only just got dressed!' Lily

ushered her in and indicated the teapot under its knitted cosy. 'I'll get you a cup.'

'I'm on my way to church,' Gladys explained, 'I can't stop, thanks. But I've got something for you.'

She delved in her bag. Lily took the envelope her friend held out to her, knowing exactly what it was – a wedding invitation – her second in a couple of days. The envelope was the usual Utility stuff, a far cry from the white vellum she'd handled the other day, but the contents meant so much more.

'I can't guess,' she flannelled, opening the flap. 'What can it be?'

She took out the card, as thin and discoloured as she remembered. But at least there were silver bells, and there were ribbons.

On it, Gladys had written in her very best hand-writing:

Miss Gladys Huskins and Mr William Webb invite you to join them on the occasion of their wedding, on Saturday July 10th at 1 p.m. at St Mary's Church, Hinton, and afterwards at the Parish Hall

Then she'd written: *Please reply to:* and her address, even though she must know that everyone she was inviting would accept.

'Hm . . . let me think,' mused Lily. 'Have I got anything else on that day? I'd better check my diary.'

'Oh, stop teasing!' smiled Gladys. Then her face clouded.

Something was wrong – and Lily sensed it was something a bit weightier than apricot roses versus sweet peas.

'What?' she probed. 'What is it?'

'Can I tell you something?' Gladys said slowly. 'And ask you something, too.'

Lily nodded. 'Of course.'

'I wrote the invitations last night,' Gladys began. 'Sat up late. There's one for your mum, and Jim, and my gran, and Les and Beryl, and Sid, of course. And I wrote one to Bill. It might seem a bit funny inviting the groom to his own wedding, but he can pin it up by his bunk. He'll want to do that, won't he?'

Lily nodded, wondering when Gladys would get to the point. Unless that was the point and was all Gladys had wanted to ask. Deciding it must be, she'd opened her mouth to reply when what her friend said next almost made her gasp.

'You're going to think I'm mad,' said Gladys without further preamble. 'But I want to invite Bill's mum. I want to find her.'

'What? I thought you said it was impossible—'

'I know I did, I know.' Gladys shook her head, as if she herself thought she was mad. 'But when I saw the words written down, my name and Bill's, and "wedding", it was like . . . I dunno. Her little boy's all grown up, he's out there in this war, risking his life day and night, God love him, and he's going to get married and she doesn't even know? She doesn't even know he exists, if he's alive or dead? Just think of that!'

Lily thought, but all she could think was—

'How? How are you going to do it? You don't know the first thing about Bill's mum! Where she is, or if she's alive or dead, or anything!'

'That's what I wanted to ask you. You're cleverer than me. You'll think of a way to track her down. Oh, Lily, you will help me find her, won't you?'

'What do you think, Jim?' asked Lily later. He was planting broad beans in the raised beds they'd made in the yard – everyone was still digging for victory. 'Do you think we could?'

'There isn't much to go on, is there?' Jim considered. He was running a trowel through the earth, making tiny trenches for the bean seeds. 'Just that Bill was dumped in a children's home in Stepney. Barnardo's, wasn't it?' Lily nodded, watching the earth part like waves as the point of the trowel sliced through it. 'I suppose you'd have to start there. If it's still there, if it hasn't been bombed, if it still has its records going back twenty years, and if they're prepared to give you the information.'

'Thanks, put us off before we start, why don't you?'

Lily had been daunted at first, and not at all sure it was a good idea, but thinking about it, and always keen on a challenge, she'd got quite excited by the prospect.

'I'm not trying to,' soothed Jim. 'But I don't want Gladys to get her hopes up and be disappointed. Or you, for that matter.'

'Neither do I, but it means so much to her. Apart from her gran, who's not exactly loving, it's not as if she's got any family of her own – that's why it's so important to her. So it's worth a try, surely?'

Jim straightened. He looked at Lily with a not unfamiliar mix of affection, exasperation and patience.

'You really want to do this?'

'Yes – oh, I don't know. All I know is, Gladys does, and I can't let her down.'

'OK. But it's not going to be easy.'

'I know that!'

'You can't just nip off to London and expect to sort it in a day. It could take several trips. You can start at Barnardo's, but you'll probably end up having to go and look at public records. Birth and marriage registers, that kind of thing.'

As usual, Lily, carried away by Gladys's longing and her own willingness to help, hadn't thought of that.

'Yes . . . I suppose you're right.'

Jim said nothing but bent to his seed trench again. He was often right, or not so much right – more the gentle and necessary brake on the careering juggernaut of Lily's enthusiasms. But he knew that set of her mouth: this was one thing she wasn't keen to let go of. He held out his hand for the seed packet, and as she passed it, another look crossed her face.

'On the other hand,' she said, 'we do know someone who lives in London, so if we took some time off, we could stay over and do a couple of days' worth of hunting at a time.'

Jim looked up.

'We could take a Saturday off to start with,' mused Lily. 'He's at work in the week.'

Jim gave her a grin.

'Clever you,' he said. 'Of course. Sid!'

Chapter 11

'Well, Sis, that's a bit of a blinder,' he said when she got hold of him and explained what she and Gladys wanted to do. There was a telephone at Sid's digs, and they spoke as often as they could, Lily from the telephone box by the chip shop.

It wasn't just because Reg was away that Lily had become closer to the brother who was still within reach: she'd always been closer to Sid. They looked alike, tall and blue-eyed with their mop of fair hair, while Reg had their mother's soft brown hair and eyes. But that wasn't all. Reg was quieter and more considered – also like their mother – while Sid and Lily were outgoing and adventurous – a personality inherited from the father Sid could hardly remember and Lily had never known, who'd died when she was a baby. It was Sid who'd let Lily use the go-kart he'd made from an old orange box and a set of pram wheels and had picked her up and been kind rather than cross when she'd flipped it over and bent the frame; Sid who'd taken her scrumping apples from the big houses up on Cavendish Road and had taken all the blame when their mum had found out; and more recently Sid who'd entrusted her with some of his secrets, secrets that no one else knew.

'I know it's a lot to ask, but could we stay with you? Or if not, could you find us, I don't know, a hostel or something? Anything!' she hazarded. 'I know you're at work in the week, and so are we, but if me and Gladys can get a Saturday off together, we could come on the train very early, stay over Saturday night and come home on the Sunday.'

Saturdays off were highly prized by the Marlow's staff.

'I see you've got it all worked out! What a surprise!'

'It's just an idea, Sid. I haven't told Gladys yet. You know what she's like, she'll get all excited.'

'I know exactly what she's like!' She could tell Sid was smiling. 'But look, it's a sweet thought of Gladys's, and, well, Bill's a mate.'

Sid and Bill had trained together before going their different naval ways.

'And you did introduce them in the first place!'

'Oh, blackmail now – nice one!' But she could tell

111

Sid was smiling again down the phone. Lily smiled too. 'Leave it with me. I'll have a think and see what I can come up with.'

Lily didn't say anything to Gladys, not wanting to disappoint her if it came to nothing, though she had every faith Sid would make sure it came to something. And she was right. A few days later, a letter arrived:

Hello Sis,

Looks like you're in luck. My landlady and her daughter are going away the weekend after next. As I'm her favourite lodger – could be my handsome face and sunny outlook, more likely those eggs Mum sent for her last time I'd been home – she says you can use her daughter's room. You'll have to bunk in together, but hope you won't mind that.

Sid went on to say he'd meet them at the station when they knew what train they'd be getting. He also offered to come with them on their quest.

I can't have you two innocents wandering round London Town on your own. What would Mum say?!

Mum, thought Lily, wouldn't say anything, because she had no intention of telling Dora what the plan was. Gladys had begged her not to – she wanted as few people to know as possible, in case they had to admit defeat. But Lily was sure she wouldn't mind Sid, of all people, being in the know. Gladys loved Bill, but she idolised Sid and when she heard what he'd offered to do for them, she welled up.

'You're a true friend, Lily,' she sniffed. 'And Sid . . . well, I can never thank him enough!'

Lily didn't point out that they hadn't even got to London yet, still less found Bill's mother. She'd let Gladys enjoy the moment.

'Another one?' said Peter Simmonds in mock surprise. 'Are you sure? Where are you going to put it?'

'In my tummy,' declared John proudly.

His mother burst out laughing.

'There's your answer,' she said. 'But really, John—'

'Oh, let him,' said Peter, adding quickly, 'if that's all right with you. He's done a lot of running around this afternoon.'

'And catching and throwing,' added John.

Eileen nodded at her son and he helped himself to another rock cake.

The cricket lesson had been a big success.

Her suggestion had been something of an experiment. John did want to learn the game, but she'd also wanted to see how he and Peter got on before she allowed herself to get any more involved: she wouldn't have dreamt of letting any man into her life unless he could accept her son – and even more importantly, that John took to him. She had no such worries now. When they'd met, Peter had shaken John solemnly by the hand and on the way to the park had tactfully let Eileen do most of the talking, only chipping in when invited, respectful of their existing bond.

Once in the park, though, he'd gently taken charge and had proved a natural teacher, starting off with a game of throw and catch. Eileen had seen how in a short time John's concentration and co-ordination had improved, but before he could get bored or tired, Peter changed tack and had him running between the wickets (his jacket and her cardigan laid on the ground) and trying to intercept balls before they rolled over the boundary (the path).

Seated watching with her back against a plane tree, Eileen had felt positively left out. After showing John the correct way to pick up a bat ('Like you would an axe. . . . What do you mean, you've never picked up an axe?' Peter had teased) he'd bowled him a few impossible-to-miss balls before announcing it was time for tea.

'One more thing to remember,' he declared as they both flopped down. 'Cricket teas are a very important part of the game.' Eileen had already set out the flasks of tea and lemonade, some ham sand-wiches and the rock cakes she'd spent the previous evening making. 'And I can tell you, John, this one looks top-notch.'

Later, as they packed away the things, John having run off to look for 'treasures' to add to his collection, Peter turned to Eileen.

'Do you think he enjoyed it?'

'You know he did!' she smiled. 'And knowing him, he won't leave it there. He'll want to practise. Every Sunday, probably.'

'Fine by me,' Peter replied quickly, then, worried he'd shown a bit too much enthusiasm, covered it with: 'Oh, there's something I meant to tell you. It's a work matter.'

Eileen secured the cover over the wicker basket without looking up. She knew what he was doing – steering them back onto neutral ground. Oh, well, one step at a time.

'So what do you think, Miss Collins? Do you accept?' Miss Frobisher asked next day.

Ever since it had become known in the store that Miss Naylor had left 'for personal reasons' there'd been speculation about her job. With profits down because of rationing and lack of stock, Marlow's wasn't keen to engage any more staff, but the last thing Lily had expected was that she'd be asked to cover. She swallowed hard and found her voice.

'If you're sure I'm up to it, Miss Frobisher . . .'

'I wouldn't have suggested it otherwise,' her boss replied crisply. 'You're more than ready for the responsibility at second sales level. And I'll oversee

Schoolwear as well as this department. You won't be totally on your own.'

'Well, in that case,' stuttered Lily, 'thank you! You know I'll do my best.'

'Good, so—'

'There's only one thing,' Lily began. 'When would you like me to start?'

She held her breath. She'd filled in her leave form asking for the following Saturday off for the London jaunt with Gladys: it was in the pocket of her uniform dress for Miss Frobisher to approve. Gladys had already had her form signed: was this unexpected shove up the ranks going to scupper it for Lily?

'Well,' Miss Frobisher reflected, 'I need to have a good look at Schoolwear first, properly assess the stock levels, look at the targets and so on. So perhaps next Monday – a week today?'

Lily's exhaled breath of relief sounded so loud to her she was surprised the windows didn't rattle.

'In that case, Miss Frobisher, could I possibly take leave on the Saturday before? I've got an offer to see my brother in London.'

'London! Quite an expedition!'

'Yes. And it's taken a lot of planning,' she added hopefully.

'I'm sure it has. All right, give me your form. There won't be many Saturdays off once you start your new role!'

* * *

'Well, I'll go to the foot of our stairs!' The expression was one of Dora's favourites, employed when a simple 'Well I never!' just wasn't enough. 'Our Reg a sergeant, Sid with his fancy job at the Admiralty, and now you, running a department!'

'Not quite, Mum! Miss Frobisher's still in charge.'

'Maybe, ordering the stock and that,' pooh-poohed Dora, as if it was nothing. 'But day-to-day, it's you, isn't it, Lily, stood there saying what's what. And with a junior to work under you, as well! That'll rock Sid back on his heels, always swanking about the Wrens he gets running around for him!' Lily smiled at her mother's delighted pride, relieved that her news had distracted her from asking any more questions about the trip to London, and why Gladys was tagging along if the point was to see Sid. Lily had come up with a white lie about Gladys being on the lookout for a fancy corsage like the one Ava Gardner had worn at her wedding, and, as a truthful person, it was a lie which was refusing to lie down quietly.

She closed her eyes briefly in silent prayer. Just let them find Bill's mother. Then all the effort and all the evasions would be worth it.

Chapter 12

Lily had made a few train journeys, including a couple on her own, but Gladys was something of a novice and stood meekly by on Saturday morning while Lily bought the tickets and led her to a third-class carriage. It was the first train out of Hinton and, mercifully, empty. They even managed to get a seat, till Lily gave hers up to an elderly lady with a cat in a basket and Gladys sacrificed hers to a solider in battledress who came hobbling on with sticks.

Sid was waiting for them at the barrier wearing his uniform which, he said, he'd put on to add 'a bit of clout'. He hugged each of the girls in turn, and with Gladys already thanking him, though they hadn't achieved anything yet, took the small overnight bag they were sharing and hustled them out beneath the huge Euston Arch into the bustle of London. He'd worked out the buses; they were going to go straight to Stepney.

Lily had visited Sid in Birmingham and in Liverpool. She was used, she thought, to what Hitler's Blitzkrieg had done and was still doing, but London was something else again and both girls sat silent as the bus passed bombsite after bombsite. Ravaged churches, offices, restaurants and shops near the station gave way to warehouses and factories as the bus wove eastwards via 'Road Closed' signs and craters. Then it was whole streets razed, houses sliced in half and stripped bare but for shreds of wallpaper or a cobweb of curtain flapping at a window frame.

It made them realise just how much their small Midland town had been spared – there'd been frequent warnings, but actual bombs had been relatively few. The bomb before Christmas, everyone agreed, had been a mistake or a misjudgement on the part of the pilot. There was no mistake about the devastation in London; anything and anyone was a target. Lily shivered. She'd been so pleased when she'd learnt Sid wasn't being sent abroad; one brother to worry about was enough. How could she have thought he was safe here?

Not that Sid seemed bothered. He kept up a lively conversation all the way, pointing out such sights as there were. Lily supposed he was used to what he was seeing. There was nothing unusual in his chatting up the conductress either, or the hopeful look in her eye when he said cheerily 'See you on the way back, maybe?' as they got off. He'd looked up Dr Barnardo's home in the telephone directory: they were aiming for Stepney Causeway.

It was a bit of a walk from the bus stop, through a market, over slippery cabbage leaves and rolling potatoes, dodging children playing tag and harassed mothers with their shopping bags, then under a dripping viaduct with a train thundering overhead. Gladys was already trailing behind – convinced she was going to be meeting Bill's mother that same day, she was in her best dress and shoes, which rubbed. Lily had had the good sense to wear her work shoes which she knew she could stand in all day, but she was feeling pretty weary herself thanks to the early start.

They couldn't miss Dr Barnardo's – it occupied almost all of one side of the street and half of the other, with the name etched in the stone pediment across the top. They also couldn't miss the fact that the windows were boarded up and the doors barred with corrugated iron.

'Ah,' said Sid. 'Looks like they've shipped out, moved the kids somewhere safer. Let's see if there's anyone we can ask.'

Sure enough, almost at the corner where the Causeway met a busy road, there was something called a Boys' Hostel – and it was still open. They mounted the steps.

Inside, it was all brown linoleum and a smell of disinfectant, but at least that meant it was clean, Lily supposed. What had she expected, carpets and a vase of flowers? It was a hostel, not a hotel. There was a little cubby hole with a window and a brass bell. Sid made it ping and a middle-aged woman in a neat black dress appeared. She was slightly over made-up and brought with her an overpowering whiff of cigarettes, but her smile was friendly enough.

'Can I help you?'

'Good morning!' Sid said brightly, in his winning way. 'I'm sorry to trouble you, but I wonder if you can. We're looking for some information about a boy who, er, was in your care. His name's William Webb.'

'Now look here,' she said, and the initially refined accent dropped into a broad East End drawl. 'We get a lot of people asking this kind of thing. I can see you ain't police, but who are you exactly? Is it trouble?'

'No, no,' Lily butted in. 'We're his friends.'

'More than friends,' Gladys piped up. 'I'm his fiancée!'

'Congratulations,' the woman replied tartly, folding her arms. 'Well, I can't help you, anyway. I'm only temporary while the matron's in hospital, and all our records is locked away in the basement next door. And that's shut up for the duration, and the kiddies gone to safety.'

Gladys's face fell, but Lily wasn't giving up that easily. This was exactly why she was here.

'Look, you might not remember him, but there must be other people who do – other staff who might?'

'Other staff? You having a laugh? There's me and the cook and a maid of all work, to look after twenty lads all working . . . I say *they're* working! We work our fingers to the bone and not much reward—'

Sid put his hand in his pocket and jingled a few coins.

'I'm sure you do a wonderful job. But these young ladies have come a long way, and it'd be a shame to send them home disappointed, wouldn't it?'

He took his hand out of his pocket and examined a palm full of silver, as if idly counting it.

The woman licked her lips and Lily noticed her yellow-stained fingertips. The only cigarettes in the shops were the dreaded 'Spanish Shawl'. They were advertised as 'perfumed', but Lily had heard smokers say it was to cover up the fact they tasted like stable sweepings. To get hold of Players or Craven A you had to pay black market prices.

'I suppose you could ask Miriam,' said the woman. 'She's been here since the year dot, first the children's home, then here. That's the cook,' she added graciously.

'We'd be very grateful.' Sid laid a couple of coins on the cubby hole's little counter and the woman pocketed them swiftly. She moved to the door at the side of the window and opened it.

'Come through,' she said.

Then she left them squashed together in the cramped office while she went to another door and hollered.

'Miriam! Miriam! People to see you!'

For a long while nothing happened. Behind Gladys's back, Lily raised her eyebrows at Sid. He gave her a sort of waggling thumbs up, thumbs down.

The woman shouted louder.

'MIRIAM!'

'Deaf as a post,' she huffed. 'Got an aid, but she won't wear it. It's a wonder I've got any voice left.' It was certainly hoarse, but Lily had put that down to the smoking. 'Oh, here she comes.'

They heard the heavy tread of feet, then some puffing as Miriam heaved herself up some steps. She was a storybook cook – fat, florid and her face dabbed with flour. She was like a half-risen loaf herself, bulging doughily in her white overall. But it was immaculately clean, and her frizzy grey hair was secured under a net. She looked from one to another.

'I'm sorry to interrupt you at work,' said Sid, speaking loudly and clearly. 'But we're hoping you remember one of the boys. Name of William Webb.'

Miriam shook her head and Gladys gave a cry of disappointment.

'She won't have heard you,' said the other woman.

'Her left ear's the better one.' She moved towards the door. 'I'll leave you to it. Laundry to sort.'

Sid repeated what he'd said into Miriam's good ear, adding,

'He was a Barnardo's boy all his life – he must have spent the last couple of years here in the hostel. He worked the lighters on the river, then the pleasure boats, till he joined up. William Webb. Bill.'

Light broke over Miriam's face.

'Bill?' she said. 'Billy Webb? Blond, well, ginger-blond – strawberry blond they call it now, don't they, since that film! And a face full of freckles! You're friends of his?'

'Yes, we all are.'

'I'm his fiancée!' Gladys was like a stuck record.

'Young Billy? Getting married? Well, blow me down!' Instead, Miriam sat down, squeezing herself into a captain's chair. Her doughy middle bulged between the arms and the seat. 'Joined the Navy, didn't he, bless him, the minute he could, even though he was only seventeen. What's he doing now? I'd love to hear how he's getting on.'

So they explained, enunciating clearly, how Sid and Bill had met in training, how Sid had introduced the happy couple, and all about the forthcoming wedding.

'That's why we're here,' said Gladys urgently. 'I want to find his mum and invite her.'

'Bless me, well, that's a different matter.' Miriam looked doubtful.

'We don't know anything about her,' Gladys added 'Nor does Bill. I suppose – he's always supposed – she wasn't married and had to give him up.'

'Oh, no, duck, you're wrong there,' said Miriam. 'It wasn't like that at all!'

Then she explained.

Bill's mother had been married. Bill's father had had a perfectly good job – 'a porter down the market – Billingsgate – you know, the fish' – but he'd been wounded in the Great War and couldn't go back to heavy work. Like so many maimed ex-servicemen, he was reduced to selling matches on the street and the couple had fallen into poverty. When his father contracted pneumonia and died, Bill's mother had no way of supporting herself, let alone a child.

'That's why she brought him here.' Miriam shook her head. 'Breaking her heart, she was, to leave the little mite, he can't have been much over a year. Now, the manager in them days of the kiddies' home, she was a good sort, not like her you just met.' They all knew who she was talking about. 'Sent her to me for a cup of tea, that's why I remember, and I'd seen her around, up the market and that. She told me she'd be back as soon as she could afford to keep Billy. But we never saw her again.'

Tears had begun to leak from Gladys's eyes halfway through Miriam's story; now they flowed. Lily reached for her hand.

'I'm not crying for me,' sobbed Gladys. 'It doesn't

look like we'll find her, but I'm not crying for me, I'm crying for her! We always thought Bill was abandoned by a mum who didn't love him, or at least didn't care, or couldn't care, for him. But to find . . . to have a baby and love him for over a year, to know everything about him, his favourite toy, what he likes best to eat, to teach him to say mama and dada, watch him take his first steps, and then to have to give him up . . .'

She gulped a noisy sob. Sid nudged Lily and passed her his handkerchief; Lily passed it on to Gladys, who pressed it to her eyes.

'We're not giving up, Glad,' he said. 'It's good news! We know she was *Mrs* Webb; it wasn't her maiden name. So it should be easier to find her.'

It was still a vain hope, but Lily didn't say anything. Twenty years had passed and the disappearing Mrs Webb could be anywhere by now. Even if she'd stayed fairly local, this part of London, near the river and the docks, had been bombed to destruction. Whole neighbourhoods had disappeared overnight and the people who lived there at best evacuated and resettled, at worst, killed. And given that Bill's mother had never come back for him when he was younger, she could have died well before the war anyway.

But Sid had turned back to Miriam and spoke into her good ear.

'I don't suppose you remember where she'd been living? It'd be a start.'

If Miriam thought the same as Lily, she didn't say so.

'She must have been local,' Sid persisted. 'You said you'd seen her around.'

'Well, yes.' Miriam sounded doubtful, as well she might. 'Like I say, they'd come down in the world. A long way down. One room it was, on Steel's Lane.'

'And where's that?' asked Lily.

'Not far, duck. Runs along the back of the Commercial Road. That's where he used to sell his matches and all.'

Sid didn't produce any money this time; they could tell Miriam wouldn't expect it and might even have been offended. She eased herself out of her chair like a cork from a bottle – Lily almost expected a 'pop' – and spoke to Gladys.

'Don't be crying for what's past, love. He wasn't unhappy here – it was all he ever knew, see. But you make sure and give him a happy marriage and happy future, eh?'

Gladys sniffed and flung herself at Miriam.

'Thank you!' she snuffled. 'I will! I will.'

This time it was Sid who raised his eyebrows at Lily, thanking Miriam and hustling them out into the street.

Blinking in the sudden sunlight, Lily asked, 'Steel's Lane next?'

'No,' said Sid. 'You must both be worn out. I know I am, after that lot, the She-Wolf and the Fairy

Godmother!' Sid had always had a habit of giving people nicknames – Bill had been 'Cobby' Webb when he'd first mentioned him to Lily as a possible boyfriend for Gladys. 'Right now, I suggest some dinner!'

Chapter 13

As they were in the East End, Sid said it had to be jellied eels, but when Gladys quailed, found them a pie and mash shop. Everyone agreed they felt a lot better for being outside of something hot and having asked in the pie shop for Steel's Lane, they set off in reasonably high spirits – until they saw it.

It wasn't much more than an alley, with tiny lock-ups and dingy doorways leading to tenement rooms above. Dustbins stank with rubbish and a gutter down the middle ran with water – at least, Lily hoped it was water. She was beginning to think Bill's mother had made the right decision. Putting a child in a Barnardo's home didn't sound ideal, but it had to be more hygienic surroundings for a young child than a filthy hovel here.

Sid told them to wait by a grubby little shop offering electrical repairs while he went to 'make some enquiries'. Gladys was looking about in a mix of fascination and horror. Lily watched Sid go in and out of various tiny establishments – a cobbler's, a tobacconist's, a pawn shop – with their dirty windows and faded lettering. He worked his way all up and down the street. It must have taken him over forty minutes, but when he came back, he was shaking his head.

'No joy,' he said. 'No one remembered her and young Bill. Mind, it was twenty years ago. I got some interesting offers though. I could have had thirty bob for my watch in the pawn shop. Cheek!'

Lily had noticed it: it was new – an oblong gold-coloured face with a brown crocodile strap.

'That's that, then,' said Gladys.

She was over her outburst at Barnardo's and seemed perfectly calm. Perhaps, thought Lily, simply finding out that Bill had been loved and wanted was enough for her, and she was going to take Miriam's advice and look to the future. But she hadn't reckoned on Sid taking the search so much to heart.

'Oh no,' he said, 'We're not leaving it there! I sit at a desk all day, shovelling bits of paper from one side to the other. This is the biggest challenge I've had since I bust my ankle and had to give up my training! Come on, girls!'

He led them back to the Commercial Road and

the pie and mash shop. It was still busy, even though dinnertime was long gone.

At the counter he ordered three cups of tea, and as the man went to the urn, asked casually, 'We're looking for someone that used to live round here – on Steel's Lane. A Mrs Webb. Remember her at all?'

The man, occupied with not scalding himself, shook his head and brought the cups to the counter.

'Can't help you, mate, sorry,' he said, flicking a fly away from an open jar of pickle with a filthy tea towel.

Sid paid for the tea.

'Never mind,' he said brightly. 'Worth a try.'

They took their cups to a shelf fixed in the window at the front of the shop. Gladys went off to find a WC ('No more to drink till I've been – I'm desperate!') and Sid and Lily hitched themselves up on two high stools.

'How much longer are we going to carry on?' she asked. 'We can't go in and out of every shop and café in Stepney.'

'Not like you to fall at the first fence, Lil.' Sid sipped his tea, making a face at the taste. There was no sugar, of course.

'I know, but if Gladys is happy with what we've found out – that Bill's mum did at least love him—'

'Let's give it another hour, eh? If we haven't struck gold by then, we'll call it a day.'

'Only a day?' Lily was aghast. 'You mean we're going to come back tomorrow and try again?'

She looked at the scummy film on top of her tea. She wasn't from a fancy background herself, nor was Gladys – their homes were simple two up, two downs in a terrace, but they were clean and – though she hated the word – respectable. Women whitened their steps and polished their door knockers and washed their nets. Hinton had its less desirable areas but they were nothing like this. Even before the war had battered it and covered it in filth and dust, it must have been grim, and the people depressed and dejected and not even shabby – ragged, almost, some of them. So much for jolly Cockneys in their Pearly Queen outfits having a knees-up round the old joanna. Oh, there were good people in the East End, she was sure, kind people who looked out for each other and helped in time of trouble – people like Miriam – but how she stayed so cheerful in this place was a mystery. Lily felt ashamed as she realised what a sheltered life she'd led. There were slums like this in all big cities; she'd known that, but had never seen them for herself, not close to, and if she never saw Stepney again it would be too soon.

Sid shushed her as Gladys came back and drank down her tea, her eyes fixed glassily on the street. Lily and Sid let her be; she had a lot to think about.

An old man had followed Gladys back in – well, limped in after her on a crutch held under his good arm; the other sleeve hung empty. A threadbare Army cap showed he'd fought in the First War – no medals, but he'd probably had to sell those to stay alive. He was going round the tables begging for coppers for a cup of tea. No one had given him any, but he was coming towards them now and Lily reached for her bag. She could spare a few pennies – he looked as if he could do with a square meal, let alone a cup of tea. She fished threepence out of her purse and gave it to him. He gave her a terrifying grin out of a mouth of broken teeth, touched his forehead and shuffled off out again.

'I thought he wanted a cup of—' she began.

'Straight to the pub, I imagine,' said Sid drily. 'But hang on – stay here!'

'Sid! What are you—?'

Surely he wasn't going to go and demand her money back?

Lily and Gladys craned through the window. Sid caught the old man up easily and touched his arm: she saw them have a conversation, then they went off together out of sight. Lily turned to Gladys and shrugged. What was Sid up to now?

'Elementary, my dear Watsons,' he said smugly when he got back. 'We were so hung up on finding Bill's mum – the elusive Mrs Webb – we'd forgotten about his dad! When we knew all along he was a war veteran who sold matches on this very road! Well, you know how those old pals stick together – one of them would surely remember him!'

'And that old bloke did? Remember him?'

'Yes, or he said he did – but he took me to the bloke who'd taken over Bill's dad's pitch. He'd known them well, remembered Bill being born, and her having to give him up. She had to go looking for work, the idea was to come back for Bill when she'd got enough put by to be able to give him a good home.'

'But where is she now?'

'That he didn't know.'

'Oh Sid! I thought you were going to say—'

'But we can find out easily enough.'

'How?'

'She got a job as a housekeeper to some people called Quartermain. Not round here, "up West", he said.'

'That could be anywhere in London!' objected Lily. 'Everywhere's west of here!'

'Yes, but with a name like Quartermain – that's why he remembered – it's hardly common, is it? All we've got to do is look in the telephone directory!'

'If they're on the telephone.'

'If they can afford a housekeeper, they most likely will be. If not, there's the electoral roll.'

With all this to take in, Gladys seemed in even more of a trance, but Lily felt herself perk up again. Sid had an answer for everything, and 'no' wasn't one of them. She smiled at her brother. She was so glad she'd got him involved.

There were still a lot of ifs and buts. If they were in the telephone directory. If Mrs Webb was still with these Quartermain people. If the Quartermain family were still in London. If the whole household hadn't moved somewhere safer, been bombed out or injured or killed . . .

'Drink up,' said Sid, swilling down the last of his tea. 'We'll go back to my place, a bit of work with the directory, and then I think an early night. The search resumes in the morning!'

Sid's lodgings were in Marylebone, another long journey by several buses, and just as shocking as they wove through the destruction around the miraculously intact St Paul's in the City. Gladys fell asleep, her head against the bus window, but Lily looked eagerly right and left as they passed along Oxford Street, marvelling at the size of Selfridges and thrilled to see Marshall and Snelgrove's, where Miss Frobisher had worked as a buyer.

Sid's lodgings were off Lisson Grove – 'where Eliza Doolittle lived', he'd informed them – and though it wasn't grand or smart, the white stucco peeling and the window frames needing painting, after Stepney it seemed like a palace. Sid let them in through a door with coloured glass panels. There was a Turkey rug in the hall and a vase of flowers on a small polished table; most importantly a telephone fixed to the wall. Lily smiled, happy to see where the calls she made to her brother were received. Sid extracted the L–Z directory from the shelf beneath before leading them up to his room on the top floor.

Again, it wasn't luxurious, but scrupulously clean and tidy – part a conscientious landlady, part Sid's naval training, Lily supposed. There was a single bed with a plain oak headboard, a chest of drawers with a Roberts radio, a small wardrobe, a table and upright chair and near the fireplace an easy chair with wooden arms. On the hearth was a small gas ring with a kettle and on a shelf, propping up some books, tea and coffee tins and a few mugs. Sid explained drinks were allowed, but no cooking.

On the mantelpiece, below a bevelled mirror, were Sid's shaving things, a bottle of pomade, and, Lily was glad to see, a photograph of their mum and a snap of the three children, herself, Sid and Reg the last time they'd all been together, before Reg joined up. Sid grinned at her ('Not forgotten, see!') and went to the window. Lily followed him and saw grey rooftops, chimneys, and below, a soot-blackened yard. Sid lifted the sash and brought in a bottle of milk from the sill.

'All mod cons,' he said, waving it.

He brewed up some tea – rather better than the tea they'd had in Stepney – there was even some sugar, and a whole new bag of biscuits he produced from the top of the wardrobe. When they'd all revived, he opened the telephone directory on the table and Lily and Gladys crowded round as he ran his finger down the 'Q's.

There were four Quartermains listed, but Sid could tell from the addresses that two were too far out to be strictly speaking 'up West'. Of the remaining two, there was one in somewhere called Pimlico, and another in Kensington.

'Perfect,' said Sid. 'Not too far. I'll show you where you're going to lay your heads, we'll have a wash and brush-up, get ourselves a bite to eat and turn in early. Tomorrow – to fresh woods and pastures new!'

Sid went out to fetch them cheese rolls from The Globe, the pub on the corner, and chips from the chip shop which was handily opposite. Gladys yawned throughout their makeshift meal, then took herself straight off to bed, though it was only just past eight o'clock.

'You stay up as long as you like, Lily,' she said. 'The way I feel, a direct hit wouldn't wake me! But shove me over if I'm taking too much room.'

'And I was going to show you a night on the town!' Sid told Lily as he made her some hot milk on the little gas ring. 'But I could see Gladys was whacked.'

Lily gave her brother a wry glance.

'I'm not sure Mum'd approve of the kind of night-life you mean.'

'I meant a show!' said Sid defensively, taking the pan off the heat and pouring the contents carefully into a mug. 'A musical. *Flying Colours*, maybe – I hear Douglas Byng doesn't disappoint, and Binnie Hale's always a treat.'

Lily took the mug he handed her. Sid had insisted she had the armchair; he sat cross-legged on the floor with a bottle of beer. The names meant nothing to her; she was more interested to hear if there was anyone significant in his own life.

Most people would have been fooled by Sid's easy charm. He could get round any woman with a bit of chat and a smile, like the bus conductress on the way to Stepney and even the She-Wolf at Barnardo's. Only Lily knew that that wasn't where his natural inclinations lay. The secret he'd shared with her, and which, with his permission, she'd shared only with Jim, was that her brother's real affections were for men.

Lily had been shattered at first, unable to believe it, but she'd come to see that that was simply the way Sid had been made, and it had never altered her feelings for him. She still loved him for the person he was, and that would never change.

But it was the reason Sid had been so keen to work in London. For all that his tendencies were illegal and dangerous and could have got him thrown out of the Navy and imprisoned with hard labour, Sid could meet others like himself and lead the sort of life he wanted – needed – far more easily there.

She didn't need to frame the question. Sid knew she'd been waiting for them to be alone to find out whether his move to the city had worked out as he'd hoped.

'There is someone, since you didn't ask,' he said, taking a swig of beer.

'Oh, Sid!'

It was what Lily had been desperate to hear. It had been nearly a year since Sid's first love: she felt able to call it that now. Anthony, a pilot in the Fleet Air Arm, had been killed when his plane had been shot down over the North Sea.

'It's early days,' said Sid. 'But . . . well, we get on great. He's bright, funny. Makes me laugh.'

'Oh, Sid, I'm so pleased for you! Is he . . . another serviceman?'

'Yes.'

Lily hesitated. There was so much she wanted to ask. His name. What he looked like. Where they'd met. But all she really needed to know was that Sid was happy – she didn't need to know any more. It didn't stop her being curious, but she was also trying to be discreet. It was Sid's business – but then he volunteered something anyway.

'He gave me this watch, actually. For my birthday.'

The smart, expensive-looking watch that Lily had noticed.

She made a face that said 'impressed'.

'He must think a lot of you.'

139

'I think a lot of him.' Sid took another swig of beer. 'Blimey, no wonder they call this stuff "arms and legs". No body to it at all.'

He was changing the subject; Lily knew him well enough for that, and she conceded. He'd tell her more – if he wanted to – in his own good time.

Chapter 14

When Lily took down the blackout next morning, it was to more May sunshine, and when she and Gladys had washed and dressed they presented themselves at Sid's door, ready for another day of detective work. First though, Sid found some Elastoplast for the blisters Gladys had got from all the walking yesterday. That had them marvelling – none had been seen in Hinton for months.

With Gladys patched up, and after breakfast in a café, they set off. Sid had suggested they try the Kensington address first as it was nearer. It was a pity they couldn't take the Underground, he added, but being Sunday, there were no trains, and after a twenty-minute wait, it didn't look as though there were any buses, either. There was nothing for it but to walk, Gladys gamely saying that she could manage.

Their progress was slow, with lots of stops for Gladys to adjust her plasters, but Lily thought it was probably a good thing. These Quartermain people might be church-goers, so there was no point in getting there too early.

It was after eleven by the time they turned into the street where the Quartermains lived. The houses were similar to the one where Sid lodged, but discreetly different – bigger – four storeys – and smarter, in a curving terrace. Having said that, there'd been a hit on the end of the street, where the corner house had crumbled like a chalk cliff. To stop people plunging down in the blackout, the houses had been allowed to keep their basement railings, but they'd had to sacrifice their wrought-iron porches, leaving only a faint outline of where they'd been. The Quartermains had covered up some of the scarring with pots containing red and white geraniums and blue lobelia.

'Patriotic types, anyway,' Sid observed. 'All set?'

Gladys and Lily nodded and the three of them climbed the steps to the front door. Sid raised the lion's head knocker and let it fall, giving them an encouraging grin.

The door was opened by a maid in a black dress and apron, far too young to be the housekeeper – Bill's mother. Lily suddenly wondered if they should have gone down to the basement, to the servants' entrance, but if Sid was having the same thought, it was too late now.

'Good morning. I'm sorry to trouble you. We're looking for a Mrs Webb. She is, or was, the house-keeper here.'

The maid's eyes widened. She said nothing, but turned as another woman, well dressed in a light summery frock, obviously the lady of the house, came out of a door on the left of the hall.

'What's this?' she said.

'They're asking for Mrs Webb, madam,' replied the maid.

The change was instantaneous.

'That'll be all, thank you, Lizzie,' said the older woman. The maid nodded and disappeared, and the older woman came towards them.

'I can't talk to you here,' she said, looking over her shoulder. 'Come with me.'

Without even putting on a coat, she stepped out of the house and closed the door behind her, then led them across the road to a little garden square. Before the war, it would have been fenced and gated and only residents would have had a key; now the railings and the gate had gone. A tramp was asleep on one of the benches and the grass was unkempt. There was a pagoda-like structure in the centre and the woman led them to it. They all sat down.

'Why are you here?' she asked. 'Who are you?'

Sid explained. He spoke about how fond they all were of Bill, and their search for his mother over the past day and a half. Before Gladys could chip in, he mentioned that she was Bill's fiancée and her hope that Bill and his mother could be reunited by the time of the wedding. The woman listened in silence, her hand at her throat. Lily noticed her rings, a wedding band and a sizeable ruby and diamond engagement ring.

When Sid had finished, there was silence, then she spoke.

'I am Mrs Webb,' she said. 'That is, I was. I came as housekeeper here nearly twenty years ago, that much you know. Mrs Quartermain was already ill – TB. There were no children. She died when I'd been here about two years, and Ernest asked me to marry him six months later. I'm Mrs Quartermain now.'

That was a facer! After all the frustrations the day before, there was Bill's mother right beside them! None of them had expected it to be this easy.

Gladys was staring at her – her future mother-in-law – in amazement mixed with awe. Sid grinned broadly and glanced at Lily.

'That's taken the wind out of our sails!' he exclaimed. He'd explained that he and Bill had met in the Navy. 'I mean – that's wonderful! To have found you!'

Mrs Webb – Mrs Quartermain – looked anguished.

'It's not wonderful at all!' she said. 'You don't understand – I've never told anyone I had a son!

I can't . . . I simply can't . . . Ernest would never accept . . . I know that! He must never know! You have to go!'

'And to think I felt sorry for her!' said Gladys when Mrs Quartermain had gone back in. 'All this time, I thought she must have been torn up inside for having to leave him. I thought she'd be desperate to see him, and over the moon that we'd come!'

They were still in the little pagoda, too stunned to move.

'"I had a son",' Gladys went on. 'That's what she said. Not "I have". She doesn't want to know Bill. Her own son. How can she possibly not? How can she possibly say that without even meeting him?'

Over the top of Gladys's head, Sid caught Lily's eye.

'Look,' he said. 'It was a hell of a shock for her, us turning up out of the blue. Maybe when she's had time to have a think, she'll change her mind.'

'Exactly,' cried Lily. 'She might come round.'

'You saw her,' said Gladys. 'You heard her.' She gestured across the square. 'Look at the life she's got here. She doesn't want to give that up. That's more important to her than her own son. Ask her to the wedding? I hate her! I hate her! I wish we'd never come!'

This wasn't how Lily had seen things working out at all.

'Oh Gladys . . . I'm so sorry,' she said.

Then Sid put his arm round Gladys and she burrowed her face in his shoulder.

There was nothing else they could do. They sat there while Gladys had another cry, then trailed sadly back to Marylebone. The May morning was still bright; this part of London, despite the sandbags and occasional signs of bomb damage, was looking pert and spring-like. The plane trees were in leaf, making wavy patterns on the pavement, and pink blossom drifted down from the cherry trees. Thrushes and blackbirds had already hatched their first broods and were out and about, looking for food for their chicks. People were out and about too, smartly dressed London people, and the smell of their Sunday dinners floated up from basement kitchens. For once, though, even Lily wasn't hungry.

When they got back to Sid's lodgings, Gladys went off to wash her face and Lily flopped down in the armchair.

'What time's your train?' Sid asked.

'Not till ten past six. But I think, if you don't mind, Sid, we might get an earlier one.'

'I think that'd be a good idea,' Sid agreed. 'I mean, we could fill the time, go to a concert, see the sights – the ones that haven't been bombed. But we've got to get there and back and apart from her blisters, well, Gladys is beyond herself, isn't she? She's not going to enjoy anything now.'

'I don't think any of us would. I'm sorry it's ended like this, but I think we may as well get home.'

Sid suggested they take a taxi to the station: they'd done enough walking, he said. He tried to give them the money for the fare, but Gladys insisted she'd pay, and for the new train tickets.

'I made you do this,' she said sadly, 'Both of you. And it's not your fault it hasn't worked out. I was ready not to find her, especially after the setbacks yesterday – but I never expected that when we did, she'd flat refuse to do anything about it. She said we don't understand – well, I don't understand her!'

Sid gave her a hug.

'We often can't understand other people, Glad, and there's not much we can do about it. But there's one thing this doesn't alter and that's how much you love Bill and how much he loves you. Or the fact you're going to have a wonderful wedding and a wonderful married life. Bill's never missed his mother up to now, has he? Never shown any curiosity about her that I know of. So put this weekend away. Put it in a box and don't open it again.'

Lily looked at him and thought again how glad she was she'd got him involved – she'd been groping for the past hour for what she could say to Gladys, but Sid had summed it up perfectly.

They didn't get back much sooner than if they'd taken their original train. The one they caught was shunted into a siding while troop trains passed, then there was a delay at Rugby when the engine broke down and had to be changed. It was well after dark when they finally stepped on to the blacked-out platform in Hinton.

They hadn't talked much on the way; there was no more to be said about Mrs Webb, or Mrs Quartermain as she now was. Lily took her toothbrush from the overnight bag they'd shared; Gladys could bring the rest of her things to work in the morning.

'I'm sorry it didn't work out like we hoped, Gladys,' she said. 'But Sid's right. You've got to look forward now.'

'Oh, I am,' said Gladys. 'I've thought about it all the way home. I'm not giving up.'

'What?'

'I've got her address,' said Gladys defiantly. 'I'm going to invite her to the wedding anyway.'

'Gladys!' Astonished by Gladys's unexpected determination, Lily was also appalled. 'Isn't that a bit risky? I mean, we don't know anything about what goes on behind that front door. From what she said . . . if her husband – this Ernest . . . if he wouldn't – if he *won't* – countenance the idea of her having had a child before, even though she was a widow and it's perfectly respectable, well . . . he might be the sort who – I don't know – opens her post or something!'

'If he does, that's her lookout, isn't it?' said Gladys. Lily had never heard her sound so harsh. 'Never mind leaving Bill in that home all those years while she was living in the lap of luxury, if she'd been a bit more welcoming to us, if she'd even acknowledged she had a son when we gave her the chance . . . but she never even asked about him, beyond what Sid told her! I don't know how she can live with herself!'

She probably won't be able to, thought Lily, if her husband turned out to be the post-opening sort. He might even throw her out.

'I had a photo of Bill to give her, you know,' Gladys went on, more in sorrow than in anger. 'I've only got four myself, and I was going to give her the best, the one of him in his uniform.'

Poor Gladys – Lily's heart went out to her. They'd invested so much effort in this whole enterprise and Gladys had invested so much hope. Lily wasn't at all convinced that sending a wedding invitation was a good idea, in fact, a very bad one, but her only hope was that maybe Gladys would calm down. It had been a very emotional weekend; she was over-wrought. Perhaps she'd see things more clearly in the morning.

Next morning, though, Lily had other things to think about – her first day on Schoolwear. Miss Frobisher, as she'd promised, had had a good look at the depart-ment and found plenty that in her view needed attention. But she had no intention of telling Lily what to do – she was backing her hunch that the new second salesgirl would see for herself what could be done differently – and better.

She left Lily introducing herself to the junior, Minnie, and swept off, saying she'd be back later to see if Lily had any thoughts.

Lily gulped, but one quick look at the oak-and-glass display drawers behind the counter gave her lots to think about straight away. Why was the games kit here, in the centre? Where were the standard school shirts? And why would the ties and caps be where they were and not . . . ?

By mid-morning, with Minnie obediently sorting socks, Lily already had a long list of 'thoughts' to pass to Miss Frobisher, who smiled and nodded approvingly. Just as she'd hoped, Lily had spotted straight away what needed to be done.

Lily had been so keen to get to her new department that she hadn't seen Gladys first thing, but they crossed in the canteen at dinnertime, Gladys leaving as Lily arrived.

'How's it going?' her friend asked at once. 'Are you enjoying it?'

'It's a bit too soon for that!' Lily replied. 'But once I've got used to it, do you know, I think I might!'

'Good.' Gladys sounded warm, friendly, her usual self.

'And how are you?' Lily ventured. 'Do you feel any better about things now you've slept on it?'

'Better?' said Gladys rather tartly, for her. 'It's a

bit too soon for that and all! But I'm sending the invitation if that's what you mean, see if it pricks her conscience.'

'Ah.'

There was a mulishness in Gladys Lily had never seen before.

'I haven't changed my mind and I'm not going to,' Gladys went on. 'I know you don't agree with it, Lily, but I don't always have to do what you say.'

'No, of course you don't,' said Lily quickly. 'Let's not fall out over it, please. I won't say any more. Subject closed. You send it.'

'Thank you,' said Gladys with an air of finality. 'It's my wedding, and I will!'

The difference of opinion over the invitation was soon smoothed over. It was impossible to fall out with Gladys for long, Lily knew, and she also knew she was needed as a sounding board while Gladys burbled on about her latest idea for the flowers – pink roses and white carnations. Lily did her best, but despite her resolve, she was getting very weary of flowers, and so was Beryl.

'I think the dresses are a bit more important!' she said.

Then, one day – triumph!

'I've got them!' she told Lily, who'd called in at the shop after work.

With a conjuror's flourish, Beryl whipped the

sheets off two mannequins to reveal first a bridal gown, and then a bridesmaid's dress in the same style. With a deep scooped neck, a satin bodice, a chiffon over-skirt and a corsage at the waist, it was a tender soft green.

'Like it?'

'Like it?' Lily exclaimed. 'I love it!'

'Green, see!' Beryl beamed. 'She can't argue with that – it'll go with any flowers!'

'Beryl, you're a genius!' Lily touched the skirt. There was more material in it than she'd seen in a dress in her life, never mind since two years of clothes rationing. That was the beauty of second-hand. 'It's beautiful, I can't wait to wear it. And you bought them specially, one for me as well? That must have cost you!'

Beryl shrugged.

'I promised you two you'd knock spots off Evelyn Brimble and I meant it. Now the business is doing better, it was time I had some new stock, anyway.'

Lily held the filmy chiffon skirt to one side and let it fall.

'I'm going to feel like Ginger Rogers! Oh, thank you! I'll wait till Gladys has seen hers and we'll try them on together.'

'Your mum'll have to let out the darts and lift the hem a bit on Glad's, but as long as she wears a decent heel . . . oh, please God, she likes it!'

'She'll have to! Time's ticking on!'

'If she doesn't,' declared Beryl, sheathing Lily's dress in its cover again, 'I don't know what I'll do. Strangulation's looking tempting.'

But murder wasn't necessary. Gladys loved Lily's dress and was ecstatic about her own, Dora slightly less so when she saw the work involved. But she got on with it with her usual good grace.

Chapter 15

There wasn't a cloud in the sky on the day of the Red Cross fete – perfect midsummer weather.

'Just what we need for the wedding!' Gladys exclaimed as she and Lily walked arm-in-arm in the dappled shade up the drive of 'Holmwood' – the Brimbles' house.

'How many days is it now, Gladys?' asked Jim innocently, though Lily knew he knew perfectly well. She aimed a kick at his ankle, but he anticipated it and stepped neatly out of range.

'Sixteen,' replied Gladys breathily. 'And only fifteen till Bill arrives.'

Bill had confirmed the dates using the secret code which he and Gladys, with remarkable ingenuity, had designed. If a letter had a PS, that PS contained a coded message. All the signals courses Bill had done on his way to becoming a Wireless Operator hadn't gone amiss.

Lily understood well enough how her friend must be longing for her big day. Bill had been away at sea for almost a year and Gladys had been so brave and uncomplaining, but the endless wedding plans had almost driven her to distraction. The dresses were ready, the veil and even the flowers finally chosen, the reception menu decided on. There were no balloons to be had, so Gladys had settled for strips of lametta and streamers to decorate the hall. But every time Lily thought that was it, there was something else: Gladys was now on the hunt for a lucky chimney sweep to greet them when they came out of church. Big day or not, and much as she loved her friend, Lily had had it up to here. And there'd still been no reply from Mrs Quartermain, because she knew Gladys would have told her in triumph if there had.

'What shall we do first?' she asked to change the subject. 'Going to win me something on the hoopla, Jim? Or have a go on Test Your Strength?'

'Straight to Splat the Rat,' said Jim decisively. 'I've had enough practice keeping them away from the hens and the veg in your back yard—'

He broke off. The house had come into view. A huge Victorian Gothic pile in terracotta brick, it looked as though the architect had flipped open his book of designs and stuck a pin in every page. There were round windows, pointy windows, carvings, reliefs, curlicues, gables and even a tower with a steepled roof. As they blinked at the sheer excess, a uniformed Red Cross official appeared from a make-shift booth, checked their tickets and waved them round the side.

'Fete that way,' he said.

On the lawn behind the house, between shrubberies and flower beds, the fete was in full swing. Dora had been there all morning helping to set up, but Jim, Lily and Gladys had delayed their arrival, not being bothered about the official opening by the Mayor. Their first commitment was to meet Beryl and Les at half past three for the Bonny Baby contest – naturally, Bobby was going to win, at least in the eyes of his doting parents.

It was everything a proper fete should be. The bunting was up, the stalls were busy, and the band of the Boys' Brigade was tootling away merrily on the wide stone-flagged terrace. Gladys wanted to head for the White Elephant, anticipating choice pickings for her bottom drawer, and Lily wanted to say hello to her mum in the tea tent, so they left Jim examining tomato plants on the plant stall.

'Afternoon!' Jim started in surprise and saw Robert Marlow behind him. 'I was wondering if you'd be here! I don't think you've met Mr Bigley? Of Bigley's the hauliers? Barry, this is Jim Goodridge.'

In flannels and a stripy blazer, Bigley had dressed up to his image of the English gentleman at leisure: all it needed was for the band to break into the Eton Boating Song. But what sprang to Jim's mind was a favourite phrase of Dora's – 'There's no varnish can hide the grain of the wood.'

Grudgingly – what was Robert thinking? – but with no choice, Jim held out his hand. Bigley was the last person he'd expected to see – let alone be introduced to.

'How do you do.'

'Pleased to meet you.' Bigley pumped his hand. 'I gather you're Robert's cousin.'

'That's right,' said Jim cautiously.

He wondered what else Robert had said – surely not that he worked at Marlow's? Lord knew what ideas that might put into Bigley's head. Robert's eyes signalled panic and Jim understood. Robert thought Bigley might resume his campaign and expected Jim to get him out of it if he did. What a hopeless character Robert was, the backbone of an earthworm. But Bigley was all smiles.

'Well, this is very splendid, isn't it?' he beamed. Close to, his face was a mass of red veins, and he gave off a sickening waft of hair tonic which failed to cover up a heavier waft of perspiration – or, thought Jim sourly, the stench of corruption. 'First time I've been in Hinton for a while.' He winked. 'Business interests, you know, they've been taking me away.'

'Oh yes?' asked Jim coolly.

Bigley lowered his voice.

'Robert knows this, and as you're family, I don't mind telling you. I had a few little . . . shall we say "off-ration" interests going. But some joker must have found out and tipped off the police. Luckily, I, um, well, let's say I have contacts.'

He managed to not quite actually tap his nose as he said it. Jim shot a glance at Robert, who frowned and gave a warning shake of his head. Bigley was so carried away with his own importance he didn't notice anyway.

'Let's say I got wind of it,' he went on, 'and I'm all right, the paperwork's gone in the incinerator. They can't pin so much as a parking fine on me, but I thought I'd cool it round here for a while even so.'

'A narrow escape.' Jim was amazed the words could come out through his grinding teeth.

'Did me a favour, really,' smirked Bigley. 'It was small fry in Hinton. There's bigger and better fish elsewhere. You have to have your eye to the main chance these days, don't you, Robert?'

'Indeed,' gulped Robert. 'Talking of which, have you had any tea, Barry? Before the tea tent gets too busy?'

Bigley shot a flashy watch from his sleeve and consulted it.

'Blimey, yes, I said I'd meet the good lady wife five minutes ago! Excuse me, fellas. Good to meet you, Jim.'

Jim smiled thinly and turned to Robert, who was puffing out his cheeks in relief.

'Looks like you've had a lucky escape.'

'I know. My heart did a double back-flip when he showed up – I wasn't sure what he wanted. But if I'm off the hook, it's thanks to you, Jim. I am grateful.'

'I don't want your thanks,' said Jim frostily. 'I'd rather Bigley had been caught. You know why he got away with it, don't you?'

'I think I've worked it out,' said Robert slowly. 'He's invited me to join his lodge.'

'The masonic lodge? Oh, I get it.'

So DCI Gregson and the Golf Club Ball were the least of it. Everyone knew that the police and the masons were as thick as – well, thieves.

'Are you going to join?' Jim asked.

'I'm already in a lodge in Birmingham,' said Robert. 'Through Sir Douglas.'

Of course. He would be.

'Anyway,' said Robert. 'All water under the bridge, eh?'

'It might be for you!'

It was dirty water, in Jim's view, but Robert was right. He had to let it go. With his suspicions confirmed about Bigley being so well in with the police, there was no more he could do.

'I'm sorry you can't come to the wedding, by the way,' Robert went on.

Jim wasn't, but he answered politely.

'Prior engagement, I'm afraid. Another wedding, in fact.'

'There's a lot of it about.' Robert brushed a stray leaf from the sleeve of his linen jacket and gave a sly smile. 'So when are you going to pop the question to your girl, eh?'

'I beg your pardon?'

'Well? You've been together a while, haven't you? Don't you think you'd better get on with it?'

'I don't need lessons in how to run my love life from you, thanks very much!' Jim was incensed. 'Or in anything, come to that!'

Robert looked at him sharply for a moment, then shrugged.

'Suit yourself. But you heard what Barry said – you've got to have your eye to the main chance in this life.'

With a friendly pat on the shoulder, he sauntered off, leaving Jim staring wordlessly after him.

The fete was over. Jim was on ARP duty, so he'd had to leave early, but Lily and Gladys had stayed behind to help wash the tea things because Gladys was keen to 'have a nosey' inside the big house, even if it was only as far as the kitchen and the servants' hall. They were impressive enough – the flagged kitchen with its long scrubbed table and two ranges was as big as the entire ground floor of Lily's modest home. Emboldened, Gladys had managed to get as far as the servants' WC and had reported that even that had a polished pine seat and a porcelain wash-hand basin.

Now they were on the carriage sweep in front of the house, waiting for Dora to collect her cake tins before the trek home. Beryl crunched towards them, struggling over the gravel with Bobby's pushchair. Lily and Gladys rushed to help her: Les, who was a volunteer fireman, had already left with their winnings from the stalls, including two turnips, which had stood in for coconuts on the coconut shy.

But Beryl was fixated on another of the afternoon's events – the Bonny Baby contest.

'Second place! Second! What a blooming cheek!'

Bobby didn't seem bothered, happily chewing on his second-place rosette, but his mother was seething.

'Don't take on, Beryl,' soothed Gladys. 'He was obviously the bonniest there. What does Evelyn Brimble know about babies, for goodness' sake, it was ridiculous asking her to judge.'

'Yes, she was bound to choose the frilliest girl.' Lily poured more balm on Beryl's wounds. 'And if you think about it, Bobby was obviously the bonniest boy.'

This consoled the proud mother, and she conceded.

'That's true, by a mile,' she nodded. 'Not like that poor little mite in the sailor suit bawling his head off.' She removed the rosette from Bobby's clutches and gave him his dummy. 'Lovely dress she had on, mind. Not the winning baby, Evelyn.'

Lily wrinkled her nose. Her thorny side masked, Evelyn had looked the perfect English rose in a wide-brimmed straw hat and a pink halter-necked sundress.

'One way to save on material, I suppose,' she sniffed.

As if in agreement, the second-bonniest baby spat out his dummy and started to grizzle.

'Tired,' said Beryl shortly. 'Give me a hand with his chariot, will you?'

Together Gladys and Lily helped to carry the push-chair to where the tarmacked drive began and, as they turned from waving Beryl and Bobby goodbye, Dora appeared with a clanking bag of cake tins. Lily took it from her and they began walking down the drive.

'You must be exhausted, Mum!'

'I'm fine.'

It was her mum's automatic response: she'd be saying that on her deathbed, Lily often thought. In fact, Dora would probably get off her deathbed to dust down an imaginary cobweb from the corner of the room.

'I don't know how!' objected Gladys, used to the selfish demands of her carping gran. 'You can't have sat down since you got up!'

'Oh but I did,' Dora smiled. 'I had half an hour off to go round the stalls. I sat down to have my fortune told.'

Madame Zuleika, alias Mrs Wimbush, stalwart of the WI and a champion jam-maker, had had a little tent all of her own, and an eager queue of customers all afternoon.

'Did you? Well, go on!' Lily was intrigued by this sudden frivolity on the part of her usually sensible mother. 'Tell me you're going to meet a tall, dark, handsome stranger!'

'That's right, and there'll be pigs flying past a blue moon,' tutted Dora, her usual common sense restored. 'If you really want to know, she said there'd be good news in the post – another circular from the Ministry of Food, more like – oh, and some unexpected news in person. So if you've got anything to tell me, Lily, you'd better spit it out!'

Lily laughed.

'Nothing I can think of! But I'll do my best to come up with something.'

'Don't try too hard,' retorted her mum. 'I know what you're like for getting yourself mixed up in things you shouldn't!'

Yes, thought Lily ruefully, like Robert Marlow's pea-brained schemes that Jim always seemed to get involved in, and that – her mum was right – Lily always seemed to get dragged into as well. The only good news she wanted to hear was that Barry Bigley had been arrested, and she couldn't see that arriving in the post – or the chief constable popping round to announce it in person, not after what Jim had told her about the way the brazen black marketeer had been boasting that very afternoon.

But Gladys nudged her and made a face, mouthing, 'Bill's mum, maybe?' Lily smiled fondly at her friend:

it was no surprise that Gladys would immediately think of that. But Bill's mum or no Bill's mum, and despite all her frustrations with the preparations, Lily was determined to make sure Gladys and Bill had their day to remember.

A day to remember? There was no chance of anyone forgetting – Gladys made sure of that. The day after the fete, she appeared at Lily's with a huge scroll of paper – actually a tattered old sales poster from Marlow's, paper being in short supply. On the reverse, she'd noted everything to be done in the run-up to the wedding – the final feeding of the wedding cake with its tot of rum and its covering with cardboard icing, her gran's home perm, the collection of the flowers, the precise arrival time of the wedding car. There was more, lots more, and day-by-day Gladys ticked things off as they happened. Her gran had to be kitted out, and a navy crepe dress smelling only slightly of mothballs was brought round for Dora to let out under the arms. Gran's straw hat was steamed back into shape, her cracked black patent shoes polished and an ancient fur tippet hung on to the line to air in case of a chilly day. On and on it went: the decoration of the hall, who'd sit where, the number of hoarded hairgrips, Sid's best man duties, the colour of Jim's tie. Something old, something new, something borrowed, something blue. . . .

Dora was endlessly patient ('It's her big day, bless her, and goodness knows she's waited long enough!') but Lily was dizzy with it all and Jim was almost beside himself. He'd taken to volunteering for extra ARP and fire-watching duties to escape Gladys's regular visitations.

'I'm sorry,' he told Lily, 'But if I hear one more word about this wedding—'

'Don't tell me.' Lily reached to smooth down his hair where he always ruffled it up when he was agitated. 'You'll scream.'

'Worse than that,' said Jim. 'I'm not sure I'll be responsible for my actions.'

Bill wired on the Monday before the wedding to say his ship had docked, which removed one worry – at least he was in the country. But to make the most of their time together after the ceremony, he'd arranged his forty-eight-hour pass from the wedding morning, not the night before, something of a risk with the trains so unreliable. Bill, however, had no qualms, as he wired:

SEE YOU AT THE CHURCH! I'LL BE THERE, RAIN, SHINE, HELL OR HIGH WATER!
LOVE YOU

So the bridegroom was confident – but there was still no word from his mother. She didn't feature on Gladys's wedding chart and Gladys didn't mention her or the invitation again. Lily certainly wasn't going to bring up the subject. Maybe she'd simply turn up on the day.

Chapter 16

Finally, finally, the wedding day dawned. The weather had been warm and sunny all week and Lily had been praying it would hold. Along with the trains – and Mrs Quartermain, of course – it was the only thing that was beyond Gladys's control.

Lily crept out of bed and, hardly daring to look, took down the blackout: had she heard rain in the night, or had she imagined it? She had. The dawn was pearly with the promise of real heat before the day was through. Lily opened the window and breathed in the fresh morning air. She knew it was the only moment of calm she'd have before nightfall.

By nine thirty, having 'not slept a wink', Gladys was at Lily's, her usually poker-straight hair softly waved and her make-up done. Gloria, of fashion show fame, had developed a little sideline doing make-up for special occasions. It was another good thing that had come out of the fashion show for Beryl, who took 10 per cent on any bookings she got for Gloria. This time, however, Gloria had given her services for free, in the same way as Beryl, who wasn't, of course, charging Gladys or Lily for their dresses.

'And they say there's no sentiment in business!' Les had said wryly.

Coiffed and made-up as she was – Gloria had even painted her nails – Gladys could do nothing to help, so while she sat in Dora's dressing gown staring dreamily into space, Dora and Lily charged back and forth to the hall with the food, while Jim was detailed to transport the cake, a heavy responsibility – literally, with its rum content. When they'd laid out the hall according to Gladys's meticulous plan, they tore home to get ready, Dora into her claret-coloured dress and fawn jacket, Lily into her soft green bridesmaid's dress. Then she helped Gladys, by now pale under her make-up and visibly trembling, into her dress and veil.

It was a perfect fit. Lily did up the little covered buttons at the back, fixed the veil, and fastened Gladys's rope of imitation pearls. Then she turned her friend to face the mirror. Gladys stared disbelievingly into the glass.

'It doesn't seem real,' she murmured. 'It doesn't look like me.'

'Well, it is, and it does,' Lily said firmly. 'It's here, Gladys, your big day. And you look so beautiful. Bill won't believe his eyes!' Then quickly – 'Ooh, I didn't mean that like it sounded!'

But it was a good thing to have said because suddenly the unreality of it all dissolved. They weren't two people they hardly recognised in their fancy frocks and unaccustomed make-up – Gladys, learning from Gloria, had brushed Lily's eyebrows and added a dab of powder and slick of lipstick. They were back to being the friends they'd always been from Lily's very first day at Marlow's.

'Oh, Lily, thank you!' cried Gladys. 'I'm sorry if I've nearly driven you mad over the wedding – no, I have, I know I have!' she insisted as Lily started to deny it. 'But it means that much to me. I just want it to be perfect – for Bill!'

Lily felt a rush of love for her friend, and everything, the balloons, the chimney sweep, the plate tea placement, the obsession with the tiniest detail, was forgiven. More than that, Lily understood in a flash the fuss over Bill's mother.

'Bill has you now,' she said. 'He won't need anyone or anything else. Ever.'

There was so much that could have gone wrong – Sid's train to be late, or not run, or worse still, Bill's. But when the wedding car with Gladys, Lily and Jim drew up at the church two minutes early – Gladys couldn't wait a second longer – the first person Lily saw outside the church was her brother. All she could do was wave as he gave her a thumbs-up; she had to help Gladys out of the car and arrange her dress and veil while Jim conferred with Les, today's photographer.

Then Sid was there, shaking Jim's hand and trying to hug Lily and Gladys without creasing their frocks. He reassured Gladys that Bill was in the church 'as white as a sheet and shaking like an arboretum'. Bobby, Les added, was chewing happily on a prayer book and Beryl couldn't wait to see 'her' bride. Then Sid scuttled back inside and Lily, Jim and the blushing bride posed by the wych-arch with Les telling them to 'Say cheese!' while the vicar waited tactfully in the porch. When he had greeted them and gone back inside, the three friends stood on the threshold of the church, dim and blessedly cool, its stained glass behind the chicken wire scattering jewels on the rich blue carpet. Jim winked at Lily.

'All set?' he mouthed.

Lily smiled back. Almost two years ago, she'd been Beryl's bridesmaid and Jim had been Les's best man. In his speech, Jim had paid her a compliment which had been, really, the first inkling that he might rather like her. And now here they were again . . .

They heard the first notes of the organ. Gladys was clutching Jim's arm. He gently prised her fingers apart and covered her hand with his own.

'It's going to be fine, Gladys. Relax. It's your big moment. So enjoy it.'

Gladys took his advice – and a deep breath. She turned to look at Lily and gave her a radiant smile. Truly, she did look beautiful.

'Thank you, Lily,' she whispered 'And you, Jim. For everything.'

Jim smiled at Gladys, then at Lily. Lily smiled at Gladys, then at Jim.

The organ crashed into the opening bars of the Bridal March. They were off.

One minute it had seemed as if the wedding day would never come – then suddenly it was not just there, it was nearly over – and it had all gone to plan, right down to the appearance of the chimney sweep as the happy couple left the church. If Gladys could have borrowed a black cat to cross their path as well, she doubtless would have done, but Dora had sewn a scrap of blue ribbon into the hem of her underskirt *and* embroidered a tiny horseshoe, so surely that was luck enough? As if they needed it, anyway, both of them radiating happiness.

When the kisses, handshakes and photographs were over, they'd taken the snaking mossy path to the church hall, Bill and Gladys brushing the dried rose petals she'd spent all summer collecting from their shoulders. Now the famous plate tea had been eaten and enjoyed and it was time for the speeches. Without

171

her parents there, Gladys had told Jim that, grateful as she was that he was giving her away, she'd prefer not to have a stand-in 'father of the bride' speech. So Jim was off the hook and on the beer – or so he threatened, but Lily knew Sid and Bill, more hardened drinkers, would get through most of the limited supply they'd managed to smuggle past the hall's caretaker.

Sid, as best man, got to his feet and chinked his knife on his glass.

'Pray silence for Mr William Webb, the blushing groom!' he announced.

To applause and catcalls, Bill stood up. He produced a sheet of paper from his pocket. He looked down at Gladys, who looked up at him adoringly, then met the eyes of their guests around the long table. He held up the sheet of paper.

'It's all here,' he said. 'Taken me weeks, it has, to write. To tell you the truth, I didn't know where to start. I got most of it out of a book called "How to Make a Wedding Speech" – then all my shipmates started chipping in – not that I could include any of what they wanted me to say!'

'Shame!' That was Sid.

'But do you know what?' Bill went on. 'Now I'm here, I know exactly what I want to say, and I don't need any of it.'

He put the paper down.

'My wife and I—'

He got no further. Everyone started cheering and clapping, and Les wolf-whistling, while Gladys blushed scarlet and hid her face in her hands. When the flurry had died down, Bill resumed, quite composed now.

'My wife and I only met thanks to my mate Sid here. In fact, the first time we met was at another wedding.'

Here he nodded towards Les and Beryl, who nodded in agreement.

'Sid had set me and Gladys up as pen pals,' Bill went on, 'but the minute I set eyes on her I thought to myself "Pen pals! Blow that!" I knew from the first she was the only girl for me, and in – what is it now, Glad? – nearly two years, we've never had a cross word. She's been the best girl and most loving fiancée any bloke could want, with her letters and cards – I can't tell you what they mean when you're away – and I know she's going to be the best wife a man could want as well. Glad, this is for you.' With that, he picked up his knife and began to tap something on his glass.

Gladys looked mystified – they all did – till Sid translated.

'Hah! Morse Code for "I love you"! Blimey, Bill, you great sloppy date!'

Cue deafening cheers, foot-stamping and applause. And, inevitably, tears from Gladys – of joy.

* * *

'It's all gone so fast!' she lamented later.

She and Lily were in the Ladies so that Lily could help her change into her going-away frock. Soon Bill would be able to reveal the surprise he'd booked for their wedding night – the bridal suite, no less, at the White Lion. As he'd remarked to Sid, he hardly wanted to go back to Gladys's, with her gran putting her ear trumpet to the wall. He had no intention of them going down to the hotel dining room that evening either – he'd arranged for sandwiches and a half-bottle of champagne in the room, so, he said, they could just be together. When Sid told her all this, Lily felt a new rush of affection for Bill. He was so thoughtful, just like Jim, just like Sid. He deserved Gladys and she deserved him. He was a husband now, but he was also a son any mother would, or should, have been proud of.

Of Mrs Quartermain there'd been no sign. Lily hadn't really expected it, though she still dreaded that Gladys had. But as she helped her friend out of her wedding dress, Gladys brought the matter up.

'I thought our day wouldn't be complete without Bill's mum,' she said, standing in her slip. 'But I was wrong. We don't need her. Not at all. Not now we're together.'

'Oh, I'm so happy you can see it like that at last,' cried Lily, taking her hands. 'She's the past, Gladys, and you and Bill, you're the future.'

Gladys nodded and stepped into the going-away frock that Lily was holding ready for her.

'That's the way to look at it,' she confirmed. 'All he's got to do is get through this war safe, and we'll be home and dry.'

Then, giggling at what she'd said, given that Bill would be going back to sea, Gladys buttoned her frock while Lily stood by, ready to tidy her hair.

They might have giggled then, but when Bill pulled Lily to one side just before they left, her smile faded.

'Look, Lily,' he began. 'You know I can't say much about what I've been doing, but I can tell you it's no pleasure trip out there. I'm below decks in the wireless room or jammed in the carpenter's cupboard on the coding machine with God knows what going on above, knowing that if we got hit and holed I'd have not a cat's chance of getting out.' It was the first time Lily had ever heard him speak seriously about his life at sea and it sounded grim. Bill glanced towards Gladys, who was saying goodbye to Beryl and Les. 'There's been times when I thought this day'd never come, and thank God it has because if anything does happen to me, well, at least Glad'll get some kind of a pension and' – his voice cracked – 'I know you'd do this anyway, but if I can't look after her, you will, won't you? You and your mum and Jim and Sid? Promise me you will. I'd die happy – well, happier – knowing that.'

'Oh, Bill!'

It was the longest and most serious conversation

they'd ever had – almost the only conversation, he'd been serving away so much – and Lily could have hugged him. In fact, she did.

'I promise we will – we would, I mean. But it's not going to happen because you're going to come through this, and you'll be together for ever, you have to be!'

Bill hugged her back.

'That's the plan!' he confirmed, sounding more robust. 'Let's hope Adolf sees it that way too.'

Gladys arrived then to claim him – they'd been apart for five minutes after all – and off they went in a hail of 'confetti'. They'd used up all the rose petals at the church, but Gladys produced bags of tiny paper circles she'd had the secretaries at Marlow's save from their hole punches. She really had thought of everything.

'Goodbye! Good luck!' they all called after the taxi, as if Gladys and Bill were emigrating when the reality was that Gladys would be back at work on Monday, and Lily would see her then: Bill would have taken the first train back to Portsmouth. The best news, though, was that his ship would be under refit for about two months, so he and Gladys could be together as often as he could get leave.

'Blimey,' said Sid, when they all trooped back inside. 'I could do with a drink!'

In their traditional gesture, Marlow's had given Gladys a Marriage Grant and a bottle of champagne, which must by now have been coming from Mr Marlow's own cellar. They'd cracked it open to have with the cake, but even with Dora having 'just a touch' to leave more for the others, Gladys's gran had scorned warnings about her dyspepsia and had held out her glass for a refill. So, nice as it had been, one bottle hadn't gone very far.

'That'll have to wait, I'm afraid,' Dora told him. 'We've got to leave this hall as we found it!'

'Worse than blooming deck inspection!' Sid muttered, but he and Jim set to, taking down Gladys's decorations and stacking the chairs, while Lily and Dora heaved Gladys's gran, red in the face and burping gently, into another taxi (Gladys's masterplan again).

'Nothing left but for us to go, I suppose,' Dora concluded, when the hall met with her approval.

Sid said his goodbyes. He'd warned them all along that he'd have to get back to London that same night. Lily hoped it might be for a date with the fellow he'd told her about, but the reason, he said, was that he was on duty at 6 a.m. the next morning – there was 'something pretty big' afoot.

'An invasion?' Lily asked.

The papers were always speculating – one week the Allies were planning to land in Normandy, then it was the South of France, then Greece, then Italy. It could have been any or all of them; they were all under Nazi occupation.

'I could tell you,' Sid replied smugly, 'but then I'd have to kill you, wouldn't I?'

Brothers, even when grown up, Lily concluded, had an endless capacity to annoy.

Chapter 17

At home, not knowing quite what to do with themselves, Dora and Lily changed out of their finery. Dora wondered what, if anything, to do about tea.

'It's thrown me out, eating in the middle of the afternoon,' she said. 'My stomach doesn't know what to think.'

Lily didn't know what to think either, or how she felt. Happy for Gladys, of course, but also somehow deflated.

'I expect Jim will want something,' she said, peering in the bread bin. He'd promptly taken off his suit, climbed into his old clothes and was out in the yard, lovingly examining his carrots and beans.

The day's early promise was holding out in a

beautiful sunset. Lily could see it, apricot and amber, as they sat round the table with bread, dripping and the tomatoes that Jim had brought in, still warm from the sun. She wondered if Gladys and Bill were watching the sunset from the bridal suite as they had their sandwiches and champagne, though thinking about Gladys's wedding night gave her a funny feeling.

Beryl had always seemed older and more worldly-wise, from the first time Lily had met her outside the staff entrance on her very first day at Marlow's. But of the three of them, Gladys had always been the innocent, and though older than Lily by six months, had seemed the youngest. Now sweet, simple Gladys was a married woman too, and tonight for the first time she'd undress in front of her husband and slip under the covers with him. When Lily next saw Gladys she'd be a changed person, a woman, experienced in a way Lily wasn't. She glanced at Jim, absorbed in the *Chronicle*'s crossword.

She knew what she felt for him was love. She knew he was fond of her – more than fond. She knew from the way his breathing got faster and he held her closer and tighter when they kissed that the strong physical attraction was there too. But would he ever act on his feelings?

He was chewing his pencil, thinking. He looked up to see her looking at him.

'What?'

'Nothing,' she fibbed.

'OK, so help me with this clue. As we're all feeling a bit soppy today – "Soft melodies for couples". Five letters, second letter "a".' Then as usual, he answered his own question before Lily had had time to think. 'Oh, I get it!' He filled in the squares rapidly. 'Pairs.'

Lily looked blank.

'Airs – that's your melodies, put a "p" in front, as in *piano,* the instruction in music for playing something quietly – soft, you see? And you get "pairs" – that's couples, isn't it?'

She did now he'd explained it. It was easier when you had the crossword in front of you, as she'd complained to Jim many times. But he'd moved on.

'Which means five down is second letter "r" . . . And the clue is "Don't stop, although a person's upset". Two words, five letters and then two. So if upset means an anagram of "person's" . . .' He scribbled the letters randomly on the side of the page. 'Got it! "Press on".'

He entered it on the grid triumphantly.

Well, if that wasn't a message, thought Lily, standing up and stacking the plates. She hoped she and Jim might be a pair permanently, one day. But for now all she could do was press on regardless. Who needed Morse Code?

She took the plates out into the scullery and ran the regulation inch of water into the sink to wash up. But as she sprinkled in the washing soda, she had a sudden thought.

181

Next year – 1944 – would be a leap year. If Jim hadn't made a move by then, well, she could always take matters into her own hands. That'd show him!

All the time they'd been at the table, Dora had been watching them. That they were in love was plain to see. Jim might not show it – not in front of her, anyway, but time and again she'd seen the lovingly indulgent looks he gave her daughter as she elaborated on the nerve of the customer who'd demanded a refund on a baby vest that wasn't even a brand that Marlow's sold or even more so as Lily struggled with the stocking she was darning and stabbed her finger for the twentieth time. As for Lily – well, Dora knew she wasn't the soppy, hearts and flowers type, far from it, but if she was going to give her heart to anyone it would be someone like Jim. He was quieter than she was, not so fierce or outspoken, but he shared the same quick intelligence, the same curiosity about life, the same sense of right and wrong and the same generous heart. Just like Lily, he'd go halfway around the world to help anyone in a fix – like the way he'd helped Beryl with her accounts for the shop. He was responsible and thoughtful too – look how devastated he'd been when the Army had rejected him on account of his eyesight, and how he'd agonised over whether he should move back to his home village to look after his invalid dad when his mum had died. Luckily, Les's mum, Ivy, had been looking for a way to get out of

Hinton and had leapt at the role, taking Les's younger sister, Susan, with her.

Yes, thought Dora, as she shook out the tablecloth in the yard, Lily and Jim were a good match. Funny that her youngest should be the first to be, or at least seem, settled. But maybe it wasn't such a surprise. What chance did Reg have to meet a nice girl, stuck out in the desert? And as for Sid . . .'Oh, you know, still keeping his options open,' was what she said when friends asked if he had a steady girlfriend, as they often did – he was such a good-looking lad. But Dora knew she was fibbing. The real truth, a truth that as his mother she'd always known deep down, was that Sid was not the marrying kind.

'The news is coming on, Mum!'

Lily was calling her from the doorway.

'Coming!'

She quickly folded the cloth and hurried in, seating herself just as the chimes of Big Ben faded and the news began, as always:

'This is the BBC *Home and Forces Programme*. Here is the news and this is Alvar Liddell reading it.'

Mr Liddell took a breath. If they'd known what was coming, the three of them gathered round the wireless in the small back room – in fact, everyone in the country listening on that warm and stuffy night – might have taken a breath as well.

The wireless set hissed and popped. The newsreader's clear tones rose above it.

'*The armed forces of Britain, the United States and Canada have landed on the Mediterranean island of Sicily, the first major landing of British troops on European soil since the fall of Crete two years ago. Initial resistance has been weak against the British with little anti-aircraft fire and no enemy naval intervention.*'

Another breath from the radio set. Silence in the room.

'*Late last night airborne troops in parachutes and gliders – many of whom fought in North Africa – were dropped over the island. American paratroopers were the first to land at 2110 hours. They were followed by British airborne troops two hours later. There is little news about them at present, but all the aircraft carrying them returned to base in North Africa safely.*'

Usually, by now, Dora would have stood up, the mention of North Africa having clutched at her heart, and Jim would have leapt to turn the radiogram off.

When Reg had first been posted out there, Dora had bravely stuck it out through every bulletin, but after a couple of scares about his safety and one chilling telegram from the War Office when he was missing, she could only take so much. Since then, she often needed time before she could face hearing what he might be going through. But when Lily looked at her mother, she was sitting forward, drinking in every word.

The airborne assault, it appeared, had been followed by a huge invasion force – hundreds of ships from North Africa carrying troops, equipment and heavy artillery. The Americans had met some resistance at their landing point, but the British had been luckier at theirs. The Canadians, poor things, had faced choppy seas, but the British, again, had been protected by their designated bay. The troops were now, Mr Liddell assured them, despite some heavy sniping, making steady progress inland.

Finally, and with a sense of reluctance, the bulletin dwindled into domestic news – industrial production figures and hopes for the grain harvest. Interest in the room immediately waned, and Jim reached to turn off the set.

'Sicily!' he mused. 'This is it, then. The push to take back Europe.'

'It explains one thing anyway,' said Lily with grim satisfaction. She liked a reason for things, and if there wasn't one, had a tendency to make up her own, often far more complex than the reality. This time, however, there was no need. 'That was why Sid had to shoot off, like an oily rope on a wet deck, as he put it. And why he and Bill went into such a huddle at the reception.'

Working at the Admiralty, Sid would have known all about the invasion plans. So would Reg, not that they'd heard from him lately – and not that he'd have been able to tell them if they had.

Lily looked at her mother, wondering what to say. Even after a couple of narrow escapes – and those were only the ones they knew about – it was no good trying to pretend that Reg was invincible, protected by some sort of invisible force field. He was in danger every minute of every day, and now that he was no doubt part of an assault force, every second of every minute. She voiced the only thing she dared.

'It sounds good so far though, Mum, doesn't it?'

Dora nodded absently.

She was thinking about Reg, of course. He was with her every waking moment, and often when she was sleeping too. In church that day she'd prayed to God to keep her boy safe – she'd prayed for every mother's son, but Reg first and foremost. But in a separate prayer she'd named someone else, Hugh, the Canadian she'd met, the man that Lily and Jim knew nothing about and could never have suspected.

Not for the first time, she replayed in her head the few chance meetings they'd had from their first encounter at the WVS tea bar to the moment on that broken pavement when she'd lost her footing. Hugh, like a guardian angel, had emerged from a shop and saved her from falling. He'd pulled her up against his uniform tunic and held her there, safe, close, warm, and Dora knew the giddy, fizzing feeling she'd had was nothing to do with the shock of the fall.

But Dora was a sensible woman. Even then, beyond

a wonder that she could feel that way again after her long widowhood, Hugh Anderson might have remained nothing but a fantasy figure, a mirage, and the falling and the being held something she must have imagined. But then, a few weeks later, he'd appeared at the tea bar again – and not by chance. He'd sought her out deliberately – to say goodbye. He was being posted away.

'Down south,' he'd explained, 'and then, who knows where?'

Now, in her own back room among her own familiar things, Dora knew exactly where he was. The broadcast had named the First Canadian Armoured Brigade – Hugh's lot – as part of the invasion force. He'd been on those choppy seas, she was sure. He'd waded ashore at the head of his men, led them up the beach to the shelter of the rocks, and now he, and they, were making their way through . . . here her imagination let her down. What was Sicily like? Sandy scrub? Forest? Ravines? Always assuming he'd survived and would go on surviving. That his tunic hadn't been ripped by a sniper's bullet or by shrapnel . . .

With the smallest of sighs, she stood up. She knew what she had to do. Push down the worry, grit her teeth, pin on a smile, keep calm and carry on.

'Well, this won't knit the baby a new bonnet,' she said. 'Or get the cocoa made.'

'Reg will be OK, Mum.' Lily gripped her hand as

she passed. 'I'm sure he will. I said a prayer for him in church.'

'Me too, love, me too.' Dora squeezed her daughter's hand in return. 'Anyway, we'll know when we know. Nothing we can do about it from here, is there?'

Lily shook her head.

'No,' confirmed Dora. 'So I'd best get that cocoa on and we'll get to bed. It's been a long day.'

Chapter 18

There was no need to buy a Sunday newspaper – a child of five could have written the front-page story. All the headlines were the same, or variations on a theme.

ALLIES INVADE SICILY! shouted one.

INVASION BEGINS! yelled another.

SICILY INVADED stated a more sober paper, more soberly.

But it was the only one. Even Hitler's feared propaganda chief Joseph Goebbels would have had a hard time trying to play down the jubilant mood in Britain. *OPERATION HUSKY A ROARING SUCCESS!* and *FIRST LINE OF AXIS DEFENCES CRUSHED!*

crowed the sub-headings in the noisier papers, while the *Sunday Pictorial* even dared to claim:

HITLER – THE END IS IN SIGHT!

Really? Could they dare to hope?

Maybe they could, thought Lily, poring over the family's tattered atlas with Jim: from Sicily the toe of Italy was within striking distance. And then, and then – if the British and Commonwealth troops and the Aussies and the Kiwis and the Americans and the Canadians could do it, and together they surely could; if they could fight their way up, whatever resistance they met . . . Lily traced the route they might take. Naples, Rome, through or over the Alps . . . then all of Europe would be before them. With the Russians pushing back on the Eastern Front and if, in time, there were other invasions – into Northern France maybe . . . well, yes, maybe they could dare to hope.

After the flatness they'd felt in the immediate aftermath of the wedding, it was exciting but unsettling – too much emotion for one weekend. Jim sensed Lily's mood.

'Come on,' he said, closing the atlas and pulling her to her feet. 'Let's go to the cricket.'

As editor of the *Marlow's Messenger,* the staff newsletter, Jim had to report on matches. Peter Simmonds had appointed himself manager-coach of the football team and captain of the cricket, and always wrote up an account, but Jim thought it wise to attend the occasional match himself. Though Mr Simmonds couldn't fiddle the final scores, Jim didn't trust him to be entirely unbiased. He didn't want to find himself condoning a ball-tampering scandal or some footballing foul which his colleague had conveniently failed to mention.

'Who are we playing?' asked Lily as they walked to the cricket field, which the council had been unable to plough up for allotments because it was protected by some sort of covenant.

'Tatchell's Second XI,' said Jim with a raised eyebrow. 'Let's hope Barry Bigley isn't the umpire.'

By the time they got there, the match had started, but thankfully the umpire was no one they recognised. Jim and Lily found a place on the boundary and Jim put down his jacket so they could sit on the grass. Lily leant against him, the sun on her face but, filtered through a fringe of trees, not in her eyes. Marlow's were batting and, already absorbed in the game, Jim put his arm round her and kissed the top of her head while she scanned the crowd.

A good number of Tatchell's employees from the factory floor had turned out in support ('Probably a condition of work, knowing that place!' scorned Jim) but there was no one Lily recognised from Marlow's, just what she presumed were a few long-suffering wives and a sprinkling of children playing tag behind the sight-screens. Suddenly, though, she sat up and nudged Jim in the ribs.

'What is it? A wasp?'

'No! Look!' On the other side of the pitch, coming across the grass, were Miss Frobisher and a small fair-haired boy in shorts and an Aertex shirt, presumably her son. 'Look who it is!'

'Well, well, well,' said Jim, for once not adding, 'Three holes in the desert', a weak wartime joke that was doing the rounds.

'What's she doing here?'

'What do you think?' Jim teased. 'You were the one who told me Simmonds was sweet on her. Beryl spotted it at the fashion show. And you said they'd been going on their breaks together.'

'Some of the time. And at work is one thing, but coming to the cricket in her own time . . . ?'

'Well, there it is. And there she is. But it's a black mark for you, Lily, so much for your detection skills!'

'I've been stuck in the corner on Schoolwear lately, remember!' Lily retorted. 'You can't see a thing from over there!'

'Can't stick your nose in, you mean!' grinned Jim. 'Now if you don't mind, I'm trying to watch the match.'

Lily wasn't. She watched, fascinated, as Miss Frobisher, in fawn slacks and a crisp pale blue shirt, scanned the field. Her little boy – John – was scampering ahead. Mr Simmonds, next in to bat, was strapping on his pads at the pavilion steps. He must have been waiting for Miss Frobisher to arrive, because he looked up, saw her, and broke into a grin. He waved; Miss Frobisher waved and smiled back and pointed him out to her little boy. He windmilled both arms and started capering about.

'Well!'

Sighing, Jim turned to Lily.

'Not again! Well what?'

'Do you think they're – you know – properly going steady? Courting? I mean, if they don't mind being seen in public . . . do you suppose it's been going on all this time?'

'How would I know? Funnily enough, when Simmonds and I are banged up in that airless hole he calls his office, we're discussing stock levels, not our love lives. Why don't you go and ask her?'

'Don't be daft! As if I could! I don't even know whether to go and say hello.'

'Why ever not?'

'Well . . . it's a bit awkward.'

'Who for? We're all adults.'

Lily still wasn't sure, but Miss Frobisher solved the problem for her.

Her son had attached himself to an older boy and, having spoken to him and presumably told him where she was going, Miss Frobisher walked round the boundary to where Lily and Jim were sitting.

'Good afternoon,' she smiled, as cool as a cucumber kept in an ice house. Jim got politely to his feet and

Lily scrambled to hers. 'I didn't know you were a fan of cricket, Lily.'

'I'm not,' Lily said quickly. 'I came with Jim; he's writing it up for the *Messenger*.'

'Ah. Then perhaps you won't mind missing the next few overs and helping with the teas. The urn takes forever to heat up.'

So this wasn't the first time she'd been to a match! Following her meekly, Lily found herself in the tiny pavilion kitchen, assembling cups and laying out sandwiches according to Miss Frobisher's instructions.

Miss Frobisher didn't say anything about herself and Mr Simmonds – she hardly needed to. But they were a couple all right – it was as plain as – well, as if it had come in a note wrapped round a cricket ball and thrown through a plate-glass window. Lily didn't say anything either, but she felt honoured, as if she'd been entrusted with a secret.

Tea laid out and the urn hissing like a demented cobra, the two of them went out into the sunshine and stood on the steps. The score had crept up.

'Ten to make and the match to win,' murmured Miss Frobisher.

It sounded like a quotation – it was a quotation, but Lily didn't know that. She could see from the scoreboard, though, that Marlow's did indeed need ten runs to crush their rivals. Mr Simmonds was still in to bat, though the other Marlow's player had changed – twice, Miss Frobisher, displaying some

194

arcane knowledge, informed her. Lily screwed up her eyes. The sun was lower now. The other batsman was, she was sure, Gloria's boyfriend, the much-maligned Derek from Shirts and Ties.

'And Peter's made a half-century, look!'

Now Lily did look, it was recorded on the scoreboard. Peter! she thought. Just like that!

Till now, Lily had never quite seen what all the fuss was about with cricket. On the wireless it had always seemed interminable and mindlessly dull, but as this game neared its end, it had her gripped, especially as Miss Frobisher proved an expert commentator.

'There are six balls in each over, and the bowler changes ends after each ball,' she explained. 'Peter's by far the better player – Derek's a decent pace bowler, but no batsman, that's why he's in last – so Peter's got to judge how many runs he can take on each ball, especially with the last ball of the over, to keep Derek in.'

She might as well have been speaking Swahili, but Lily nodded sagely. Miss Frobisher must have been taught all this by Mr Simmonds and she'd actually bothered to take it in! If that wasn't love . . .

As they watched, the runs mounted. Two . . . another two . . . a 'No ball'. Miss Frobisher's hands were clenched, willing her hero on. Finally, a resounding whack from Peter Simmonds – a six! He threw down his bat and punched the air as if he'd won the Ashes. Miss Frobisher ran down the pavilion steps to cheer from the boundary while John, beside himself, had raced across the field and was bouncing around the victorious captain, who picked him up and threw him high in the air.

'Well!' as Beryl would have said, and Lily so recently had.

Well!

When the players came in to tea you could see how comfortable Miss Frobisher and Mr Simmonds were with each other. It showed in so many small ways – she knew that he took his tea without milk and Lily noticed she gave him an extra-large piece of cake. He, too, was chivalrous towards her, shielding her from an over-excited Derek who was unwisely demonstrating his pace-bowling moves in the middle of the crowd. But it showed most of all, Jim said, in the confident and fluid way Peter Simmonds had played – Marlow's very own Douglas Jardine, he was thinking of writing.

On the walk home, Lily was still marvelling.

'I see Sicily's old news,' Jim observed drily, 'and poor Gladys'll be lucky to get a word in tomorrow about her wedding. As for the weekend's other big story . . .'

'What's that?'

'Come on! Who else got married yesterday?' prompted Jim.

It took Lily a moment to think.

'Robert and Evelyn!' she exclaimed. 'I wonder how it went!'

'We'll find out soon enough. It'll be in the *Chronicle,*

won't it?' said Jim scornfully. 'The usual forelock-tugging "local bigwigs marry", with a blurry photograph of the loving couple.'

'You can mock,' warned Lily. 'You'll have to give it a big splash in the *Messenger*.'

'You reckon?' Jim sounded even more scornful. 'I've got much better stories. I shall be breaking the big scandal – "Love Among the Sale Rails" – Eileen Frobisher and Peter Simmonds!'

'Jim!' Lily stopped dead. 'You can't! Don't you dare!'

Jim stopped as well.

'Honestly, sometimes I think I could say I'm actually a secret agent who's going to be dropped into France by hot-air balloon dressed as a gorilla and you'd believe me! I'm teasing. I'm leading on the night watchman's clairvoyant dog, then the tug-of-war between Marlow's and the volunteer firefighters. Then I might have room for a wedding – Gladys and Bill's!'

Another couple were on their way home too, a little boy walking between them. From time to time he tugged on their hands, and they swung his hands back and forth, chanting 'A one . . . a two . . . and a three!' On the three, they swung him up in the air to his great shrieks of glee.

'So what now?' Peter Simmonds asked when John had tired of that and was running ahead, kicking a stone along the pavement.

'Meaning?'

'Meaning that after this afternoon, cats are out of bags and among the pigeons, hares'll be running . . .'

'About us, you mean? Because of Lily Collins being there?'

'Well, yes! It's bad luck really,' he went on, 'one of your own staff turning up. You know the blokes on the team'd never say anything at work – they're not interested.'

'Maybe they should be,' Eileen observed wryly, 'instead of obsessing about their forward strokes and silly mid-off or whatever.'

'What?'

But she was teasing: she smiled and called to her son. 'John! Not too far ahead, please! And slow down, you'll fall!'

'Aren't you concerned about Lily saying something? You know what the salesgirls are like for gossip.'

Eileen stopped walking. He stopped too and turned to face her.

'Two things,' she said patiently. 'First, Lily is the last person to gossip. And secondly, even if she were, our . . . friendship . . . is the worst-kept secret in the store as it is!'

'Do you think so?' He was genuinely amazed. 'But we've been so discreet!'

Eileen could see she'd have to spell it out.

'Peter, let me tell you something, in case you haven't

noticed, which you obviously haven't. Women have a sort of sixth sense about these things.' She took a breath. 'The whole reason the anonymous letters started when they did was because Jennifer Naylor had sensed there could be something between us.'

His face was a picture of disbelief.

'No!'

'Yes! And trust me, so have most of the female staff at Marlow's. I think it's about time we came clean. I'm tired of pretending, aren't you?'

'Well, yes, of course,' he stuttered. 'But given that everyone thinks you're married—'

'I'm sick of that as well!' Eileen burst out. 'Pretending to be married, that is. Look, we – I – don't have to go into details. But I'd like it to be known that I've parted from John's father, I have been for years and that . . . well . . . oh, do you really need me to say it?'

'You don't mind people knowing that we're a couple? In fact you want them to?' He couldn't keep the delight out of his voice, and there was another emotion there too. 'If you knew how long I've wanted to be open about it—'

'Really?'

Now she was the one to be amazed. He was always so restrained.

'Yes! And we're not going to flaunt it at work, are we? But we need to tell Mr Marlow. You know what he's like about "staff liaisons".'

'At least we don't work on the same department – though you are technically my manager,' Eileen reflected.

'I like "technically"! Thanks! But look—' He found he couldn't take the grin off his face. 'I'll ask to see Mr Marlow first thing in the morning.'

'And I'll deal with Lily,' Eileen confirmed. 'Knowing her, she's probably tying herself in knots about seeing us anyway.'

Peter touched her cheek, then bent and kissed her briefly. She glanced towards her little boy. He was happily tapping his stone along with a stick. She slid her arms round Peter's neck.

'And if Mr Marlow huffs and puffs,' she smiled, 'just change the subject to your cricketing triumph. I'm sure you'd like to crow about that – only joking!' she added as he gave her a hurt look. 'You played brilliantly. Even I could see that.'

Chapter 19

Jim and Lily were nearly home. They crunched along the cinder path which ran between the backs of the houses in Brook Street and Mill Street, though it was years since there'd been a brook or a mill anywhere near, then through the back gate with the stiff latch and the hinge that had gone back to squeaking since there was no oil to be spared. The back door stood open, and from the kitchen, Lily could hear women's voices.

'Mum's got a visitor,' she tutted. 'I hope it's not Jean Crosbie.'

Their next-door neighbour was a waspish woman with a fussy husband and an adenoidal son, but they had to tolerate her because the Anderson shelter was in the Crosbies' yard, and they shared it. But as they got nearer, Lily realised it wasn't a voice she recognised – it wasn't a local accent and it was a young voice, too.

She pushed the door open further and went in.

Dora was sitting at the table, and a young woman was washing up some teacups. Lily gaped. Was her mother ill? Washing up had always been expected of her children, and Jim as well, but a visitor?

The young woman turned when she heard the door scrape open – that needed fixing too. She pushed a lock of dark hair out of her eyes with a damp wrist.

'You must be Lily!' she smiled. 'I'm so glad I haven't missed you! I can't shake hands – look at me, making myself at home! I'm Gwenda.'

'Our Reg's fiancée,' said Dora, as if that explained everything.

Yet more tea was made, not for Gwenda – ('I'm practically afloat!') but for Lily and Jim, who were agog.

Excitedly, talking over one another – Lily had hardly ever seen her mother so animated – Gwenda and Dora explained between them. Gwenda, apparently, was a driver with the Mechanised Transport Corps based in Alexandria and she'd been sent back to England to collect a customised Daimler with a special long-range radio installed. She'd only arrived on Friday, had been given the weekend to see her family and was on her way back to an air base to fly off with the car the next day.

As she talked about life in Egypt, a whole world opened up before Lily. She knew there were women bus and tram drivers in Hinton, and all over the country. She knew about the women of the MTC who drove Government officials and visiting foreign dignitaries. She knew they drove ambulances too, but she'd never thought about them working abroad. She gazed at Gwenda in awe.

'Of course,' Gwenda was saying in her slightly sing-song accent, 'my dad having the garage business, he taught me to drive – me and my sister – on the lanes and the fields by us from when we were about twelve. So when the war came – well, there was only one choice for me.'

'Her sister's out there as well,' Dora put in. 'Not a driver though. She's a plotter with the WAAF.'

'That's my twin, Bethan,' supplied Gwenda.

Bethan . . .

'Where's your home?' Jim was intrigued for a different reason: he'd been trying to place the accent. His family home was in Worcestershire, but it was north of that, he sensed. 'There's Welsh in there somewhere. Shropshire? Border country? But which side of the border?'

Gwenda clapped her hands and her dark eyes danced. Lily had never seen so much energy in such a small package.

'Very good! Just over the border – Welshpool!' she said. 'My mam's Welsh and I speak it with her.'

Dora beamed.

'Typical of our Reg, isn't it, Lily, to keep it to himself? They've been courting since Christmas! Met at a dance!'

'It's only recently we got engaged,' Gwenda leapt to her fiancé's defence. Lily liked her instantly. 'And we haven't been able to see that much of each other. Oh!' She checked herself. 'I should put my ring back on. I took it off for the washing up.'

She reached in her pocket and brought out a ring – an emerald surrounded by tiny petal-shaped diamonds.

'He had it made,' she said proudly, holding in out to Lily. 'Designed it himself and had it made in the souk. Took me out for dinner by the Nile and proposed under the stars.'

Lily was glad she was sitting down. Quiet, modest, unassuming Reg? Either the desert sun had turned his head or he had hidden depths which the murkier light of Hinton had never revealed.

'So what . . . what happens now?' she stuttered, as Gwenda eased the ring back on her finger. 'Can you make any plans? Where is Reg, for a start? Is he part of the—'

She didn't want to say the word so Jim finished the sentence for her by asking:

'Is he in Sicily?'

'No! That's the other thing!' Dora answered for her future daughter-in-law. 'Gwenda's brought a long letter from him, but she's told me anyway. He's stayed behind! In North Africa!'

'What?'

'Which means we can still see each other – well, in theory,' said Gwenda. 'But he'll be safe where he is, that's all that matters.'

'He's there for the duration,' confirmed Dora. Relief had smoothed four years' worth of wartime worry from her face. 'He's been assigned to help in the rebuilding of Libya. The fighting's moved on, but he's staying put!'

'Oh Mum! Oh Jim!'

Lily didn't know which way to turn, and Gwenda looked on smiling as she hugged each of them, one after the other.

'And Gwenda – oh!' For good measure Lily hugged her too. 'Thank you for coming! Thank you for telling us! And congratulations! Welcome to the family!'

Gwenda left soon after, resolutely cheerful about having to rely on the trains. ('No petrol rationing where I am. I've been spoilt rotten!') She promised to keep in touch ('I know what Reg is like with his letters – not very good!') and left them admiring the presents Reg had sent them – a filigree bracelet studded with tiny stones for Lily, while Dora had a pendant with the head of an Egyptian Queen, and

Jim a pair of olive wood bookends in the shape of the Pyramids.

Lily read, then re-read, the letter from Reg. They couldn't complain about that one – it was a full four pages. He told them again what Gwenda had told them, but also that they had 'a hell of a job on' as Libya was in ruins and he could see it taking to the end of the war and beyond. In the meantime, he said, he wanted them to stay well, and hoped against hope they took to Gwenda.

I hope you'll all like her, he wrote. *And come to love her* – Reg, quiet, undemonstrative Reg openly admitting it! – *as much as I do.*

'Well, they've got enough in common,' said Jim. They were finally having their tea – Dora had eked out the end of the Government Cheddar with a dab of mustard and top of the milk and toasted the result. 'Imagine their pillow talk. Oil leaks. Kinks in fuel pipes. Carburettors. It's a match made in heaven.'

But Lily's mind was running on.

'Reg'll move up there, won't he?' she ventured. 'To Welshpool. It stands to reason. He'll work for her father – maybe her dad will even take him into the business.'

She wondered how her mother would take it – Reg had always been such a homebody – or so they'd thought. But Dora seemed remarkably easy about it: Gwenda's good humour must be catching.

'After Africa, Shropshire isn't so very far away,'

she said. 'And I'll tell you another thing. That Mrs Wimbush – Madame Zuleika – wasn't so far off with her predictions. Good news in a letter and in person!'

Lily frowned.

'It's two out of three, but I'm still waiting for your tall, dark, handsome stranger!'

Dora gave a tiny smile. Hugh had had sandy hair and blue eyes, and he was gone for good.

'Gwenda's small, dark and pretty,' she said. 'I'll settle for that.'

'What a weekend!' Lily said to Jim as they took the crocks out. 'Romance in the air or what?'

Jim gave a theatrical sniff.

'I don't think so. Just the slop pail,' he said. 'I'll take it down to the pig bin in a minute.'

He saw Lily's mouth compress into a line and smiled to himself. If her dropped hints got any heavier, they'd dent the kitchen floor. They were heading towards something permanent themselves, he knew that – they both knew it, surely? – but they were still young. All in good time.

Lily clattered the plates into the sink and ran the water. It bounced up off a spoon in a vicious jet and she stepped back, irritated. Blow leap year, she thought. If Jim persisted in being so deliberately obtuse . . . well, Gwenda had given her another idea. She didn't kid herself she could learn to drive and join the MTC, let alone be sent abroad, and she was

207

still a year or so off conscription anyway. But she could always volunteer . . . What about the ATS?

They were still recruiting – there was no use pretending that the war was going to end that quickly. Yes, the invasion of Sicily seemed to be going well, but it had only been forty-eight hours, and there'd been false dawns before. Hitler was going to fight to the death – his own and that of thousands, maybe millions of others, everyone realised that now. And much as Lily loved her job at Marlow's, much as she loved Jim, she wasn't going to hang around. Marriage wasn't the be-all and end-all, whatever Gladys or Evelyn Brimble or even Gwenda might think. Time waits for no man, not even Jim Goodridge, Lily thought, as she turned off the tap with a fiercer twist than it needed.

Her own romantic life paled further into insignificance when Lily saw Gladys next day. Her friend practically floated into the staff cloakroom, a dazed and dreamy smile on her face. Lily could see that the weekend's other excitements would have to wait. Mr Churchill might have talked about the country's finest hour after the Battle of Britain but this was Gladys's, and she deserved to savour every minute.

'Shall we both try to get on early dinner?' Gladys breathed. 'I've got so much to tell you, Lily, about Saturday night and Sunday!'

Lily smiled and nodded, hoping Gladys would draw

more of a veil over proceedings than Beryl had in describing her honeymoon. But that was Beryl for you. Gladys would surely be more discreet.

And talking of discreet . . . Lily still hadn't decided how to broach yesterday's encounter with Miss Frobisher at the cricket. Was it up to her to say anything?

She needn't have worried. Within half an hour of the store's opening, Miss Frobisher breezed over to Schoolwear, where Lily was organising a drawerful of gym knickers in size order.

'Good game yesterday, wasn't it?' she said easily. Then she gave a faint frown. 'Sorry, that should be "match". Mr Simmonds would soon be picking me up on that!'

He had reverted to being Mr Simmonds, of course, in the store. Lily had expected that much. But she hadn't expected what Miss Frobisher said next.

'In case you're wondering, Lily, you needn't feel compromised. You won't have to treat anything you saw as a secret. Mr Simmonds and I have been seeing each other for a while, and it'll soon be common knowledge. As will the fact that I'm perfectly free to conduct a relationship because I no longer see anything of my son's father and I haven't for years. To all events and purposes, he doesn't exist.'

Lily gulped. Whatever she'd expected, it hadn't been an out-and-out confession.

'I'm sorry. Have I embarrassed you?' Miss Frobisher

smiled. 'But as you're the only witness . . . with Mr Goodridge of course, but, well—' She raised a shapely eyebrow. 'Men! I doubt he even noticed. I don't think any of the cricket team have.'

Lily refrained from repeating Jim's joke about putting the story in the staff newsletter.

She wasn't sure what to say next. A simple 'thank you for telling me' would have done, but relief at having the issue taken out of her hands and the affection she felt for her boss won.

'Thank you,' she managed in her usual voice, before her beaming smile got in the way, 'for telling me. And I'm . . . I'm very happy for you!'

'How did the happy couple get on after they left us?' Dora asked when Lily got home from work that night. 'Gladys has still got her head in the clouds, I dare say.'

Lily's entire dinner hour had been taken up watching Gladys draw her fork back and forth through her mash, inscribing the letter 'B', and arranging her peas in a heart shape as she eulogised about her wedding night.

'Not the clouds,' she grinned. 'Gladys is somewhere in outer space. Another galaxy, maybe. Poor Mr Bunting – we're supposed to be getting ready for the sale but in the end he had to take the red pen off her and mark down the dominoes himself.'

She added that Gladys couldn't be happier, that

Bill had got safely back to Portsmouth, and that the new bride was going to go down and see him as much as she could over the summer.

'Well, that's nice,' said Dora.

'Yes,' agreed Lily.

She glanced out of the window at Jim, who was earthing up the potatoes. She looked at his long back with its untucked shirt, at the way the late sun touched his hair and brought out the chestnut in it, at his hands in the warm soil, hands which gave her little electric shocks when they ventured into her blouse or pressed her against him. She wondered if they'd ever have a wedding night that she could tell Gladys about – discreetly. The way things stood, she couldn't be sure. At least she had more than one idea about how to move on. If there was one thing better than having a plan, it was having two.

'By the way,' her mother went on, 'I shan't be here tomorrow when you get in. I've had to swap my shift at the tea bar to help Mrs Venables out. Her daughter's baby's come early . . . Lily, are you listening? You'll have to do your own tea tomorrow. Or get your Jim to take you out!'

My Jim, thought Lily. Is he? Time, she supposed, would tell. Depending how much time she gave him.

Chapter 20

There was one snag with the swapped shift, and Dora had realised it from the start. She'd be trapped at the tea bar with Jean Crosbie, a sitting duck for her neighbour's endless diatribes.

'I said to him, I said, "Who do you think you're fooling?" Can you believe it, Dora, thinking he could get that past me, using sugar paper to weigh out my butter ration, when we all know it weighs heavier than greaseproof! I said to him, I said, "If you think I'm bringing my custom here in future, Bert Dodds, you've got another think coming!" I mean, you'd think he'd be grateful, I've been with him since rationing first came in—'

'Where are you going to go instead?' Dora managed to slip in a quick question as Jean drew breath.

'I shall go up Fishwick's, on the Tipton Road,' declared Jean. 'They've got a better selection anyway. I wish I'd gone there from the off, but I thought I ought to support the corner shop. What a fool! Cling peaches, I heard Fishwick's had the other week.'

'I see.'

'You go to Baxter's, though, don't you?' Jean named another grocer nearby. 'What do you reckon to them, 'cos you're choosy about your provisions, I know – oh, look at that!' Jean was off on another tack. 'Nasty stray! Go on, get off with you!' A dog had appeared and was sniffing round a curling sandwich crust on the ground. Jean leant over the counter-flap and banged a spoon on a tin plate. 'Go on! Shoo!'

'Just a minute, Jean, don't!' Dora touched her shoulder.

'What's up with you?' Jean shook her off. 'Probably full of fleas! Putting the customers off! Shoo! Shoo!'

'No, no stop it, please!' Dora insisted. 'I don't think that dog's a stray.'

Jean stopped the plate-banging – if anything would put customers off, it was that – and wheeled round to look at her.

'He's got no collar on,' she said accusingly.

'No, but he looks pretty well fed. And – well, I think I might know him.'

'Know him? How? I didn't know you were a dog-lover, Dora Collins!'

'I'm not especially, but . . .'

Dora moved to the door of the van and went down the steps. Crouching down, she curled her fingers and held them out to the dog.

'It's you, isn't it,' she said softly. 'It's you, Buddy. You've come back.'

It was just after four when the bus dropped Dora – and Buddy – in Nettleford village. The journey had only taken half an hour once she'd found out which bus to get, but to Dora, never a great traveller, it might as well have been a camel train to Samarkand. She'd never been out this way before: she rarely strayed from the web of streets around her home in Hinton. The countryside was as alien to her as if she'd tracked what was left of Hugh's former company not to its base in the heart of England, but to the wilds of Canada itself.

Standing uncertainly on a small triangle of green, she glanced around. The village was hardly picture-postcard pretty – too far north for half timbering and hollyhocks, and the main road ran straight through it. Instead there was a row of red-brick workmen's cottages and a couple of shuttered shops, casualties of a wartime drop-off in trade. But the post office and general store looked to be open: Dora made for it to ask directions. Buddy, on the length of string she'd slipped round his neck, trotted meekly after her.

The postmaster was serving someone to War Savings stamps, but his wife bustled out from behind the shop counter to point the visitor on her way.

'It's quite a walk,' she warned her. 'Turn left at the church, down Tanners Lane, bear right where the road forks, then straight on at the crossroads – there's no signposts of course – half a mile on your right you'll see the gates to Nettleford Manor – well, there's a barrier now, and a sentry box, for the base.'

'Thank you,' said Dora, tugging Buddy away from the vegetable display he was sniffing with worrying intent. 'I'd better get going.'

For the first time since the start of the war, she didn't even think of the shoe leather she'd be wearing out. It was a fine afternoon, a cheeky sun playing hide and seek with the clouds, and Dora was buoyed by a sense of adventure. There was something about Hugh and the memory of him, not to mention having his dog beside her, that made her feel brave and bold and quite unlike her usual self. She wasn't entirely sure what she'd say to explain herself when she got to the base. All Hugh had told her was that his batman – unnamed – who was remaining behind had agreed to take care of Buddy. And not always very good care, judging by how things had ended up!

But she'd deal with that when she got there. For the moment, Dora was just amused when she thought of the look on Jean Crosbie's face when she'd bundled her WVS overall into her bag and announced that she was off.

'Mrs Greene and Miss Turner'll be here for the evening rush and I'm sure you can cope on your own till then,' she'd said airily. 'I've done it often enough, and I dare say you have too. I'll make up the time another day, but I've got to get this dog back where he belongs.'

Now, as she set out smartly along the dusty lanes, the novelty of her situation struck her once more. No pavement here, broken or otherwise, no sandbags in front of shops, no torn posters or wire-covered windows, just cow parsley foaming in the ditches and a huge, open sky. Over the unkempt hedges, cows and sheep grazed together and beyond them, fields of corn were on the turn from green to gold. She had time to take it in because Buddy slowed her down, his nose vacuuming along the verge, pulling up sharply every time he found a particularly interesting scent. After close examination of an enticing bramble, he lifted his leg, and Dora heard the throaty rumble of an approaching vehicle. She stepped up onto the verge, tugging Buddy closer to her as a tractor lumbered past with its load of hay. It was as if all the Food Flashes and Government leaflets and Ministry of Information films had come to life and leapt into colour in front of her: there was a whole other world out here.

Dragging a reluctant Buddy away, she set off again,

only to hear another engine behind, a lighter one this time. There was a gateway ahead; she hurried towards it for sanctuary and waited to see what it would be this time. A van with a pig in the back? A few crates of chickens? A rattling milk churn? No – round the corner came an Army jeep – a Canadian Army jeep, with a number stencilled on the side and a maple leaf on the bonnet. It passed her, slowed, then stopped and backed up beside her. Buddy set up a frantic volley of barks.

'Excuse me, ma'am?' The driver – a corporal from his stripes – leant across the passenger seat. 'That dog you have there . . . he looks very like . . . is he yours?'

'No,' Dora said. 'Actually, he's one of yours.'

'It's Buddy, then? I don't believe it!'

He switched off the engine, scrambled out and came round his vehicle. He wasn't very tall, but spare and wiry, with brown hair turning grey in a widow's peak over a thin, mobile face. Buddy danced on the end of his string as the man crouched down in front of him, then leapt up, put his paws on his shoulders and licked his face all over.

'It's Buddy!' he repeated.

'It is,' confirmed Dora. 'And pleased to see you, by the look of it!'

'Not as pleased as I am to see him! I've been hunting all over town! I don't know how I'd have explained to the major—' He broke off and stood up. 'But where . . . how did you come to find him? How did you know who he was? And get to bring him out here? I lost him in Hinton.'

'I know you did,' said Dora. She couldn't quite believe she was having this conversation with a complete stranger in the middle of an English country lane. There was something about these Canadians and meeting them in unlikely places. 'And I didn't find him. He found me.'

A quarter of an hour later, things became even more unlikely. Feeling rather like Alice in Wonderland when she fell down the rabbit hole, although in her case she'd been whizzed there in the jeep, Dora found herself being offered a cup of tea in what had once been the library of an English stately home. As her new acquaintance summoned a private and asked him to take Buddy, who was tied up outside, to his kennel, she looked around. The former library had become the Sergeants' and Corporals' Mess – there'd been a sign on the door. The books and the stately furniture had been removed and replaced with functional chairs and tables. Now there were board games on the shelves, and packs of cards and copies of something called *The Bugle*, which she took to be the Canadian forces' newspaper. Most pleasing to her eye, though, was a trolley with an urn of hot water and cups on it.

The private dispatched on his task, Sam – he'd given his name as Sam Cassidy – came over to her.

'Would you like a cup of tea? There's coffee as well' – it was 'carfee', the way he pronounced it – 'but I guess . . .' He grinned. 'I know you British and your tea.'

Dora gave him a smile.

'A cup of tea would be very welcome,' she confirmed.

She watched him as he set to with cups and a milk jug and wondered what he was doing in the Army. Now she'd seen him close to, there were quite a few threads of grey in his hair. She guessed he was around her age, so just about on the limit for the draft. A regular soldier, maybe? Or simply a good citizen determined to do his bit?

He approached with her cup and saucer – and a sugar bowl.

It was a long time since Dora had allowed herself more than a few grains of sugar in her tea, and now she watched a full spoonful fall into her cup with something like reverence. She stirred and drank. It was delicious.

Sam, sipping his coffee, was watching her.

'So . . . tell me all about it. How you met Buddy and the major,' he began.

Conversation in the jeep had been limited; with the top down, Dora had been too busy holding on to Buddy with one hand and her hat with the other.

Now she explained – in a somewhat edited version – how she'd encountered Hugh Anderson and his dog.

'Seems Buddy's got a knack for introductions,' Sam observed. 'Doing his bit for Anglo-Canadian relations. Maybe a dog should be standard issue to each platoon.'

Dora couldn't help smiling. It was the way 'dog' sounded like 'daag' and 'platoon' became 'pladoon' and the way everything he said lifted slightly at the end of the sentence, as if it were a question even when it wasn't.

'Good idea. If they didn't all have Buddy's knack for getting into mischief.' She knew, because Hugh had told her, that Buddy had disgraced himself by chewing an Army blanket, and she could have bet that was the least of it. 'But how did you come to lose him?'

Sam gave a sigh.

'I had a couple of hours to myself, and a few errands to run in town. I took him with me, tied him to a lamppost. I wasn't away more than ten minutes, I come out of the store and he's gone. Some boys told me he'd seen a pigeon, slipped his collar and – vamoosh!' Sam grinned. 'But he must have caught that pigeon's homing instinct to have found you at your tea bar again.'

'Ah, but they're gun dogs, aren't they, spaniels?' said Dora. When she'd first encountered Buddy she'd casually asked Jim who, being a country boy, knew these things, what spaniels were known for. 'Retrievers. And he retrieved perhaps the only other person he knew in Hinton.'

'Even so, clever of him to remember you. And where to find you.'

Dora blushed. In her account, she'd implied that she'd only met Hugh and Buddy once.

A silence fell. A couple of soldiers looked in, saw Dora there, and hurriedly went out again.

'Nothing personal,' Sam explained quickly. 'But unaccustomed to seeing a lady hereabouts. So, your turn. Tell me about yourself.'

Dora was nonplussed. Not used to talking about herself, she hardly knew where to start.

'There's not much to tell . . .' she faltered. 'I'm very ordinary. I do my voluntary work, parcels for prisoners, comforts for refugees, knitting, of course, lots of knitting. And the tea bar—'

'Ah, the tea bar. The fourth emergency service.'

She couldn't tell if he was joking or not.

'The rest of the time,' she went on, 'I do some sewing for a friend who has a shop. I queue, I cook, I do my housework, like everyone else. I do a bit more knitting. I write letters to my two boys in the Forces—'

'Two boys.' His interest seemed to quicken. 'Where are they? I mean – we're on the same side, you can tell me. If you want to.'

'I'm lucky,' said Dora, knowing she was. 'Sid's in London, and likely to stay there, or in this country, anyway. My elder boy, Reg, is abroad, but where he is, he's not in any immediate danger. Not now.'

'You are lucky.'

'I know.'

'So that's it?'

'No – my daughter, Lily, my youngest, she's still at home. And I have a lodger, Jim. They both work at Marlow's.'

He seemed impressed.

'Oh, I know it. The store. Very smart.'

'They like it. And they're doing well there.'

Dora hadn't talked so much about herself in years, if ever, but Sam's interest was encouraging; he followed everything she said with bird-like nods of his head and little compressions of his mouth. His next question was a natural one, in view of the one thing she hadn't mentioned.

'And your husband – is he doing war work?'

Dora shook her head.

'I'm afraid he died.'

Sam was immediately apologetic.

'I'm sorry to hear that, ma'am.' He knew her name but seemed shy of using it. 'I'm sorry I asked. I didn't mean to upset you.'

'It's all right,' said Dora, and it was. 'It was a long time ago. Lily was only a baby.'

'Even tougher then.'

There was no answer to that.

'And what about you?' she asked. 'How do you come to be in England?'

'Ah, that's a long story.' He glanced at the clock

on the wall. 'So long, I can't start it now. I think you'll find you've missed the last bus back from the village, and I need to be back here for roll-call, so if I'm going to run you home—'

'Would you? Well . . . if you're sure . . . ?'

'Come on!' he grinned. 'It was my fault you had to make the trek in the first place. I owe you that at least.'

Chapter 21

Dora tried to make him drop her in town, but Sam insisted on driving her right to her door and she had no choice but to accept. It was a different jeep, a closed-in one this time, so her hat wasn't a problem, but the bench seat was slippery and Dora had a job to stop herself sliding into him as he took the corners and to keep her knee away from his hand when he changed gear. That would have been embarrassing – it was bad enough the way her skirt would keep riding up. But Sam kept his eyes on the road as he told her his story. It wasn't what she'd expected at all.

He was married, with one son. When Canada had declared war on Germany, a week after Britain, his son, Bruce, had announced he was going to enlist in the Commonwealth Air Training Plan. His mother had been distraught, but there was no stopping the boy – he was eighteen, after all. He was accepted straight away ('Naturally – 20/20 vision, A1 fit,' said Sam) but within six weeks of starting to fly, his plane had come down on a training exercise. He'd suffered severe burns and had died twenty-four hours later – before Sam and his wife could get there.

Shaken, Dora put her hand to her throat. She'd had some scares with Reg, but never that grimmest of news.

'Oh, I am so sorry,' she said. 'How terrible. I can't imagine—'

'No. You can't,' he said simply. 'No one can. No one should have to.' They stopped at a crossroads and he met her eyes briefly, then looked left and right and drove on. 'They didn't want us to see him in the mortuary because of the injuries, but Grace – my wife – she insisted. And well – it broke her. She . . . I had to . . . she's in a place . . . let's call it a sana-torium.'

Dora shook her head. There was nothing to say.

Sam gave a minute shrug.

'So – I was home alone. We ran a store together, as it happens – a small hardware store – and well, my heart wasn't in it. It wasn't in anything much any more. I carried on for a while. But after Pearl Harbor there was more of a drive towards enlisting, we could see the Japs aiming for British Columbia next. I was just within the age range to sign up and I thought – why not? What have I got to lose?'

What he meant was what did he have to live for, Dora thought. Still she said nothing. Now he'd started, she thought it best to let him carry on.

'I don't know what I was expecting. I had this romantic idea that I could make a difference, avenge my boy somehow, give his life and his loss some kind of meaning. But of course, with my background, at my age, I wasn't headed for a combat role – I was always going to be one of those who only stand and wait.'

He gave a short laugh.

'Stores orderly, that's me – I might as well have stayed back in Alberta! But at least I managed to get myself posted to the UK. And when the vacancy came up for a batman to the major, I was first in line. I knew he was well thought of and I figured they wouldn't keep him hanging around the British Midlands for ever. So I'd get posted with him. Some place where the action was.'

Talk of the major made Dora sit up straighter.

'But he was posted away,' she put in. 'And you're still here.'

Sam slid her a look.

'Oh, you know that, do you?'

Careful, she told herself. She was feeling far too comfortable with Sam. She was going to let slip that she'd met Hugh more than once if she didn't watch out.

'He did mention in passing he'd be leaving.' She added haltingly, as if trying to remember, 'The south of England, I think he said.'

'Yes, well, there's the irony for you. OK, he's a regular soldier, but a fine man like him – and a family man – wife, two children—'

So Hugh's background, happily married, was just as Dora had imagined it. Of course it was. Oblivious, Sam carried on.

'So they posted him to an operational unit, but they kept me back – sent a younger guy to be his batman.' He threw her another look, then returned his eyes to the road. 'I can't tell you where they are now, but if they win through, they'll be eating a lot of spaghetti!'

So she'd been right about that, as well. Hugh's unit had been part of the invasion of Sicily.

'I'm so sorry, Sam.' She was shy of using his name, too, but it felt right here. 'You've been through so much.'

He shrugged.

'Not as much as some folks. A lot of folks. I should be thankful, shouldn't I? Looks like Jesus doesn't want me for a sunbeam just yet.'

Would it be crass to say it? She did, anyway.

'And you've got Buddy to look after. You wouldn't want to abandon him.'

It had been the right thing to say. It lightened the mood. He gave a nod of acknowledgement.

'Yes, and he's a pretty big responsibility!'

They were on the outskirts of Hinton now and she realised she'd better direct him. There was no chance for much more conversation, what with the closed roads and the potholes. They wove through the centre of town and out again and within a few minutes, the jeep had turned into Brook Street. Sam slowed and the houses slid past till he pulled up outside number 31.

'Home sweet home,' he announced.

'Thank you for the lift,' said Dora. 'And the tea. And talking of sweet, the sugar!'

Sam hadn't missed her rapturous expression when she'd tasted her tea. He'd disappeared and returned with a box of sugar lumps, which he'd tucked discreetly in her bag.

'No protests,' he'd said. 'We have more than enough.'

Now he jumped out, came round the front of the jeep and opened her door for her. Dora clambered out, trying not to show too much leg. Sam swept off his forage cap and chucked it on the seat. He closed the door and held out his hand.

'It's been a pleasure meeting you, Dora,' he said.

'You too.'

'And thank you again for playing the Good Samaritan.'

'Don't mention it.'

'Oh, but I have to,' Sam insisted. 'I'd sure have

hated to write to the major and tell him Buddy was lost.'

'I'm glad you won't have to.'

Sam had his back to the row of houses, so he didn't see the door opening. He didn't see Jean Crosbie, her hair tied up in a turban, emerge onto the step with a duster in her hand.

Dora met her neighbour's eyes, but it was Jean's mouth that amused her most. It fell open like a stage trapdoor. An Army jeep in their street which hardly ever saw any traffic but the milkman's wagon and kids in their go-karts! Dora's hand clasped by a strange man, a serviceman, and a foreign serviceman at that! And hearing him say, in his strange, soft accent, that he'd be sure to pass by the tea bar to say hello next time he was in town.

Dora held Jean's stunned gaze for a moment, then turned to face her companion.

'Do,' she replied. 'I'd like that very much.'

When she got in, Lily and Jim were eating a tea of fish and chips – Lily had baulked at cooking then, thought Dora. No surprise there!

'You're late, aren't you, Mum?' Lily was sprinkling vinegar. 'Jim got some for you as well. They're on a plate in the oven.'

Dora unpinned her hat.

'Oh, Jim, you're an angel. I'm ready for them.'

'No halo needed,' Jim called after her as she went

through to the kitchen. 'It's supposed to be hake – more like cotton wool stuffed with pins! But the chips are all right.'

Dora fetched her plate and brought it to the table. Lily was in the middle of telling Jim about Gladys's reaction to the rest of the weekend's thrilling excitement.

'I didn't know where to start,' Lily was saying. 'Seeing Miss Frobisher and Mr Simmonds together, or Gwenda turning up and all the news about Reg. But it hardly mattered; Gladys was still so wrapped up in her and Bill, I don't think she took any of it in.'

Dora sat down. She wondered what they'd say if she'd told them she'd had some excitement herself that afternoon, that on a whim she'd headed off into the middle of nowhere on a bus, with a dog on a piece of string. A dog that she'd first encountered when a man had unexpectedly walked into her life, and, through the same dog, had met another.

Lily passed her the salt, and Dora thanked her with a smile.

She'd never mentioned Hugh to anyone, but she knew she wouldn't be able to keep meeting Sam quiet – there were the sugar lumps for a start, not to mention Jean Crosbie. And why should she? Lily and Sid kept urging her to have a life of her own, and if Sam was serious about dropping by the tea bar again, she just might do that. It was about time she treated herself to a proper hairdo, she thought, probing a piece of fish for bones, instead of washing and setting her hair herself at home. She might even spend some of her coupons on a blouse she'd noticed the other day in Dorothy Perkins. After all, why not?

'Sugar? Lump sugar? Mum! Where did you get these?'

When the fish and chips had been eaten, Dora freshened the pot of tea and brought it to the table with some of the sugar lumps in her best cut-glass dish.

'They're not black market, are they?' Jim tried to sound scandalised, but Dora could see he was practically drooling.

'They were a gift,' she replied, sitting down. 'Pass your cup, Jim.' He did so. 'Well, a thank you, actually,' she went on, pouring him some tea and passing the cup back. 'For doing someone a good turn.'

'Who's got sugar lumps to give away?' demanded Lily. Then: 'Jim! What are you doing? You're not taking two?'

'If they're BM, we'd better make them disappear quickly, hadn't we?' Jim stopped with his hand poised over the bowl.

'Oh, go on,' said Dora. 'Treat yourself.'

Jim did, stirred, and drank with his eyes closed appreciatively. He might have been tasting fine wine or twenty-year-old whisky.

'So – answer my question.' Never mind spaniels, Lily was a positive Jack Russell when she was on to something. 'Who's giving away sugar lumps?'

'The Canadians,' said Dora airily. 'They've got plenty.'

Lily and Jim listened open-mouthed as she told them about her afternoon, again skimming over her encounters with Hugh, and focusing on her concern to get Buddy back where he belonged.

'Hah! Arrange the words "horse", "dark", "you're" and "a" in no particular order,' said Jim. 'But good for you!'

'Yes, well done, Mum!' said Lily. 'Do you think you'll see him again, this Sam?'

'What? I doubt it,' flannelled Dora. 'I shan't be going traipsing out there again, shall I?'

'He might find you, though,' Lily observed shrewdly. 'He knows where you live. And who knows what he might give us next time?'

'Steak,' said Jim with relish. 'T-bone steak.'

'What do you know about steak?' queried Lily. 'Have you ever had one?'

'I read my Raymond Chandler,' retorted Jim. 'They live on it over the pond. In their diners.'

'Over the pond! Diners! Listen to you!' snorted Lily. 'I want doughnuts. All that sugar's given me a proper craving for one!'

Chapter 22

'Marvellous, isn't it! Smack in the middle of wedding season! My busiest period for alterations!'

It was early August, and with the summer sale now offering 'Final Reductions', Lily had been called back temporarily to help on Childrenswear. Beryl had been reeled in by a Marlow's advertisement in the *Chronicle*, promising babies' napkins 'At Prices You Will Not See Again!'

Lily stood by as her friend, after bitter experience of leaks, pulled the terry squares this way and that, testing for thickness and strength.

'You won't find anything wrong with them, Beryl,' Lily admonished. 'This is Marlow's, remember, they're good quality! And as for worrying about Mum leaving you in the lurch with your weddings—'

'It happens!' said Beryl. 'She'll be too busy planning hers!'

'Don't talk such nonsense!'

'You'll see! When an older woman has her head turned, it's all love's young dream. Your mum and this Sam'll be in the *Chronicle* next, like Robert and Evelyn were when they got married! "Love Across the Miles" – I can see it now!'

'For goodness' sake,' replied Lily, exasperated. 'She took the dog back, Sam gave her a lift home, you can't turn that into some full-blown romance!'

Beryl could.

'No? I heard you can't keep him away from that tea bar. Any excuse.'

'Who told you that?' demanded Lily. She didn't want her mum being gossiped about. 'Jean Crosbie, I suppose. She's got half the WVS spying on Mum.'

Beryl added another napkin to the pile that had passed her inspection.

'She may have mentioned it.'

As Dora had known she would, Jean Crosbie had been round to the Collinses' like a shot. On the pretence of borrowing an ounce of suet, she'd come round the very night she'd seen Sam's jeep in the street, and pointedly asked who Dora's 'man friend with the Army transport' was. She'd also accosted Beryl next time she saw her to warn her to make the most of Dora, as – who knew? – she might soon be emigrating to Canada as a war bride. As usual with Jean, a rumour could be halfway to Nova Scotia before the truth had done up its shoelaces.

'It's rubbish,' declared Lily stoutly. 'Sam's been by the tea bar a couple of times to say hello, that's all.'

'And the rest!' scorned Beryl. 'I suppose it's the dog that wants to see your mum, is it? Pull the other one! He's sweet on her!'

Over the past few weeks, Lily had already considered this possibility, so that night she screwed up her courage and tried to find the words to ask.

They were both in the kitchen, Dora doing her best to make a new Food Ministry recipe for oatmeal and lentil sausages palatable. Thank goodness for the veg bed – there was the remains of a leek and a bit of parsley to add some flavour.

Keeping her eyes on the potatoes she was scrubbing, Lily tried to sound casual.

'Have you seen anything more of Sam, Mum?'

Dora continued chopping parsley. She knew exactly what Lily was asking, and why.

'Look, Lily,' she said, laying down the knife. 'I know what Jean Crosbie's been saying. She isn't the only one with her spies in the WVS. I wouldn't give her the satisfaction of explaining myself – in fact, it makes me smile to see her so aeriated, but I'll tell you straight, love, because you deserve to know.'

Lily dropped a potato into the pan of cold water at her elbow.

'Go on,' she said, bracing herself.

'You can put any thought of anything between me and Sam right out of your head,' said her mother. 'What would be the point? He'll be going back to Canada when the war's over – that's if he's not sent away from here well before.'

Lily considered this.

'That doesn't mean you couldn't . . . well, get fond of each other while he is here. And even – well, he might ask you to go back to Canada with him!'

Dora looked incredulous.

'And you think I'd go? Me, who thinks a trip down the road to Dudley's an adventure?'

'Well, if you like him, Mum . . .'

'Oh, Lily,' Dora sounded both sad and wise. 'Sam's a nice, decent fellow, but there can be nothing between me and him. Look, this isn't for spreading about, but this is what he's told me.'

Quietly she explained the sad story of Sam's son's death and his wife's collapse.

'Oh, Mum.' Lily was moved. 'That's awful. Poor man.'

'He's stuck here in a strange country on his own. He just wants someone to talk to,' said Dora. 'Don't we all?'

'Of course we do,' Lily agreed.

So Sam wasn't a free agent. Lily wasn't sure

whether that made things simpler or more difficult, and whether she was relieved or disappointed for her mother. Maybe, if she met Sam properly, she'd have a better idea.

'Why don't you ask him over?' she suggested. 'If he's – well, lonely, like you say, ask him for tea or something.'

Lily received one of her mum's knowing looks. 'Oh, so you still don't trust him? Or me? Want to give him the once-over?'

'No!' cried Lily, then backtracked. 'Well, maybe I do. I'd like to meet him, anyway. Why not?'

Dora gave a wry smile. 'Sure you're not still hoping for doughnuts?'

'I'd like to meet him, that's all,' Lily repeated. 'He sounds nice. If you like him, he must be nice.'

'Did I say I liked him?'

'You didn't say you didn't.'

As Jim was always remarking, Dora thought, Lily had to have the last word.

'I'll think about it.' Dora turned back to her chopping board. 'When the time's right. Now get on with those potatoes, will you, and get them on the heat.'

Dora thought long and hard about issuing an invitation to Sam. As long as they continued meeting on neutral ground – the tea bar – she could convince herself he was just a friend, and not someone she might actually become quite fond of. But even just thinking that, she knew she already was.

He wasn't a fantasy figure like Hugh had been. He was a real person, humble, unassuming, ordinary. Like her he'd been quietly living his life, working hard, not asking for much, until the war had come along and taken his son and knocked him – and his marriage – sideways. Those were the great unnumbered casualties of this war, Dora thought, wiping down the tea bar counter, the marriages that had been torpedoed in one way or another, smashed to smithereens by a death, a crippling injury, an affair or simply by the strain of being apart.

Even so, she'd been truthful in telling Lily there could never be anything beyond friendship between her and Sam. He was far too honourable a person to contemplate it – and so was she.

'Well, hello!'

And there he was, suddenly in front of her, with Buddy dancing on his lead.

Dora smiled and leant over the counter-flap.

'Hello, Buddy!' Buddy barked, then seemed to smile back, his pink tongue as always seeming far too big for his mouth. 'And what have you been up to lately?'

It was how their conversations always started – an enquiry about the dog.

'Huh! You really want to know?' Sam pulled a resigned face. 'Took me the best part of twenty minutes to get him to come back after I let him out for a run this morning. In Buddy's head he's not a dog, he's some Wild West sheriff with a brief to run every pesky squirrel he sees out of the county!'

'Buddy! You're a bad boy!'

Buddy grinned and panted proudly at what he clearly took as a compliment.

Dora poured Sam his usual 'cawfee' and passed it across to him. She watched as he sipped it.

'Have you ever thought of trying tea?' she asked.

'Now why would I want to do that?'

'Well, the coffee here isn't very special.' It was half coffee essence, half chicory, and pretty foul from what other customers had said, but he'd never complained. 'It can't be what you're used to.'

'True. But I come for the atmosphere not the coffee.' He said it with an ironic grin – the tea bar was at a draughty side entrance to the station where the wind blew cigarette packets and old fish and chip papers around like tumbleweed.

Dora knew what he was saying really, and she was pleased that he hadn't been any more overt. That was one of the many things she liked about him. He never overstepped the mark. She liked what he hadn't said, nothing embarrassing about it being the company he came for, or even the conversation, and she was grateful and relieved for that. If he had, she might not have said what she said next.

'Well,' she replied. 'I was wondering if you'd like to try a bit of a different atmosphere. And tea made in a pot, not an urn like here. It tastes better that way.'

His forehead creased.

'I'm not sure I follow.'

'I wondered if you'd like to come round. For tea at mine. Sunday tea.' She took a deep breath. 'You could meet the family – well, Lily and Jim anyway.'

'Seriously?'

'Yes, why not? Next time you get a Sunday off.'

Sam replaced his cup on the counter.

'Dora,' he said. 'That would be so kind. Thank you. I'd love to come.'

The Navy hadn't pushed out more boats in four years of war than Dora did in Sam's honour and the resulting spread, when she surveyed it, met even her high standards. There was a big plate of sandwiches (sardine and tongue), scones – only plain, but with two sorts of jam – and a Victoria sponge, made with the last of Sam's sugar lumps crushed to powder. She rather hoped he wouldn't bring doughnuts however much Lily was slavering for them; there was barely any room on the table.

There was a knock at the front door and, her mouth suddenly dry, Dora went to answer it. She only got as far as the doorway to the hall: Lily had skidded downstairs and beaten her to it. She'd been more excited than Dora to hear Sam was coming and was in her best skirt and blouse.

'We're on show as well!' she'd said when Dora had commented, and Dora could hardly talk. She was wearing the blouse she'd had her eye on – oyster-pink with a scalloped collar and drawn-thread work on the yoke. She hoped she didn't look as if she was trying too hard.

'Do I gather the VIP's here?' Jim appeared from the scullery where he'd been washing his hands; he'd been re-caulking the henhouse. He stood expectantly by. Poor Sam – quite the reception committee.

But Dora needn't have worried. Led in by a beaming Lily, Sam was more than able to hold his own. There were no doughnuts – no food offering at all, but he'd brought a bunch of carnations, and once they'd been arranged in Dora's best vase, they sat round the table. Dora was fully expecting him to have to undergo an interrogation from Lily and Jim, but Sam didn't give them a chance. Easy and expansive, he was the one to question them.

First he quizzed Dora on how she'd managed to produce such a splendid meal on rations ('She's a genius,' Lily answered warmly) and then turned his attention to Jim and Lily, asking them all about Marlow's. Dora had quite forgotten that as a shop-keeper himself, he'd be interested in their line of work. She felt almost left out as Sam laughed at Lily's tales of awkward customers, capping them with ones of his own. Then he and Jim got into discussion about the overnight disappearance of galvanised buckets, mops and broom handles – the situation with supplies had obviously been the same in Canada as in Britain once the factories had gone over to war production.

Lily signalled to her mum and they began to clear the plates.

'He seems really nice,' she said eagerly, pulling the door to once they got out to the scullery. 'You have my full approval! He's welcome any time.'

'Oh yes?' asked Dora. 'And I suppose doughnuts have got nothing to do with it?'

Sam had explained that he deliberately hadn't brought any food in case Dora might feel insulted, but if they ever wanted anything, they had only to ask.

'Nothing at all!'

Dora didn't believe her daughter for a moment, but she could have cried with relief. She hadn't realised till then just how important it was to have Lily's permission to go on seeing Sam.

Chapter 23

September had arrived, and with it rich pickings in
the jungle of blackberry bushes along the embankment
– if you could beat the birds to it. The leaves on the
ash trees were still bright green under their coating
of city dust, but the limes were already blotched with
yellow and the fallen conkers lay glossily brown where
their spiny casings had split. Summer was only just
giving way to autumn, but at Marlow's, Christmas
was in full swing – behind the scenes, anyway. The
bomb last year had pretty much wiped it – and profits
– from the calendar, so this year, everyone was determined it was going to be a success.

Jim was masterminding the first-floor extravaganza
again: Father Christmas would arrive outside on a

sleigh and process up to his grotto on Toys, where he'd sit on a padded throne and dispense a small present to every child who whispered their Christmas wishes. Most children would simply be asking for their daddies back, but as that was one wish that was in the hands of Herr Hitler and not Father Christmas, buyers across the store had used every ounce of their charm and persuasiveness to wring anything out of their suppliers that might pass as a gift.

To her great joy Lily had been recalled permanently from her exile on Schoolwear – Miss Kendall, first sales on Bedlinens, had been appointed in Miss Naylor's place. Lily had to acknowledge that her time on a different department had been good experience, but she was thrilled to be back where she felt she belonged. In view of the good job she'd done, though, Miss Frobisher told her she'd be keeping her second sales status.

'Catching me up fast!' grinned Jim, who'd reached the dizzy heights of first sales on Furniture and Household.

'And coming up to overtake on the inside,' warned Lily. 'You'd better watch out!'

Gladys was delighted to have her friend back on the neighbouring department – it made surreptitious chats easier. None of the gloss of being newly married had worn off, but now, she said, in a phrase she could only have got from some film, 'the sands in the hour glass are running out'.

'We're making the most of the time we've got left,' she told Lily, sidling over when Mr Bunting and Miss Frobisher were on their breaks.

'The *Jamaica*'s refit's almost done, is it?'

'They'll be putting to sea again in the middle of the month,' mourned Gladys. 'But we've had a good run. A whole summer we've been able to see each other. Plenty of couples only get their wedding night, so I can't feel too hard done by.'

Miss Frobisher was glad to have Lily back too, and actually said so. Ever since the way her boss had managed their unexpected meeting at the cricket pitch, and the frankness with which she'd spoken the day after, Lily had even more respect and affection for her.

When it had first been made public, Miss Frobisher's relationship with Mr Simmonds had been the number one topic of conversation in the staff canteen, along with speculation about whether her husband had ever existed, but it had soon been overtaken by the sudden sacking of Mr Riley of Luggage and Travel Goods for making 'improper advances' to young members of staff, female and – it was whispered – male. The store detectives, it transpired, had been keeping a watching brief on him for months. That was much meatier fare for those who liked to chew over the store's latest scandal with their shepherd's pie.

But time and canteen chat had moved on again. Mr Riley's misdemeanours were old news and now all the talk was of Christmas.

Lily was in the stockroom to check off a delivery that Les had trundled up.

'All present and correct,' she confirmed, giving Les back his clipboard. 'Socks, slippers and boys' pyjamas. Half the quantity we'd have liked but—'

'Don't you know there's a war on,' chanted Les. It had become a very over-used phrase and no one could hear it now without a groan. He tucked his pen back into the pocket of his brown overall. 'But for how much longer, eh, now we've only got the Nazis to deal with!'

There had been some amazing news that week: the Allies had launched an invasion from Sicily to the Italian mainland and just days after they'd landed at Salerno, Italy had surrendered. It wasn't all good news though: the Germans had sent reinforcements and redoubled their resistance.

'Only?' Lily was more sceptical. 'I can't see Hitler caving in that easily.'

'Our Beryl can!' grinned Les. 'Remember that book I was running back in the summer? She reckoned the war would be over by Christmas – she thinks she'll clean up! I haven't liked to tell her there's six others that picked that date! Mind you, I'm thinking of opening another book.' He leant in confidentially. 'Simmonds and Frobisher engaged by Christmas. That's a dead cert, if you ask me. What do you reckon? You work with her.'

Lily assumed an air of dignity she didn't really feel: the notion had occurred to her.

'That's a matter for them,' she said demurely.

'Yeah? And the rest! Beryl's going to drop you in a couple of flyers about her business, even so. She's had some new ones printed.' Like his wife, Les wasn't one to be easily put off. He clanged shut the gate of the metal cage he'd brought the boxes in and prepared to rattle off with it. 'Stick one in Frobisher's handbag, can you? And in Simmonds's little cubby hole? A hint never hurts.'

Downstairs, on the sales floor, Jim was stewing over another smug Government briefing.

'All quiet on the Furniture front, Mr Goodridge?'

Peter Simmonds, more relaxed, even more human, these days, approached and saw what Jim was reading. 'Ah, the Utility Scheme.'

Jim pushed the document to one side and straightened up.

'Banging on about what a success it is. And it is – we all get the point of standard designs to save on materials—'

'If only the manufacture was standardised as well.'

'Seven hundred different factories making the stuff? Every delivery's a lucky dip. Will it be any good or will the drawers stick and the chairs have a wobble? But . . .' Jim fell back on the tired old mantra. 'There's a war on.'

'And no one's going to forget it,' commiserated Mr Simmonds. 'But I've come to take you away from all that.' Good grief, a joke, he really had relaxed! 'Mr Marlow would like to see you.'

'Oh yes?' Jim perked up. 'About Christmas?'

'He didn't say. You'd better go and see.'

Hopeful, Jim was on his way to the back stairs before Mr Simmonds had even finished the sentence.

'Go straight in, he's expecting you,' Mr Marlow's secretary smiled and turned back to her typewriter.

Jim knocked and entered. But what he saw – or rather, who – stopped him in his tracks with his hand glued to the doorknob.

'Ah!' Cedric Marlow got up from behind his desk. 'I believe you know Mr Bigley.'

The doorknob felt clammy under Jim's hand.

Bigley, amply filling one of the elegant carver chairs on the visitors' side of the desk, got to his feet and held out his hand.

'Good to see you again!' he beamed. He turned back to Cedric. 'As I said, your lad Robert introduced Jim and me in the summer.'

Jim closed the door carefully, his mind spinning like a tank turret under fire. He crossed the wide sweep of carpet and gave Bigley's outstretched hand a cursory shake. He sat down, at a nod from his uncle, in the other chair. What the heck was Bigley doing here?

'Good news!' Cedric began, settling himself in his own chair again. 'I'm delighted to say that Mr Bigley's going to be delivering the store's coal again this winter. I can't tell you the relief of knowing we'll get regular deliveries from a reliable firm!'

'You can trust me, Cedric,' grinned Bigley. Jim winced at the over-familiarity, and waited for a pained look from his uncle, but none came. Barry Bigley carried merrily on: 'And I suggested, Jim, that as we'd met, and as Robert's no longer around, and you're taking on more and more . . .' – he favoured Jim with a wink – 'more responsibilities in general, you could be my point of contact.'

'Hmn!'

To Jim it sounded like a bat squeak of disbelief, protest and horror. But a glance at his uncle told him that Cedric Marlow had heard it as acceptance – and Jim would have to accept that.

Because what could he say? Expose Bigley in front of his uncle? Bigley would promptly spill the beans about Robert's part in the nice little coal scam they'd had going last winter. Cedric had forgiven Robert once when he'd found out about the delivery racket and had been so touched when his son had dropped everything in Birmingham to come back to help out after the bomb. To reveal that Robert had cynically used the time in Hinton for his own ends, personal and profitable, might just finish the old boy off.

But at the same time . . . Bigley was about as straight as a weasel in a revolving door. And what with the grinning and the winking, he was obviously expecting to repeat the same dodge with Jim that he'd had going with Robert. The introduction at the fete must have led Bigley to think that Robert and Jim were pals – a couple of chancers together.

Bigley's tireless good humour seemed to be catching: even Uncle Cedric, usually the most strait-laced of men, was trying out a smile.

'And another thing,' he added eagerly. 'Mr Bigley's agreed to help out with part of the Christmas proceedings.'

'Oh really?'

What now? Bigley as Father Christmas?

'I know you've been having trouble, Jim,' Cedric began, 'finding a carrier who'd forgo a morning's profits and sacrifice one of his carts to be Father Christmas's sleigh. Well, Mr Bigley here has come to the rescue and offered one of his. Isn't that generous?'

'Very.' Jim squeezed the word out between teeth that were grinding so loudly he was surprised the other two couldn't hear.

'Oh, it's nothing! It's the least I can do for the kiddies!'

Bigley attempted to look modest and failed dismally. He was better when he was boasting, Jim thought acidly.

'You see!' Cedric was completely in thrall to the man. 'He won't take any credit. And that's on top of the money he raises for the Police Widows and Orphans!'

Oh, that as well, thought Jim. A nice way to disguise a few more backhanders.

'Come now, Cedric, you're making me blush!' Barry prised himself out of his chair once more and stood up. 'I'll have to get back to business. But I'll be in touch, Jim, to, er, finalise delivery arrangements.'

Jim stood up as well, every nerve ending strained in the need to be polite.

'I'll wait to hear from you.'

'And you will!'

A threat or a promise? Almost certainly both.

As the door closed behind Bigley, Cedric Marlow sighed happily.

'Such a relief to know our winter heating is in such good hands,' he said.

'For goodness' sake, Jim! Why didn't you say no right there? And tell Mr Marlow what a so-and-so Bigley is? And that he'll rip him off?'

Jim had been bracing himself for Lily's reaction all day and now they were walking home he was getting it with both barrels.

'Yes, great idea,' said Jim ironically. 'Why didn't I think of that?'

'Well?'

'Because,' said Jim patiently, 'what would it say to Uncle Cedric? You know he's not been quite the same since the bomb. Marlow's being smashed up like that took away a lot of his confidence and he's only just getting it back. If I tell him Bigley's a crook, what does that say about the old boy's judgement? It would

251

all have to come out, the scam Robert and Bigley fixed up last time, which drops Robert in the mire, and makes my uncle realise he's not even a very good judge of his own son. I can't. It's too cruel.'

'So it's kinder to let him be defrauded? And if anyone finds out, prosecuted?'

'No one's going to find out, are they,' retorted Jim. 'That's the trouble, Bigley being so matey with the police.'

'So let me get this right,' countered Lily, 'instead you're going let Bigley diddle Marlow's? Oh and, by the way, take a rake-off yourself?'

'Of course not. I'm going to have it out with Bigley, but in person.'

'Good luck with that!'

'He's a bully,' said Jim, hoping he sounded braver than he felt. 'They're always surprised when someone stands up to them. I shall tell him I'm not having any funny business. He's got to deliver the full weight of coal he's contracted to. I'm not overpaying for short weight and I'm not having anything to do with any crooked scheme.'

Lily shook her head.

'And if he laughs in your face? Or gets his heavies to punch you in it? You know it's no good going to the police and reporting an assault!'

'Let me try at least,' Jim pleaded. 'We'll see what happens.'

* * *

There was no chance to talk about it any further that evening, and perhaps that was just as well: after tea, everyone was going straight out again. Jim took his tin hat and armband off the peg in the hall and went off on ARP duty. Lily and Dora washed the pots before going their separate ways, Dora to one of Cousin Ida's knitting parties and Lily back into town. She didn't feel much like it now, but she'd promised to meet Gladys for a night at the pictures.

Her friend needed taking out of herself: the HMS *Jamaica* was already at sea on its post-refit trials and would then be returning to squadron duties. Gladys wouldn't see Bill again for many long months, maybe longer. They'd said their last farewells a week ago, and though Gladys kept repeating her mantra that she knew she was, or had been, lucky to have seen so much of him, it didn't stop her from looking pale and wan, or her eyes being dark-rimmed when she came to work each morning.

Lily had chosen the film carefully. It was a musical – she'd avoided anything war-like – but the evening wasn't a success. The inevitable Ministry of Food propaganda piece featuring Potato Pete ('I'm always getting into hot water, but there are lots of other ways of cooking me!') was met with the inevitable bored groans and was followed by something even worse, a short feature called 'Listening to Britain'. Lily was expecting a series of interviews, but it was more a sort of montage, and not a very helpful one in the

253

circumstances. It opened with a long sequence of the sea lapping on the shore and progressed through scenes at a lookout post and then a dance hall ('Members of HM Forces in Uniform Half Price!') which immediately had Gladys reaching for her handkerchief.

'They're playing our tune,' she snuffled as 'Red Sails in the Sunset' wavered from the cinema's crackly loudspeakers.

'Have a wine gum,' said Lily helplessly, taking a couple herself.

Gladys took one, but before long, the screen was filled with more shots of the sea, two tin-hatted soldiers scanning the horizon anxiously before repairing to the pub, where they joined in a sing-song with 'We'll Meet Again' accompanied by a Scotsman on a ukulele.

Gladys gulped noisily and Lily took another wine gum. Good job there wasn't really any wine in them: she'd be blotto by the end of the evening.

Lily was exhausted when she got in – being a literal shoulder for Gladys to cry on was both upsetting and wearing. Her mother's door was closed and her light off – an evening unravelling old sweaters and carding the wool in the company of Cousin Ida's drippy friends was tiring too, in its way. Jim, of course, would be sleeping at the ARP post. Hopefully he – and all of them – would get some rest. The Luftwaffe hadn't mounted any serious raids on Britain for a long while, though the RAF's campaign against industrial targets in Germany had been going on since the summer, so everyone was braced for the retaliation they knew would come.

Lily fell gratefully into bed. As she dropped off, she almost thought she heard the latch on the back gate click. But it was so faint and she was so sleepy she simply turned on her side, tucked her legs up under her and gave a huge yawn. The next thing she knew, or rather didn't, she was asleep.

Chapter 24

Jim had a reasonable night on the ARP camp bed too, and at work next day, was further heartened as he examined a newly delivered Utility sideboard. For once, the drawers slid in and out quite smoothly.

'Mr Goodridge?' The voice was hardly above a whisper, breathy, with a pronounced local accent. 'Mr Goodridge? There's a telephone call for you . . . sir.'

Jim stifled a laugh. Sir! It had to be one of the juniors – and a very junior junior, who hadn't yet had her vowels smoothed out by exposure to Marlow's required standard of speech. That's what happened to everyone, over time, Jim and Lily included.

He turned around. There were only two telephone extensions on the first floor, so incoming calls to

Furniture always ended up on another department. This time, it must be Ladies' Fashions, because as Jim had suspected, the messenger was Bessie, just a month into her job as a junior there.

'A telephone call? Is it a customer?'

'I'm not sure,' Bessie sounded even more terrified. 'Miss McIver took it. She said something about a sleigh.'

'A sleigh?'

Jim's heart took a dive, then another. Barry 'Jingle Bells' Bigley! If he really wanted to talk about Father Christmas and his sleigh, then Jim was the Flying Dutchman.

'I'll be right there.'

Bessie scuttled off on some other task and Jim sped across the sales floor. Miss Wagstaff, arranging the folds of a petrol-blue evening dress on a mannequin, glared at him malevolently as he passed. She didn't approve of men. In her view they were belligerent aggressors who liked to keep women in their place, though it would be a brave man who tried it with her.

The telephone in Ladies' Fashions was on a flimsy gilt table next to a fire bucket. The receiver was off the hook and Jim snatched it up.

'Hello? Jim Goodridge speaking.'

'Jim!' Bigley's voice boomed down the line. 'And how are you this morning?'

'Very well, thank you,' said Jim stiffly. 'You?'

'Never better!'

Enough of that, thought Jim.

'I don't imagine this is really about the sleigh?'

'Nah, of course not,' said Barry dismissively, 'you can sort that out with the foreman at the yard. No, this is a word to the wise. Take a look in the coal shed when you get home.'

'I beg your pardon?'

'Just take a look,' said Barry smugly. 'You might find something to your advantage. And that of your landlady. Oh, and your girl. To warm the cockles of your hearts.'

Jim felt his throat constrict.

'In the coal shed?'

'That's right. Just a little gesture – as we're going to be working together. Now I must get on! But don't worry, I'll keep in touch!"

Before Jim could say anything more, the line went dead. Jim replaced the receiver at his end as carefully as if it were a stick of gelignite. It might as well have been for what Bigley had thrown into the mix.

Thankfully, it was Wednesday and half-day closing, because Jim could barely concentrate on anything for the rest of the morning. As soon as all the lights under the clock on the sales floor were lit up, meaning the staff were free to go, he hurried down the back stairs, snatched his things from the cloakroom and sped off to Brook Street. Lily was again doing her bit to keep Gladys occupied, taking her for something to eat at the ABC tearoom before they joined Dora to pack Red Cross parcels for POWs. After that, it was the early show at the Gaumont. Jim had sympathised – it sounded exhausting – but now he was grateful that Lily wasn't around.

Along the familiar streets, through the park . . . the mile or so home passed in a blur until Jim clattered down the entry and through the back gate. At the back of the house was the brick-built privy and a store that was used for coal – coal which was rationed and strictly controlled. Every household received its allocation in time for the winter – never this early in the year. Jim wrenched open the door. The shed should have been empty – they'd used the last tiny scraps, and even the coal dust, long ago, in a cold week in the summer. But instead, Jim saw two hundredweight sacks of coal, the contents glinting evilly in the smoky light, along with a sack of kindling wood and a can of paraffin.

He slammed the door shut and leant against it, feeling sick. How had Bigley got it here in broad daylight? Even if Dora had been out at the shops, surely one of the neighbours would have seen? Then Jim remembered. Lily had mentioned at break that when she'd left for work that morning, the back gate hadn't been properly latched. She'd said she'd thought she'd heard it click last night before she fell asleep.

Jim had offered to have a look at it: the fault was probably with the hinge – the gate had slipped again. He'd agreed they didn't want it banging through the winter when the wind got up, but now he had a different theory. A pound to a penny that had been Bigley's 'little gesture' arriving – sneaked in under cover of darkness.

Jim glanced at the house. The back door was shut; everything looked quiet. Dora must have already left for the Red Cross depot. Thank God, he had a bit of time. But to do what exactly?

'What are you doing there, Jim?'

Jim spun round, screwdriver in hand.

Sam was standing at the back gate with Dora beside him and Buddy on his lead.

'Ah! You're back,' said Jim, stating the obvious. 'Yes, I'm – well, I've been thinking. There's so much thieving going on . . . we won't get a delivery for a while, so we don't need it yet, but I'm thinking ahead, putting a padlock on the coal shed.'

'Oh Jim! What a good idea!' Dora came forward. 'You are a good lad.'

Knowing what he was concealing, Jim felt anything but good and he waved away the praise. He'd been to every ironmonger's in Hinton to get hold of a padlock. He'd had to pay a ludicrous price when one had finally been produced from under the counter, not to mention the cost to his conscience of engaging in criminal activity in order to cover up someone else's criminal activity. But it was worth every penny if it bought him a bit of time to think.

'Sam met me from the Red Cross and we've had a lovely walk home, haven't we?' Dora went on blithely.

She was a different person these days, much more open. Buddy agreed with a short 'ruff!' and Sam hooked his lead round the post he'd driven into the corner of one of the veg beds. Otherwise Buddy tended to signal his approval of Jim's runner beans and carrots by lifting his leg on them, which might be nutrients of a sort, but didn't exactly boost your appetite.

'I'll get him a bowl of water,' said Dora. 'And put the kettle on for us.'

She moved off into the house and Sam came to inspect Jim's handiwork.

'I looked in at Marlow's the other day,' said Sam conversationally. 'Looking for a propelling pencil.'

'Oh yes?' said Jim. 'Any luck?'

'Nope,' said Sam. 'I guess you must get through a lot of coal there, though. It's a big old place to keep warm.'

'The heating's turned right down,' said Jim, trying to stop his hand shaking as he twirled the screwdriver. 'But it's a fine balance, we can't have the customers shivering.'

'And who brings it, Marlow's coal?' Sam continued.

'You need those deliveries to keep coming. Got a decent haulier?'

Jim's synapses snapped to attention. Was Sam just making conversation or was there something more to it?

'Bigley's have got the contract,' he replied cautiously.

'Oh, have they? They deliver to us at Nettleford as well!'

'Really?'

Jim's already attentive synapses presented arms. Sam had always seemed a thoroughly good bloke. From the way he'd described his work in the stores, he'd made it sound as if he dealt mostly in boring necessities – soap, toothpaste, gas masks, boots and battledress, with occasional forays into small arms. But maybe there were other forays – into fuel, for example. And into cahoots with Bigley.

'You must get through a lot of coal at the base too,' he ventured.

'Sure do. Here, let me hold that straight for you.'

'Thanks.' Sam held the hasp while Jim fumbled in the final screw. 'And you're happy with Bigley's, are you?'

'As far as I know – no reason not to be, is there?'

'No,' faltered Jim. This wasn't getting him anywhere. The screw in place, he stopped work. 'I was just . . . do you know the man? Barry Bigley himself?'

'I've seen him around, yeah.' Sam tested the strength of the hasp. 'You've done a good job there, Jim.'

Still stuck in the mire. It was no good, Jim thought, he'd have to ask straight out.

'Do you have any dealings with him directly?'

Sam took a step back and looked at him sidelong, genuinely puzzled.

'No, not my area, like I've said, I do the small stuff. Sergeant Hudson sees to the coal deliveries.'

'What's that about Sergeant Hudson?'

Dora had reappeared and was putting an old crock dish of water down for Buddy, who thanked her by drinking lustily and splashing it all over her shoes.

'He takes in the coal up at Nettleford,' Sam explained.

'Does he? It must be the only thing he does do!' She turned to Jim but nodded her head towards Sam. 'He's always going on about him. Says he's a right shirker.'

'Well,' said Sam, 'he thinks it goes with the rank – why have a dog and bark yourself, kinda thing.' Then he paused, thoughtful. 'But now you mention it . . . it's a bit odd. There's times when he's even changed his duties and his leave to be around when there's a delivery due.'

'It doesn't sound like him to get his hands dirty!' retorted Dora. 'Idle as the day is long!'

The kettle was whistling and she returned to the house. Jim was left wondering just how dirty Hudson's hands might be – and whether he dared to take Sam into his confidence. He was desperate to talk to someone. But there might be no funny business going on anyway – there was still one thing that might exonerate Hudson.

'Your coal,' Jim began. 'A big establishment like yours . . . it must go over a weighbridge at an outfit like that?'

'OK, enough,' said Sam. 'I'm not stupid. What are you getting at?'

Jim glanced at the house, but Dora was well out of earshot. Even so, he kept his voice low.

'Bigley's on the fiddle,' he said. 'He delivers short weight, gets the full weight signed for, sells the difference on the side and he and his contact split the profit between them. He tried it at Marlow's last winter, he wants to do it again with us, and I'm wondering if he's up to the same trick at Nettleford.'

'Jeez!' Sam's mouth couldn't have gaped wider if he'd been having his tonsils inspected. 'You really think – in English law that's treason, right? The guy could hang! And as for Hudson . . . our Military Police are no marshmallows either. He'd be – well, I don't know . . .'

'It's serious all right.'

'But, Jim . . . if you know all this . . . have you been to the police?'

Jim looked towards the house again, but Dora was busy arranging cups on a tray.

Quickly he explained exactly what had gone on between Bigley and Robert Marlow, how Jim had reluctantly got involved in getting Bigley off Robert's back, and the lack of success in bringing Barry to justice over the scrap metal at Tatchell's. He followed that with his horror that Bigley wanted to repeat the coal dodge at Marlow's this winter, with Jim as the contact, and with the 'little gesture' now reposing in the coal shed as a bribe.

'It's no good whatsoever going to the police,' Jim insisted. 'Barry's bunging them all the time. That's how he wriggled out of it over the Tatchell's thing. And heaven knows how many other rackets he's paying them to turn a blind eye to.'

'Well, this is where the blinkers come off!' Sam sounded truly appalled. 'I'd better take this to someone way above Hudson's head. We've got to stop the pair of them!'

'I don't want you to get into trouble,' Jim urged. 'There's no evidence – not even hearsay – it's all suspicion and assumptions. Your Sergeant Hudson sounds a pretty crafty operator and, as I found out with Robert Marlow, you don't know how high up the tree the rot goes.'

'True. Which is why we can't let it spread!'

'Jim's not got you worrying about potato blight as well, has he?' Dora was back with the tea tray. She balanced it on the little wall round the veg bed. 'He's always fretting about something attacking his precious veg!'

Jim flicked a look at Sam. If only that was the

only worry, he thought, as Dora handed them their cups.

'I'll keep you posted, OK?' Sam muttered to Jim later, as he left. 'It may take some time. I want to think it through.'

'We haven't got long. I've got the schedule from Mr Marlow. Bigley's will be making the first delivery to us next week. And I've still got to get out of being Bigley's stooge somehow.'

Sam put on his forage cap. 'Leave it with me,' he said. 'You can trust me, Jim.'

Chapter 25

'I hope we can – trust Sam, I mean.' Lily had wanted to get the bus to work ('Look at my shoes! Nearly worn through!') but now she understood why Jim had insisted on walking – they could talk without being overheard.

'Oh, why didn't I get out of bed when I heard that wretched back gate!' she cried. 'I might have seen what was going on!'

'Oh yes, and what would you have done?' retorted Jim, taking her arm as they negotiated a pile of rotted sandbags which were spilling their contents on the pavement. 'Gone down, grabbed the poker, and set about the bloke dropping the coal off?'

'Probably, yes!'

'And another fine mess we'd have got ourselves into!' said Jim, borrowing from Laurel and Hardy. 'Anyway, you didn't. I've told Sam now, we'll have to hope he comes good.'

'Do you think he'll try and set some kind of trap? Like you tried to at Tatchell's?'

'I don't know,' shrugged Jim. 'In the end . . . like he said, we have to leave it to him.' He gave a deep sigh. 'I'm sorry, Lily. Maybe I should have faced Bigley down in front of my uncle. Then we wouldn't be going through this.'

Lily squeezed his arm. They were at their best, she often thought, when they were united against a common enemy.

'Don't be sorry,' she said. 'You were only thinking of him and trying to spare him. You were in a horrible position.'

Which was about to get worse.

Jim was so keyed up all morning, he thought he'd go mad if he had to sit in the canteen surrounded by the usual fruitless speculation about the course of the war, the prospects for someone's racing pigeons and the unidentifiable contents of today's fishcakes. Lily had enlisted Brenda from Books in her quest to keep Gladys entertained, and invited him to join them at dinnertime, but Jim politely declined. Instead he got a pass out and headed for the park. Perhaps some fresh air would clear his head.

He'd just turned onto Hinton's main shopping street when a car drew up at the kerb. The driver leant across and wound down the window.

'Jim! This is a bit of luck – I was coming to find you! Hop in!'

Barry Bigley.

Jim did as he was told. When this happened in films, the innocent party would be driven out to some remote spot and have some sense knocked into him by one of the villain's heavies. Jim doubted the reality would be quite as dramatic – there was no thug whose neck disappeared into his shoulders sitting in the back, for a start. Still, it was his chance to say his piece and tell Bigley straight he wanted nothing to do with his schemes – before the painful arm-twisting began.

Bigley put the car in gear and they shot away from the kerb. It was a Rover, practically new, with real leather seats and a walnut dashboard you could have combed your hair in – a very nice motor. Jim wasn't in the least bit religious but the phrase 'the wages of sin' sprang to mind.

'We won't stop in town,' Bigley observed, his eyes on the road. 'Just in case.'

Only Bigley could have enough petrol – and swank – to drive any further, thought Jim. How he could run around in a car was itself a mystery, when petrol had been banned for private use for over a year, and sizeable cars like this taken away and converted into vans or ambulances. He must have every policeman in the district in his pay.

After ten minutes or so, Bigley pulled up in a quiet suburban road.

'If you're going to stop anywhere, stop outside a nice little semi with a diamond pane in the door and a rose bush in the middle of the lawn,' he grinned. 'We might be a couple of insurance salesman having a chat before doing the rounds.'

If only!

'Look,' said Jim, half turning in his seat. 'Before you start, you'd better understand. I don't know if you think I'm another Robert Marlow, but I can tell you now I'm not having anything to do with a scheme like the one you and he had going last winter.'

'You say that—' Barry began, but Jim interrupted.

'No,' he repeated. 'I said no and I mean it. I know what a hundredweight looks and feels like. I've worked on farms since I was a kid. I've been lifting hundredweight sacks of grain with an awl since I was fourteen, so you needn't think you can get short weight past me. I'll only sign for the weight of coal you deliver and I'll insist you bring the rest. I'm not interested in cheating anyone – not Mr Marlow, not the miners, not the Forces, not the Merchant Navy, not the Ministry of Fuel and Power!'

'Nice speech, Jim. Well said!' Barry was still jovial. 'Ever thought of going into politics?'

'Is that clear?'

'What's clear is you haven't said thank you for the little present I had dropped round to Brook Street,' smirked Barry. 'And I thought Marlow's knocked such posh manners into everybody.'

'I was coming to that,' said Jim. 'I don't want it. You can take it back.'

'That's not very nice,' said Barry. 'Ungrateful I call it. I mean, it's there now, isn't it? And it'd be a shame if the police had a tip-off about a householder having some knock-off coal. And firewood. And paraffin. Especially if that householder was a nice respectable widow like Dora Collins.'

Jim gulped.

'A nice lady like that . . .' Barry sucked his teeth theatrically. 'Of course, the defence'd bring out her previous good character, all the voluntary work she does. And the hard life she's had, bringing up her children since her old man died. Two boys, isn't it, and young Lily that you're sweet on? Yes, our Dora might get away with a fine, if she's lucky. But it depends on the charge, doesn't it? And the magistrate, of course. Might have to make an example of her. It could be prison.'

Jim looked at the man. That really would be a skunk's trick, but he had no doubt Barry would stoop to it.

'So I think you can see,' Barry went on smoothly, 'that it'd be best for everyone if you could see your way to co-operating. Like other people do.'

271

Other people – like spineless Robert Marlow and sneaky Sergeant Hudson? Nice company Jim was keeping these days.

He reached for the door handle.

'I'll walk back, thanks,' he said.

'Suit yourself,' said Barry pleasantly, which was more unsettling than any threat. 'As I say, I'll keep in touch. To finalise arrangements, you understand.'

Jim got out and slammed the car door so hard it echoed off the pebbledash. Barry gave him a cheery wave and drove off.

Jim had lost the battle. It was up to Sam to win the war.

The thing about war, they should have known from experience, was that at times, when your nerves were already on edge, everything went quiet – and this was no different.

'What do you think's going on?' Lily asked Jim when almost a week had passed. 'Sam hasn't been to the tea bar, either. He'd better get in touch soon or Mum'll be getting worried.'

'She thinks he's on manoeuvres,' replied Jim. 'That's what she told me anyway, when we were sorting salvage last night. And he is, we hope. Just not the sort she thinks.'

Then, at last, there was news – or seemed to be, when Bessie again ventured across to summon Jim to the telephone. But he was disappointed, as he followed

272

her to Fashions, to learn that the caller was only a supplier of tea trays. They'd be dented old British Restaurant things, Jim thought, or from a bomb-damaged factory – no good for Marlow's at all.

'Jim Goodridge speaking,' he said into the receiver as politely as he could. 'May I help you?'

'It's me!' hissed Sam. 'I guessed they wouldn't like you taking personal calls.'

Behind Jim, Miss Wagstaff loomed up menacingly. There was no chance to ask Sam how he'd come up with the notion of tea trays, of all things – this was going to be awkward.

'Ah!' Jim said carefully. 'Yes, indeed! Well, it's good to hear from you! Erm . . . what have you got to offer me?'

'Success!' Sam was too jubilant to register Jim's restraint. 'We've got him!'

'Really? That's marvellous!' Jim glanced over his shoulder. Miss Wagstaff was close by, ostentatiously running her finger along a spotless rail, looking for a speck of dust. 'How many trays do you think you can supply?'

'Eh?' Sam took a moment to catch on. 'Oh, there's someone there, right? OK, let me do the talking.'

'That sounds good,' said Jim blandly.

'I took it to the captain,' Sam began, 'and to be sure – because of what you said about how high it might go – I took it separately to the colonel as well. As it turned out, they were both on the level – and

273

they took it to the CMPF – that's our Military Police – your "red caps".'

'That's fantastic!' Jim let out, then remembered he was only supposed to be talking about tea trays. Maybe they were inlaid mahogany with brass handles. He forced himself to damp down his excitement. 'But go on—'

'OK, so yesterday Bigley's was due with a coal delivery at five. At three o'clock, the captain got Hudson to lead a cross-country run. He was not amused, he clearly wanted to make sure he was around when the coal came – God, I felt sorry for the poor guys he'd be haranguing round the course! Anyway, while he was gone, we tested the weighbridge. And sure enough, it was five tons out.'

Five tons! Jim did a quick calculation. At roughly eighteen hundredweight a ton . . .

'Miss Wagstaff?' A voice spoke behind him. 'Could I trouble you to come and look at something for me?'

Deliverance! Miss McIver was leading Miss Wagstaff away.

'It's OK now,' Jim said quickly into the receiver. 'There was someone listening, but they've gone. But five tons – that's the coal ration for about five households!'

'I know.'

'And if Hudson and Bigley have been knocking off that amount every time . . .'

'It mounts up.'

'So what happened?' Jim urged. He glanced over his shoulder. Miss Wagstaff was with Miss McIver and a customer, giving her opinion on the fit of a jacket. 'Was Hudson back in time to oversee the actual delivery?'

'You bet he was! Looked like he was about to have a heart attack, but yeah. So Bigley's lorry arrives, the coal goes over the bridge – and our police guys appear.'

'Caught in the act.'

'He tried to wriggle out of it, of course. Said he knew nothing about it. But our boys had had him under surveillance. Photographed him earlier in the day tampering with the weighbridge scale.'

'So what's happened to Hudson now?'

'He's in detention awaiting court martial. And I don't think they'll deal kindly with him.'

'And Bigley?'

'That's the other end of the exercise. We'd tipped off your local police. They arrested the driver.'

'Hang on, that's no good!' Jim burst out. 'He'll say he knew nothing about the short weight – and maybe he didn't! The police'll call in Bigley, but nothing'll happen because of the sway he's got at the station!'

'Not when the colonel's had a word with the chief constable.'

Sam sounded smug, as well he might.

'The chief—'

'They have a lot to do with each other at that level. They're on committees together – Civil Defence, public order, that sort of thing.'

'I suppose they are,' said Jim wonderingly.

'So I can tell you, 'cos the colonel's told me – Barry Bigley won't be getting away with anything this time – nor will the so-called detectives he's been bribing.'

'Mr Goodridge!' Jim had been so absorbed he hadn't noticed Miss Wagstaff's return. Now she was at his elbow and in full military mode herself. 'I really must insist that you end your call. I am expecting Mrs Beresford-Tate to telephone this morning about her dress for the Conservative Club ladies' luncheon and I don't want her to have to hear that the line is engaged!'

Jim spoke politely into the receiver, back in supplicant mode to a supplier of that rare commodity, tea trays.

'Would you excuse me for a moment, sir?' Hoping Sam would understand, he made a play of covering the receiver, then turned to Miss Wagstaff. 'Of course,' he said, ladling on the charm. 'I'd hate to get in the way of something as important as that.'

'I think we've got him!' he said triumphantly to Lily at dinnertime. It was hardly sunbathing weather any more, and the store roof was occupied solely by the hen coops, so it was nice and private for a confidential conversation. 'Sam's played a blinder.'

'Oh, I want to believe it!' cried Lily, her hands clasped in front of her in excitement. 'But he's such a snake . . .'

This time, though, the snake had been scotched. By the time they left the store that evening, there it was on the newsagent's placard:

LOCAL BUSINESSMAN ARRESTED FOR BLACK MARKETEERING

Jim jingled a handful of coins.

'How many copies do you want?'

Lily smiled and threw her arms round his neck.

'Enough to paper the entire house!'

Chapter 26

After the second – and successful – battle for El Alamein in the Western Desert, the Prime Minister had said something which, Jim reflected, was turning out to be very true. What you thought might be the end of something was really just the beginning of something else.

Because next day, Jim was summoned to see Mr Marlow. Looking positively shrunken, his uncle was behind his desk, a copy of the *Hinton Chronicle* open in front of him.

'Barry Bigley,' Cedric moaned before Jim had even sat down. 'Who'd have thought it? I didn't see it coming for a moment, did you?'

Jim thought it better not to say that he hadn't

just seen it coming, he'd had to stop it in its tracks, but he didn't have the chance to because Cedric hadn't finished.

'I can't believe it,' the older man muttered. 'Such a respected businessman! And a philanthropist – those generous donations to so many local organisations!'

Chiefly the Barry Bigley Profiteering Fund and the pension pots of who knew how many in the Hinton police force, thought Jim.

'What's the world coming to?' his uncle went on. It was another rhetorical question which Jim thankfully didn't have to answer, as Cedric continued, 'I hope he didn't suggest to you that Marlow's might get mixed up in anything untoward?'

On the way upstairs, guessing what this little interview would be about, Jim had wondered what to say if asked the question. He'd decided that now, at last, he could answer truthfully.

'I'm afraid he did,' he replied.

Cedric shot up in his chair as if it were electrified. 'What?'

'I told him I'd never be party to such a thing.'

His uncle sank back again.

'Thank goodness for that! And he accepted that, did he?'

'Well . . .' Jim thought of the coal, the kindling wood, and the paraffin padlocked in the coal shed at 31, Brook Street, and the threat about Dora. 'No, he wasn't keen – he put me under all sorts of pressure, to be honest, which I was resisting. But luckily this, er, operation by the police caught him in time.'

Nettleford and the involvement of the Canadian military had, evidently by joint agreement, been kept out of the press reports, which hadn't said where the fateful coal delivery had taken place.

'We've had a lucky escape,' quavered Cedric.

'It seems so.'

Yes, Marlow's had – as long as Bigley only put his hands up to the coal scam at Nettleford. And why would he admit to anything else, past, present or future? Anyone involved on the other ends of his dirty little schemes would surely want to keep their mouths shut. And the police would be far too busy digging out – and then covering up – the rot in their own ranks to start raking over every job Bigley had ever been involved in.

At least, that was what Jim had to hope – for his own sake, for Lily's, for Dora's – and for Robert Marlow's too. One thing was heartening – Jim's instincts had been right. If Cedric's reaction to this news was anything to go by, any inkling of his son's duplicity with Bigley last winter would have devastated him.

'You mustn't worry, sir,' Jim said gently now.

'But I do! We've got to find another coal haulier for the winter!'

'Mr Simmonds is looking into that already. He's lined up two possibilities who are putting in tenders.'

'That's something.' Cedric Marlow relaxed again.

'Of course,' said Jim, 'it still leaves us with one problem.'

'What's that?'

'A sleigh for Father Christmas,' said Jim. 'But I promise you I'll get him here, if I have to go between the shafts of a dog cart myself!'

Cedric Marlow might have been reassured, but there remained the problem, as Lily pointed out, of what to do about the contraband coal in the shed.

'Our own coal on the ration'll be arriving soon,' she said. 'Mum'll want the shed opened up and swept out. We've got to get rid of what's in there!'

'Oh, that had never occurred to me,' retorted Jim caustically. 'So what's your idea? Chuck it lump by lump in the canal? Wait till the *Flying Scotsman* goes through Hinton and shake it into the coal tender from the bridge?'

'Don't be daft!'

'Well, have you got a better plan? And how do we get it away, anyhow? We need a set of wheels! What do you suggest – Bobby's pram?'

Lily considered for a moment.

'That's not a bad idea . . . But no, we daren't involve Beryl. She'd want to know what we wanted the pram for, and if she hears there's some coal going begging she'd want it for herself, and if she gets caught . . .'

'We're going round in circles,' groaned Jim. 'Maybe I could get hold of a barrow and dump the wretched stuff somewhere at dead of night. Somewhere deserving – the doorstep of the children's home, or in a church porch. A gift from God.'

'No,' said Lily suddenly. 'It's all right, you won't need a wheelbarrow. We've got transport – Sam! He can take it away!'

Jim bit his lip. It was a thought. But . . .

'Hasn't he done enough?'

'Yes!' agreed Lily. 'He has. But like the war, like all of us, he'll have to do a little bit more.'

Sam had apologised to Dora for his unexplained absence ('Something came up – a kind of covert operation, you might say'), and the bunch of chrysanths he'd brought her to say sorry were still gracing the table when he next came round for tea.

Now he knew them better, and Lily had assured him they'd certainly not feel insulted, Sam had taken to bringing something tasty for the table every time. Today it was iced buns.

When they'd savoured every sweet and sticky crumb, and Dora had told them to leave the washing up, Jim lured Sam out into the yard with a supposed worry about an infestation of red mite in the hens. There, he and Lily outlined the real problem. Sam scratched his head and blew out a breath.

'I see what you're getting at,' he said slowly. 'But

if I do take this coal off your hands, I've still got to get rid of it somehow.'

'Can't you just take it to the base?' Lily had been giving the matter a lot of thought. 'You must have heaps of coal and firewood up at Nettleford.'

'True, but—'

'Bigley's been diddling you, so it's only putting back a bit of what you should have had,' she persisted, and as Sam still looked dubious: 'For all we know, what's in our shed should have been in one of Nettleford's deliveries in the first place!'

'So what are you saying? Would this be official, or do you expect me to slip it back in unseen?'

'That's up to you,' said Jim. 'But I think if you tell your superiors, even though they've been on our side, it raises too many questions. Where did it come from, how did you come to have it – all of that.'

Sam blew out his cheeks again.

'I don't know – I've got to sneak it out of here, and sneak it onto the base . . .'

'Sam, please,' Lily put a hand on his arm. 'I know it's a lot to ask.'

'Too right it is! Do you realise what could happen to me if I'm found out?'

'I do. And I'm sorry to ask. But do you realise what could happen to Mum if *she's* found out to have it here?'

Jim hadn't had to tell Lily of Bigley's thinly veiled threat: she'd worked it out for herself. And while

Bigley was still under investigation by the police, he could drop Dora in it at any time – and just might, out of spite.

'Any day now,' pleaded Lily, 'we're going to have to open up the coal shed for our own coal. If Bigley's stuff is still there . . . if Mum thinks Jim or I have been involved in anything dodgy, even though we didn't want to be . . . please, Sam. If you're not keen to do it for us, do it for her.'

'Oh, so it's blackmail now, is it? Bigley's taught you well!'

Sam shook his head wryly.

'Will you do it?'

'Do I have a choice?'

'Thank you! Oh, thank you!' Lily almost went to kiss him, then drew back: she didn't know him that well. 'And it'll be going to the war effort now, won't it, which is as good as it heating a church hall or a children's home, which was Jim's other idea. Better, in a way.'

'When you put it like that . . .' Sam was smiling. 'She's very persuasive, your Lily, isn't she, Jim?'

'Don't I know it!'

'It's the good training I've had at Marlow's,' said Lily primly. 'Accentuate the positive.'

'I must be mad,' said Sam. 'But OK.'

The next time they knew for certain that Dora would be out for the evening, and well after a grey dusk had fallen, Sam arrived as they'd arranged. They'd talked it all through. They needed cover of darkness, but in case Jean Crosbie was on one of her nocturnal prowls, they'd also decided Sam shouldn't park in the street, but at the end of the alley that ran between the backs of the houses. He and Jim would take the coal out the back way in the smaller sacks that Sam would bring with him. It would mean more trips, but they'd attract less attention that way.

'And saves me landing up in the sick bay with a hernia,' Sam had grinned. 'All questions asked.'

Now, with a weight far greater than a couple of hundredweight of coal lifting from his shoulders, Jim fitted the key in the padlock and unhooked the hasp. The door swung open and the shed's criminal contents were revealed.

'Right,' said Sam. 'A human chain's what we need – well, a production line.' He handed Lily a sack. 'Here you go!'

Crouched in the dark in her oldest of old clothes, Lily held open the sacks while Jim shovelled coal into them as quietly as possible, cursing when a rogue lump slithered away and clattered onto the brick floor. He then carried the sacks to Sam at the back gate; Sam took them down the alley to the jeep, covering them each time with canvas and carefully locking it up. It took an hour, but finally all the dreaded coal was re-bagged and stowed. Nearly there!

'You take the paraffin, Sam, I'll take the wood,'

Jim offered. 'God, I'll be glad to see the back of this lot.'

Lily held the door wide and Jim began dragging the sack of wood into the yard.

It was a night of ragged cloud, just as well for their secret operation, because the moon was waxing into a harvest moon. As Jim came out into the open, it shrugged off a ribbon of cloud and shone full on the yard. Lily put out a hand.

'Wait a minute!'

'What?'

'There's something in there! Underneath the top bits of wood – something else. I saw it. Black – or dark anyway.'

'A spider? A mouse?'

'No!' Lily was scrabbling in the sack. 'Bigger than that! And not moving.' She straightened up with a gasp. 'Oh, Jim! Look!'

She was cradling a pair of shoes, turning them over in her hands. The moon was still defying the clouds, and they could all see clearly now. They weren't black, but a deep plum colour, suede, with a wedge heel, ankle straps and a flower appliqued to the front.

'Beautiful!' Lily breathed.

'Shoes?' Sam put the can of paraffin down carefully, so as not to make a noise. 'What the devil are they doing there?'

With a sick jolt, Jim remembered Bigley's words.

He'd said there was something in the shed for Jim, his landlady . . . and his girl. What had it been exactly? *To warm the cockles of their hearts.*

'They're another part of the bribe,' he said in disgust. 'Bigley buying us off.'

'Well, it's worked!' Lily brought the shoes up to her face and laid one against her cheek. 'I'm bought and paid for!'

'Sam, tell her,' Jim appealed. 'She can't keep them.'

Sam took one look at Lily's face and put his hands up – a white flag.

'Hey, don't involve me!' he protested.

'But—'

'Look,' said Sam. 'I'm sticking my neck out for you two already. If you think I'm cruising into Nettleford with a pair of ladies' shoes as well as a load of coal and firewood, well, I'd have some very awkward questions to answer, I can tell you!'

'You won't have to.' Lily was clutching the shoes to her chest. 'These are not going anywhere!'

'Lily!' That was Jim, and she turned on him.

'If you think I'm letting these out of my sight . . . I'll lie down in front of the jeep if you try to make Sam change his mind!' She bent and placed them reverently on the ground. 'New shoes! The first new pair I've had since . . . well, virtually ever! And shoes like these, as well?'

'They might not even fit!'

Jim really was clutching at dandelions now.

'They'll fit,' said Lily, 'if I have to chop off my toes.' She slipped off the old plimsolls she'd been wearing and slid her feet into the shoes, damp from the shed, deliciously smooth and cool. She bent and did up the ankle straps, turning her foot this way and that. 'See? They do fit, anyway! Perfect!'

They were perhaps half a size too big, but she wasn't going to admit that. Easily solved with an insole.

'They'll squeak,' said Jim accusingly. 'Shoes you haven't paid for always do.'

'Superstitious nonsense!' Lily turned to Sam. 'Sam? What do you think?'

'I think I'd better get this fuel away from here,' he answered smoothly. 'That's all you asked me to take away. I'm simply obeying orders.'

Lily could have hugged him, and this time, she did. Overruled, Jim sighed.

'Fine, keep them,' he said. 'But you can be the one to explain to your mum how you came by them.'

'I'll say,' retorted Lily, 'that they were a present from an admirer. Meaning you, Jim, of course.'

'Well, Jim must think something of you, that's all I can say, sacrificing his coupons for a pair of shoes for you!' was Dora's comment. 'But really, Lily, you might have chosen something a bit more practical!'

'Oh, Mum . . .'

'No, I take it back,' said Dora, with a smile. 'You

deserve something pretty, love. And I know you'll look after them.'

'I will,' said Lily firmly. 'I know there'll be no more where these came from.'

Chapter 27

When Lily was young, it had seemed as if Christmas would never, ever come. The waiting and the anticipation had been agonising. She'd always written her letters to Father Christmas by the end of November and hoped and hoped for something special on the day, even though the most she'd ever received was a stocking of small gifts with an orange in the toe. What wouldn't anyone give for an orange now!

Even as she grew older, the season had retained its magic. Helping her mum to make the Christmas cake and pudding on Stir-Up Sunday, dropping the silver sixpence into the mixture and making a wish; carefully hoarding her pennies and planning her gifts for family and friends. She'd still written a letter to

Father Christmas in her head, even when she'd long ceased to believe in him, but instead of a doll or a *Bunty* annual, she'd wished for a dress or, more recently, stockings, always stockings.

Last year had been different, of course, after the bomb. All she'd wished for then was to get better quickly and to get back to work, but Lily was determined not to look back. There was no time for that anyway.

September had passed in a blur, trying to outwit Barry Bigley's machinations. Sam, bless him, had managed to smuggle the coal, firewood and paraffin back onto the Nettleford base undetected. When Lily and Jim had thanked him, he made light of how difficult and just how risky for him it might have been, but Lily knew that she, Jim and by association Dora could never thank him enough.

October and November sped by the same way, this time in a haze of Christmas stock deliveries. Customers had started calling in daily in the hope of pouncing on goods as soon as they were priced and put out. A stickler for tradition, Mr Marlow didn't approve of the store's Christmas decorations going up until December the first. He turned out to be superstitious, too, because he didn't want anyone staying after hours to put them up this year. Instead, he'd agreed to pay overtime for a few members of staff to come in on the final Sunday in November to get the store looking festive.

Last year Sir Douglas Brimble had donated a massive tree from his estate but again, perhaps superstitiously, he didn't repeat the gesture. Instead Jim had somehow sourced an eight-foot Norway spruce which would be delivered at the weekend and stand inside the main entrance. The boxes of tinsel and baubles were ready to decorate it and every department had their Japanese lanterns and paper chains standing by. The famous grotto – the fashion show catwalk creatively reshaped, white-washed and decorated with painted gingerbread men and barley sugar sticks – was waiting in the basement. On Sunday Les would wheel it up on a trolley and it would be assembled in its place. Dobbin, the rocking horse, would have to make way for it on Toys, so space had to be made for him on Childrenswear, and on the last Friday in November, Lily and Miss Temple were re-arranging the rails in anticipation.

Absorbed in the exact placement of a rack of party dresses to show them off to their best advantage, Lily didn't see the woman approach. It was Miss Temple who noticed her first, and said, in her best Marlow's tones:

'Good morning, madam. How may I help you?'

The 'madam' made Lily lift her head. Not a regular customer then, because they were addressed by name . . . no, definitely not! Not a customer at all! It was Mrs Quartermain!

'Erm, if you don't mind, Miss Temple,' Lily interrupted, 'I know this lady. Perhaps I could assist her?'

'As you wish, Miss Collins.' Miss Temple sounded slightly huffy. 'I'll go and see if I can thin out the boys' waistcoats.'

'Thank you.'

Lily waited for Miss Temple to walk away, then turned to Mrs Quartermain. When they'd met before, in May, she'd been in a light summer dress. Today she was wearing a silver musquash coat over a dark dress and a neat velour hat which almost covered her hair. Lily gave her a nervous smile.

'Mrs Quartermain! This is a surprise. Can I . . . What can I do for you?'

'I'm looking for Gladys,' said Mrs Quartermain simply. 'Is she here?'

Lily's heart fluttered in her chest.

'She's not on the sales floor at the moment, I'm afraid.' Gladys was busy in the stockroom. A long-awaited delivery of jigsaws had arrived, but some of the boxes had come open and she was having to try to sort them out so that on Christmas morning, eager children didn't find the prow of a naval battleship sailing into the duckpond of their farmyard scene. 'But she is in today. I'm sure she'd want to see you.'

'I hope so, now I've come all this way.' Mrs Quartermain seemed nervous too. 'I realise we can't talk here,' she added. 'In fact, you probably shouldn't be talking to me at all without showing me some

293

matinee jackets or something.' That was sensitive of her, thought Lily, but then Mrs Quartermain had been in service herself: she knew what was expected. 'But I presume you get a lunch hour? Could I meet her somewhere?'

Lily thought quickly. Lyons or the ABC would be too busy, and Peg's Pantry was too downmarket . . .

'There's a place called the Tudor Rose,' she suggested. Popular with the sort of women who shopped at Marlow's, it was an olde-worlde tearoom that did so-called light lunches. 'It's in Newton Street, not far. Gladys is on early dinner, I know. So she could be there just after twelve?'

Mrs Quartermain nodded eagerly.

'That's fine. And Lily – it is Lily, isn't it? Perhaps you'd like to come too, if you can.' She smiled, a sweet smile. 'I got the impression Gladys rather relies on you.'

Making peace with Miss Temple by offering to take an armful of boys' waistcoats to their own section of the stockroom, Lily escaped the sales floor and took the back stairs three at a time. At the far depths of the room, in the dim light from the high windows, she found Gladys at a trestle table surrounded by piles of jigsaw pieces. Breathless, Lily passed on the news.

'Here? In Hinton? Today? Oh my gawd!'

Gladys was so flustered she almost tumbled a pyramid of pieces to the floor.

'Careful!' Lily dived to save them. 'I was knocked for six as well! But how did she know where to find you?' She replaced the jigsaw pieces on the table. 'We never told her where we worked – we didn't get that far. I presume when you sent the invitation you told her your home address for a reply, but . . . do you think she went there and your gran sent her here?'

Gladys had recovered herself a bit now.

'She won't have needed to go to my house.'

'What? Then she must have been doing even more detective work than we did!'

Gladys's look was a mixture of shame-faced and defiant.

'I wrote again.'

'Again?'

'After the wedding. And I told her things.'

'What things?'

'About me. About Bill. I sent her a copy of one of the wedding photos. And I told her Bill would be here all summer while his ship was in refit, in case she wanted to get in touch.'

'Gladys! You never said!'

'No,' Gladys replied, quite sharply for her, 'and is it any wonder? After you gave me such a hard time over me sending her a wedding invitation in the first place?'

'Oh, Gladys.' Lily felt bad. 'I'm sorry . . . but what made you write again? You said the day you got married Bill didn't need his mother. He had you.'

'And he has, of course he has! But I couldn't let it go, Lily. It didn't feel right. And when Bill went back to sea, and I was on my own, well, I wrote one more time. You've been wonderful, and you are wonderful, such a good friend, and Bill may not need her, never ever, but I . . . somehow, I think I do!'

Lily felt even worse. Poor Gladys – all she'd ever wanted was a family and with her own parents dead and Bill back at sea, who did she have? Only her self-centred gran and her ailments – imagine going home to that every night!

Lily thought guiltily of her own home, where there was and always had been someone to have a chat with or share a laugh and a joke – first her mum and her brothers, now her mum and Jim and these days Sam too, and always something happening – rather too much sometimes! Mrs Quartermain was never going to be able to give Gladys that kind of company and support, but if they could at least be in touch . . .

'I don't think I've been wonderful at all,' she said ruefully. 'Far from it. But look, none of that matters now, or why Bill's mum didn't reply to the invitation or get in touch before. She's here now, right here. She's come all this way to see you. Let's see what she's got to say.'

Lily had never been inside the Tudor Rose, but it certainly played up to its name: even the ropes of tinsel and paper chains for Christmas couldn't cover it up. The oak-panelled walls were hung with portraits of Henry VIII's unfortunate wives and the plate rack was crowded with half-timbered china cottages and hung with tattered silk pennants. An aquatint of Hampton Court Palace hung over the inglenook, and on the mantelpiece costumed dolls of Elizabeth I and Mary Queen of Scots cosied up incongruously. Lily looked around for customers of Marlow's she might have to acknowledge but saw none. Twelve o'clock was a little late for coffee and a little early for lunch, and Mrs Quartermain was waiting for them at one of only three occupied tables. She gave them a wave as they stood in the doorway. Gladys was ashen with nerves and Lily had to give her a shove to propel her forwards.

Mrs Quartermain stood up to greet them. On the table was a pot of tea and a plate of dainty sandwiches.

'Gladys,' she said, holding out her hand. 'Thank you for coming.'

'How could I not?' stammered Gladys. 'I'm so pleased you're here.'

'Let's sit down.'

They each took a chair and Mrs Quartermain poured them all a cup of tea. Then everyone took a sip, more for show than for anything else, and, cups down again, Lily and Gladys looked to the older woman.

'I'm sorry not to have given you any notice,' she

said. 'I was going to write, but after I'd left it so long, I thought you might have changed your mind.'

'Never!' Gladys spoke from the heart.

'That's very understanding of you,' said Mrs Quartermain. 'But what you also have to understand is that your turning up in London like that – it shook me to bits. When you came that Sunday, and what you said . . . I could hardly think straight. But I want you to know not a day has gone by that I haven't thought about how hard it must have been for you to track me down, and what was behind it, and how much it showed you care for Billy . . .' She corrected herself. 'For Bill. I'm ashamed of how I sent you away. But as I say, it was the shock.'

Lily looked at Gladys. It wasn't really for her to speak, but Gladys was looking dumbstruck. Then Gladys found her voice.

'That was all my fault,' she said. 'I'm sorry. I dragged Lily and Sid into it. I could only see it from my point of view. And I was so fixated on that, what a good thing it'd be for Bill, and me – for everybody, I thought – that I never saw it might be like – well, like putting a bomb under your life. I can see that now, and I'm sorry, I really am.'

'Don't be.' Mrs Quartermain's rings sparkled as she instinctively put out her hand. 'As soon as you'd gone, I regretted it. I don't exactly know what I could have done differently, with things as they stood, but . . . anyway, then you sent the invitation. I took it out every day before the wedding, you know, and looked at it, but I knew I could never attend. I thought that would be the end of it, but when you wrote again, Gladys, with the photograph . . .' Her voice shook. 'It almost broke my heart. My boy. My baby. Married.'

Gladys's eyes were glassy with unshed tears and Lily swallowed hard.

'I wanted to write,' Mrs Quartermain went on. 'I started so many letters. To you, Gladys, and directly to Bill. But what do you say to your son after twenty years? And I didn't know, but I suspected, that you'd never told him you were going to look for me. So I might have been putting a . . . well, a bomb under *his* life. Under both of yours, if he'd been angry about what you'd done.'

'I don't think Bill'd be angry!' Gladys sniffed and smiled at the same time. 'He doesn't know how to be, bless him! We've never had a cross word. He doesn't get angry, does he, Lily?'

'He's a lovely chap,' Lily confirmed.

'I'm sure he is,' said Mrs Quartermain sadly. 'And it's no thanks to me.'

'Well, that's something else I've thought about, more and more lately,' said Gladys. She was surprising Lily minute by minute and Lily was starting to feel she'd grossly underestimated her friend for all this time. 'They told us at the home you'd been upset to leave him, and you were going to go back and get

him as soon as you could. When you never did, I
thought at first you were . . . well, I'm sorry, but that
you were horrible! That you must be completely
selfish and just have preferred the money and the life
you'd found for yourself to bringing him up. And I
thought I could never forgive you. But then I thought
you must have had some reason. And I thought more
about what you'd said, about your husband and that,
and I wondered what kind of pressure he might have
put you under, and what maybe your marriage was
like, and that maybe you had no choice.'

Mrs Quartermain had been turning her spoon in
its saucer. Now she raised her eyes.

'I think I'd better start at the beginning,' she said.

Chapter 28

'My husband's first wife was an invalid,' she began. 'I was asked at my interview for the job if I had, or had any intention of having, children and before I could answer I was told that that would rule me out. There had to be complete quiet in the household: there could be no question of a small child growing up there and running about. I took the job anyway. All I wanted was a secure position where I could live in, save money, and in a couple of years, set myself up again in some kind of home with young Bill.'

'It didn't work out like that, though, did it?' asked Gladys gently.

'No. After Ernest's – my husband's – wife died I was absolutely astonished when he asked me to marry

him. I had no idea he had feelings for me . . . I'm
not sure now that he really did . . .' She compressed
her lips again. 'But I thought if he felt like that about
me, and the whole question of the house having to
be quiet had been removed, I'd be able to tell him
about Bill and bring him to live with us.' Gripped,
Gladys and Lily nodded encouragement, and she went
on. 'When I fell pregnant soon after our marriage, I
was delighted. I thought that if we started a family,
it would be even easier to fetch Bill and absorb him
into it. But when I told Ernest I was expecting, he
hit the roof. He wanted me to get rid of the baby.'

Lily looked at Gladys, shocked, then back to Mrs
Quartermain. They'd gathered from what she'd said
when they'd first sought her out that her husband
was a tricky customer, but Lily had never imagined
a bully quite like this. Let alone that there might be
more children!

Now Mrs Quartermain had started, it was as if
years of dammed up emotion was coming pouring out.

'You'll have gathered by now, perhaps, that Ernest
is . . . rather a difficult man. I'd worked for him for
a couple of years by then, I knew as an employer he
liked things done a certain way, you expect that. But
it was only when I got to know him as a man . . .
he has to be the centre of his world. He likes – needs
– his own way, or things . . . well, let's just say he
makes life very awkward . . .'

She tailed off, and this time it was Gladys whose

hand went out to touch the older woman's. Mrs Quartermain squeezed it briefly, then, as if strengthened, went on.

'I stood up to him though, about the baby, and I'm glad I did. I don't know what I'd have done over the years without my girls – I had twins, you see. But after that – well, he withdrew pretty much all affection. I never dared to admit that I already had a child, let alone that I'd wanted to bring him to live with us.' She closed her eyes momentarily, as if she was trying to shut out some unpleasant scene. 'That would have been the end of it. He'd have thrown me out and made sure I never saw the girls again.'

Gladys and Lily were watching her, horrified.

'Yes, I can see what you're thinking.' Mrs Quartermain gave a sad smile. 'It sounds Victorian, doesn't it? But Ernest is quite a bit older than me. He is a Victorian, really, in his attitudes.'

Gladys seemed speechless, so Lily asked the question.

'Your girls . . . your daughters . . . how old are they now?'

'Fifteen, and away at school – it's been evacuated up to Yorkshire.'

'Bill's got sisters!' Gladys spoke at last. 'Half-sisters.'

'Identical twins,' said Mrs Quartermain. 'Iris and Rose.'

'What pretty names!'

'Would you like to see a photograph?'

'Oh yes please!' breathed Gladys.

Mrs Quartermain reached for her bag and brought out a photograph wallet. She laid a couple of snaps on the table, and Lily and Gladys bent over them eagerly.

The first seemed to have been taken in a park, or possibly, having seen the style in which they lived, the garden of the house in London. Mrs Quartermain was sitting on a fancy wrought-iron bench, a teenage girl on either side of her. Gladys picked up the photograph and examined it, no doubt looking for any likeness to Bill. From what Lily could see there wasn't much; the girls had longer faces, more pronounced eyes and darker, straighter hair. All three were smiling at the camera, but to Lily they had a sort of forced, frozen look. Sometimes that was to do with the exposure and the time it took to take a picture, but in this case she wondered if it was because of who was behind the camera, the forbidding Ernest Quartermain, perhaps.

Gladys laid the photo down and picked up the other. Again, Lily leant over to see. This one had been taken at the seaside, probably by one of those photographers who roamed the promenade. Again, Mrs Quartermain was flanked by the two girls, one on each arm, and they were well wrapped up against the wind, one of the girls holding onto her hat. But they were all smiling broadly; they looked completely carefree.

'I love that one,' offered Mrs Quartermain. 'It was only taken about a month ago. I went up to see them at their half-term. We went to Scarborough for the day and spending time with them alone, away from the house – and on top of finding out about Bill – it made me realise I had to do something.'

Lily and Gladys looked at her. So this was why it had taken her so long.

'They'll be sixteen next year, you see,' said Mrs Quartermain. 'And that's what's made the difference. They'll be able to decide for themselves what they want to do, and which parent they want to live with. I'm going to separate from Ernest.'

'What? But, but . . . will he let you?'

To Gladys, Ernest Quartermain was a modern-day Bluebeard.

'I think he'll have to.' Mrs Quartermain sounded suddenly much more confident. 'Oh, I didn't say, did I? The other way in which my husband's Victorian is that he has a mistress.'

Lily gaped. She must be naïve, but the way some people lived their lives!

'I've known about her for years,' said Mrs Quartermain, 'and put up with that as well, for the girls' sake. But I've had enough, and I'm going to tell him so. I've seen a solicitor and I intend to divorce him.'

Good grief, thought Lily. Gladys's simple quest really had put a bomb under the woman's life. Mrs Quartermain acknowledged it too.

'It's thanks to you, Gladys.' The older woman's

rings flashed again as she touched Gladys's hand. 'You getting in touch, and more than that, not taking no for an answer, not letting go, and restoring Bill to me, if you like. I've missed so many chances. I've missed another while he was in the country over the summer and goodness knows I'm torturing myself over it, but God willing, if he survives this war, I'm not going to let it happen again. I want to do what's right, what's always been right, and now – or very soon – I can. That's if you'll let me – if you feel sure that Bill would want to know me.'

The tears Gladys had been holding in coursed down her cheeks and she brushed them away with the back of her hand. Unable to speak, she nodded her head vigorously. Lily knew she could speak for her.

'I'm sure he would!'

Time had sped by, and it was a good job Lily looked at her watch. Gladys had produced the photographs of Bill that she always carried with her and she and his mum were poring over them, Gladys explaining every detail right down to the colour of Bill's shirt and how it suited him. Lily nudged her friend.

'I'm so sorry, Mrs Quartermain,' she said, standing up and collecting her things, 'but we've got to get back.'

Mrs Quartermain understood at once.

'Of course, I don't want you to get into trouble! But you've had nothing to eat – I'll get them to wrap the sandwiches for you.'

She signalled to the waitress, who took the plate away and came back with two greaseproof parcels. While she'd been gone, Gladys and Mrs Quartermain – Agnes, as she'd told Gladys to call her – had been discussing how best to tell Bill. They decided that Gladys should prepare the ground in a letter, and his mother would only write once he'd responded.

'It'll take a while,' Gladys warned her. 'I write to the *Jamaica*'s shore base, you see, but it can take weeks – months, sometimes – before letters even get to him, let alone a reply come back.'

'Don't worry about that,' said Mrs Quartermain. 'Things aren't going to move very fast at my end either.' She shrugged her coat back on. It was a beauty, but from what she'd told them, she'd paid a high enough price for it over the years. 'My solicitor's told me that to stop Ernest simply denying everything, I have to be sure of my facts. I need to find a private detective to follow him and get photographic proof. Pretty sordid, but there you are, it's how it's done.' She spoke frankly enough, but she looked rueful. 'I've wasted so much time.'

'You had your reasons,' said Lily. 'Your daughters. You were protecting them.'

'Yes,' urged Gladys. 'To be a mother to them and give them a home. Like you would have done for Bill, if you could have.'

Before the two of them could start going over it all again, and getting weepy, Lily butted in.

'I'm sorry,' she said, 'but we really do have to go.'

As they stood outside saying their goodbyes, Gladys took a deep breath.

'There's one more thing,' she said. 'I haven't told anyone this, not even Bill. Not yet. I was going to wait a bit longer, till I could be a million per cent sure, but now, since you're here, I'm going to say it. Fact is, I'm expecting!'

'Gladys!' Lily burst out.

'Oh my dear—' Mrs Quartermain's voice shook. 'Really? This is too much!' She took Gladys in her arms and pressed her against her coat. 'When will you—'

'In June,' said Gladys, tears welling once more. 'So you're a mum again and a grandma all in the same day! How about that?'

There was a lot to talk about on the way back to work, and no chance to say any of it because they were in such a rush. But now it made sense, thought Lily, as they dodged the shoppers and the shop and office workers hurrying to and from their own lunches – the way Mrs Quartermain had rebuffed them, and her silence ever since despite Gladys's attempts to make contact. And that wasn't all.

'Now I understand!' Lily said as they turned into the relative quiet of Brewer Street and headed for the staff entrance. With that in sight, they could afford to slow down a bit.

'About Bill's mum?'

'That, yes, but about you, too – looking so rough the last few weeks!'

Gladys's wan appearance and hollowed eyes hadn't just been about missing Bill, they'd also been down to morning sickness and the exhaustion of the first few weeks of pregnancy.

'Oh, thanks very much!'

'You know what I mean! You haven't been yourself. But I'm so happy for you – and Bill. Everyone will be.'

'Yes. And I'm starting to feel a bit better now,' Gladys confided, as they passed through the swing door into the behind-the-scenes part of the store.

'I wish you'd said though!' Lily signed back in with the pencil tied to the timekeeper's ledger. 'You must have known for a while. But I suppose you wanted to tell Bill first.'

'Well . . . yes, I do, but I wanted three months to go by before I even tell him.' Gladys took the pencil from her and signed back in too. 'My mum miscarried quite a few times before she had me, I was scared I'd do the same. But I should be twelve weeks next week, the doctor says. Baby's due in June.'

'It's such good news! I'm sure you'll be fine,' Lily assured her as they hurried to the cloakroom to drop off their bags and gas masks. 'And I promise I'll keep mum till you give me the OK . . . oh!' They both giggled at the turn of phrase. 'It's your news to tell, anyway.'

'Perhaps in a few weeks, at Christmas,' said Gladys with satisfaction. 'A little extra surprise for everyone.'

'Perfect! That still leaves Mum plenty of time to knit!'

They were stuffing their things in their lockers now, but as Gladys went to stow her packet of sandwiches, Lily stopped her.

'I'll make an excuse to Mr Bunting,' she said. 'Explain you'll be a bit late back. If I call it "feminine problems" he won't dare ask any more.'

'But I won't be late,' Gladys protested. 'We can make it.'

'Oh, no,' said Lily firmly. 'You are going to go to the canteen and eat your sandwiches. I can last till afternoon break, but you've got to keep your strength up. You're eating for two now. Or,' she added wickedly, 'now we know there are twins in the family, it could be three!'

Chapter 29

Lily had already felt that Christmas was rushing in on her – now it seemed, in the nicest of ways, to have come early. She dashed off a letter to Sid, telling him that the agonising weekend they'd spent looking for Mrs Quartermain had paid off in the end, and she told Jim in person as they walked home that night. He was pleased, of course, for everyone's sake, but Lily could tell he was much more preoccupied with getting the store dressed up for Christmas on Sunday, and even more so with the arrival of Father Christmas the next day.

After scores of phone calls, he'd managed to persuade a local brewery to convert one of their drays into a sleigh for the occasion, and though

Mr Marlow had baulked at the idea of Father Christmas perched on an empty beer crate, Jim had explained it was their only option. The crate, in any event, would be covered with sacking. Mr Marlow had finally given way, bought off with the happy news that Peter Simmonds had found another haulier who'd guarantee the store's coal deliveries over the winter.

In the event, Monday's grand entrance of Father Christmas was everything Jim could have wished for. Posters had gone up well before, and a good crowd of mothers and excited children were gathered behind the red ropes set up on the pavement. A pale December sun was shining against a wintry blue sky, and when the dray-cum-sleigh rounded the corner, horse clip-clopping proudly, bridle bells ringing merrily, an excited cheer went up. Albert, one of the store's retired carpenters, his costume padded out with a pillow, beamed and waved and 'ho-ho-ho'd' till his jaw must have ached but the children loved it. As he descended, bulging sack on his back, and made his way through the store – Jim had had him in to rehearse the route, he wasn't taking any chances – the children and their mothers followed behind. Then they patiently queued again to enter the grotto, pay the small entrance fee and receive a gift from his sack.

'Well done, you!' said Lily to Jim halfway through the afternoon. The grotto was still busy; older children had evidently nagged their mothers to bring them in after school. 'It's been non-stop, and this is only the first day. There's weeks to go yet!'

'Hm, well, let's see,' Jim replied. 'As long as it makes headlines in the *Chronicle*—'

'Oh, you're never satisfied!'

'High standards, that's all,' said Jim piously. 'Isn't that what Marlow's teaches us?'

But Lily could tell he was pleased. She was on her way to her afternoon break when they met on the stairs and he dragged her into the cleaners' cupboard for a surreptitious smooch.

Next day, Lily got a dinnertime pass out just so she could get the *Chronicle*'s lunchtime edition for Jim. Gladys came with her: she wanted to post her Christmas parcel to Bill to make sure it arrived on time.

Gladys was chuntering on about the special green ration book issued to all pregnant women, and how, as such, she'd had first pick of some Bramley cooking apples the grocer had had in.

'I'd eaten a whole half of one before I got it home. It was that sharp and fresh, it was lovely, but I didn't half pay for it later on – ooh, the indigestion . . . Lily, you look like you've seen a ghost! What is it?'

Lily had stopped dead in the middle of the pavement.

'Nothing,' she improvised quickly. 'Sorry. I saw something that . . . We need to go our separate ways here, Gladys. You get off to the post office.'

'All right,' said Gladys doubtfully. 'If you're sure you're OK.'

'Oh, I'm fine,' said Lily, smiling now. 'Very fine. Don't worry about me.'

What she'd seen was the newspaper seller's placard. In huge black letters it read:

LOCAL BUSINESSMAN CHARGED

That could mean only one thing – Barry Bigley! And it did. Lily bought two copies of the paper – one for salvage, one to keep – and shot straight back to work.

She knew Jim was having lunch with Peter Simmonds: if the grotto proved a success, they were hoping to capitalise on it to reintroduce some of their other ideas to keep the customers coming and to keep Marlow's moving with the times. Jim's pet project was to get Cedric Marlow to drop the apostrophe from the name ('So old-fashioned!' he constantly lamented). None of their plans could be raised with Mr Marlow till the New Year, of course. The grotto had to prove its worth first.

Lily scanned the canteen – ah, there they were, in the corner. She wove her way to their table. Both had pushed away their plates and were poring over sheets of figures. They looked up, surprised to see her.

'I'm sorry to interrupt, Mr Simmonds,' Lily began. 'But I thought you'd both like to see this.' She held out a copy of the *Chronicle* with the Bigley story deliberately uppermost. Jim's eyes widened.

'Sorry, silly me,' said Lily, as if to correct herself. 'Our Father Christmas story is below, so not the main headline, but still main news – and a lovely photograph!'

Jim dutifully flipped the folded paper, scanned the Father Christmas piece and handed it to Peter Simmonds. While he was reading it, Jim met Lily's eyes. They shared a look of disbelieving triumph.

'Thank you,' mouthed Jim. 'And thank God!'

It wasn't till the evening that they had the chance to really enjoy the outcome of the whole sorry saga. Lily was washing her stockings in the scullery sink, her hands all soapy.

'Read it out!' she begged. 'I want to hear it again!'

'Tch!' tutted Jim. 'Talk about enjoying someone else's misfortune!'

'Can you blame me?'

'What do you think?'

He began to read: '*Prominent local businessman Mr Barry Bigley of Bigley's Hauliers, Stoney Road, Hinton has been formally charged with conspiracy to effect black market sales of coal, petrol and sheet metal across this and neighbouring counties. He has been remanded in custody—*'

'Custody!' shrieked Lily.

'*Remanded in custody pending trial,*' Jim continued.

'I suppose they thought he might interfere with witnesses. And they were probably right.'

Lily shivered.

'Ugh! That man!'

Jim carried on reading:

'"*This is a shocking example of racketeering and exploitation,*" *said Chief Constable Mr James Carruthers in a statement, which went on:* "*There can be no doubt that such activities seriously undermine the war effort and make a mockery of the sacrifices both of our brave fighting men and the millions of law-abiding citizens of this country.*"'

He lowered the paper. 'That's pretty strong stuff from the police.'

'Well it's about time!' Lily squeezed the suds from her stockings. 'But there's still nothing there about how many police have been charged with dereliction of duty or corruption or whatever, is there?'

'That's a bit much to expect,' said Jim. 'But you notice it's not Bigley's pal Detective Chief Inspector Gregson giving the statement. He usually does. It looks to me like this whole thing has gone over his head, which was exactly what Sam said would happen if he took it to the Canadian top brass.'

'I hope Gregson's not going to get away with it!'

'We'll just have to hope there'll be a full internal enquiry at Hinton police and the next headline we'll read – or most likely won't because he'll be quietly retired – is that Gregson has been removed from duty.'

'Hm.' Lily lifted the bowl of soap suds to one side – Dora wouldn't stand for them being thrown away after only a couple of pairs of stockings had been washed in them. She ran cold water into the sink for rinsing. 'Read me the editorial as well, Jim. That really gives Bigley a kicking.'

'Your blood's properly up, isn't it?' Jim grinned. But he turned the page and began:

'*Shocked as we are by the wicked crimes perpetrated by one of Hinton's formerly most respected citizens, the* Chronicle *can only agree with the Member of Parliament for Manchester Platting, the Right Honourable Mr J. R. Clynes, who stated last year that such actions amount to "treason of the very worst kind".*

The Chronicle *has no hesitation in calling for the strongest possible penalties to be exacted. A fine and a long term of penal servitude are only to be expected: some would wish to go further. Interment, flogging and even making such acts a capital crime are, in the opinion of this newspaper, not too harsh a punishment for such heinous behaviour which truly threatens the very safety of the country we are fighting for.*'

He put down the paper and pulled a face.

'Hang 'em and flog 'em, that's going it a bit. I'm not sure I'd want to see Barry Bigley hanged. Would you?'

Lily thought about it. She thought about how Robert Marlow had piled the pressure on Jim to sort

317

out the mess he'd got himself mixed up in and how Bigley himself had tried to get Jim even more embroiled. The bribe of the coal and the firewood and the paraffin arriving by dead of night, and the threat about Dora. Having to drag Sam into the equation and get rid of the stuff by dead of night as well, and the consequences for any of them if they'd been found out. Of course her blood was up! But, but – Bigley obviously hadn't dropped any of them in it – he'd only owned up to the coal scam they'd arrested him for, up at Nettleford, and the business about the scrap metal and the petrol must have come to light through paperwork the police had found in his office that he hadn't had time to destroy. It could have been so different if Bigley had confessed to the business at Marlow's as well, and Lily supposed she should feel grateful to him for that. And then there was the question of the shoes. The plum suede uppers and the leather soles didn't squeak, but Lily still felt a bit self-conscious wearing them. The wages of sin? But they were gorgeous, and who did she have to thank for them . . . ?

'No,' she said reluctantly in answer to Jim's question. 'I can't say I would. I think hanging's barbaric and a horrible way for anyone's life to end, whatever they've done. But I never want to see him round here again. I hope they lock him up and throw away the key.'

'Me too,' Jim agreed. 'But heavens, I'm glad it's over.'

Chapter 30

Now she was in on Gladys's secret, Lily watched, and watched over, her friend with extra affection in the weeks before Christmas. She made sure Gladys ate up all her dinner and checked that she was getting the fruit and drinking the full pint of milk a day which her special green ration book entitled her to. She couldn't help noticing how good Gladys was with the little ones queuing for the grotto, keeping them chatting as the line inched forwards, earning grateful looks from parents already wearied by their children's over-excitement. She helped toddlers up on to Dobbin the rocking horse, fitting their feet gently into his stirrups and making sure they didn't rock too wildly. She enthused as they came out of the grotto clutching

319

their little present, telling them to 'keep on being good for Mummy' until the day itself, and earning yet more grateful looks.

Gladys was going to be such a good mother, thought Lily warmly. Now the first three months had passed she'd got her colour back and was already looking fuller in the face and more rounded of figure. She wouldn't announce her pregnancy in the store till after Christmas, she'd decided, and would work as long as possible, but Lily had to face the fact that her best friend would still be leaving. Of the three of them who'd been shop girls there in the beginning, Lily, Gladys and Beryl, only Lily would be left – and Jim, of course.

Jim was busy in the pre-Christmas rush, inevitably, but Lily still wondered as he took her hand for their walk home or kissed her goodnight on the landing if he ever thought, as she did, about where their relationship was going. Was he ever going to give her any indication? He loved her; she loved him. She'd said so, he'd said so, and she knew he meant it. So what was holding him back? Lily wasn't a patient person. She liked to make things happen. Even her own self-imposed deadline of next year's leap year day seemed too long to wait, and her next birthday, and possibly joining the ATS, which might wake him up a bit, was even further off.

She could always join up under-age; lots of people did, but she'd have to go away for training and then very likely be posted away. If that happened, and with Bill away at sea, who'd support Gladys when the baby was born? And then there was Marlow's . . . only a year ago her beloved store had been half-ruined. She and the rest of the staff had worked so hard to restore its shine and reputation – and she'd had her promotion to second sales.

If she left for the ATS, would she get her old job back after the war when other Marlow's staff would be returning too? She didn't want to leave everything she loved with the risk of it not being there when she returned – and the same applied to her and Jim.

As the store closed on Christmas Eve, Lily breathed a sigh of relief. It had been an exhausting day. Last-minute shoppers – mostly men, it had to be said – had raced in, panicked, after a business lunch, to buy gifts for their wives and secretaries, and to pick up the toys they'd promised weeks ago they'd take care of. The grotto was still doing a brisk trade right up to closing time, and as Gladys was busy serving, Lily had taken over crowd-marshalling and Dobbin duties.

When all the customers had finally left, there was more work to do, but with something of a festive atmosphere. Miss Frobisher took off her jacket; Miss Temple eased her bunions out of her shoes and padded around happily in stockinged feet. Lily tidied the rails and the drawers behind the counter as the other two moved around the department, noting which goods would be heading for reduction in the sale. On Toys next door, the grotto had to be dismantled and taken away. Jim, Les and Mr Simmonds loaded it onto a trolley for Les to trundle off.

'Put it somewhere safe till next year!' Jim called after him.

Takings from the grotto had far exceeded their expectations and, even after deductions for Albert's wage and the cost of the small gifts, it was showing a healthy profit. As hoped, it had benefitted other departments too. With their children pacified, the mothers had gone on to spend time and money in Perfumery and Cosmetics, Toiletries, Accessories, even Small Household, a satellite of Jim's department, treating themselves to a new tray cloth or tea towel – the excitement when those had come in! – to impress seasonal visitors.

Mr Simmonds had decreed that re-siting Dobbin and restoring Toys and Childrenswear to their usual layouts could wait until the store opened again after Christmas, and by seven o'clock, Lily, Jim and Gladys had joined the rest of the staff in the canteen for the traditional glass of punch, a mince pie and a 'thank you' from Mr Marlow himself.

The canteen had had its Christmas garb on for weeks – paper chains and strips of lametta. Now several of the tables had been pushed together to form one long row, swagged with red crepe paper and laden with food and drink. It was also the tradition that the canteen staff were off duty for the occasion. There were two huge vats of punch at one end of the table: Mr Simmonds stood behind one and Mr Bertram, the ground-floor supervisor, behind the other. Miss Frobisher, Miss Kendall and Miss Drake were stationed behind the trays of sandwiches to serve them out with tongs, and Miss Wagstaff, a rictus smile on her face, was holding a tray of mince pies, ready to circulate with them.

When everyone had a glass and a plate of food, Miss Garner clapped her hands and called for quiet. Mr Marlow, who'd greeted everyone as they came in, but after that had stood quietly chatting to Jim's boss, Mr Hooper, stepped forward.

There was no doubt that the last year had aged him and looking at his uncle Jim knew he'd done the right thing in shielding him as much as possible from Barry Bigley's – and Robert's – misdemeanours. Lily could see the change in Mr Marlow too. Standing next to Jim, she felt for his hand and squeezed it as the older man started what Mr Simmonds called his address to the troops.

'Thank you, everyone,' Mr Marlow began. 'It's been quite a year. I don't want to dwell on what happened last Christmas, but I have to mention it, because I want to pay tribute to you all for your supreme efforts to rebuild Marlow's. When I say rebuild, I mean in the literal sense, of course, but even more importantly to rebuild our reputation.

Today, our customers can once again look to us to supply the best we can in these trying times – the best quality at the best possible prices we can negotiate. For that I would like to thank our hard-working buyers, every one of them.'

Everyone shuffled their plates and glasses so they could applaud; there were a few 'hear hears' and murmurs of agreement. Lily caught Miss Frobisher's eye and smiled. Miss Frobisher smiled back. She was wearing one of the outfits that Lily most admired, a navy dress in spotted voile with a white collar and cuffs. She'd undone the top two buttons and turned back the cuffs for her duties serving the food. Along with a few strands of her usually immaculate hair which had come loose, it made her look even prettier and less severe – not that she really was, as Lily knew. She turned her attention back to Mr Marlow.

'Those customers would not, however, shop here unless they could also be assured of the most attentive service at all times. So I want to thank every member of staff, from the most experienced salesmen and women . . .'

Lily glanced over to Miss Temple and Miss Thomas, who between them had almost eighty years of service. They looked both pleased and proud.

'. . . to the very newest junior, who I believe is . . .'

Miss Garner whispered something in his ear.

'Ah, yes,' Mr Marlow continued. 'Miss Miller, on Ladies' Fashions.'

Poor Bessie blushed and nearly dropped her glass, but Mr Marlow hadn't finished yet.

'So when you receive your wages for this week, or your salary for the month, you will find a slightly larger bonus than has been paid in recent years. That's my way of saying thank you for all your hard work in this most difficult year.'

There were louder murmurs this time, of appreciation and thanks. Some brave soul even shouted 'hurrah!'

Mr Marlow acknowledged this with his fleeting smile.

'Thank you,' he said. 'Now, there are two other members of staff I'd like to single out. They've worked beyond the call of duty to get the store back on its feet, building on a challenge I set them some time ago, to come up with ideas to . . . well, to keep Marlow's a going concern. They are Peter Simmonds and Jim Goodridge.'

Lily flashed Jim a smile. He'd turned as crimson as Bessie and was shaking his head in embarrassment.

'I asked them for ideas to keep up staff morale, hence our very successful football and cricket teams, and the staff newsletter, *The Marlow's Messenger.* They both give up a lot of their free time to make these a success.'

There was a pause and a smatter of applause – mostly from the cricket and football teams punching each other on the arms and congratulating themselves.

'The female members of staff aren't forgotten – several take part in rounders and netball matches. Many more take advantage of the hairdresser who comes in fortnightly.'

No one could disagree with that. Lily's hair had benefitted hugely from the 'relaxant' that had calmed down her flyaway curls – for a while, anyway.

'In recognition of the hard work these two gentlemen have put in, and because Mr Bertram, our ground-floor supervisor, will shortly be retiring, I am creating a new post of senior supervisor. Mr Simmonds will in future oversee both floors. Miss Frobisher will become first-floor supervisor, but as she will retain her responsibilities as the buyer on Childrenswear, I'm appointing Mr Goodridge as her deputy, retaining his role on Furniture.'

There was a moment's silence while everyone took this in – a development no less of a surprise to Lily than to everyone else – and to Jim as well, it seemed, from his stunned look. Miss Frobisher and Mr Simmonds, however, must have been in on the plan; they looked as though they'd been practising their pleased-but-modest faces.

Another, louder round of applause broke out. So many people crowded round Mr Simmonds and Miss Frobisher and even Jim that Lily found herself pushed away from him and pressed up against Gladys.

'Jim promoted! How about that!' exclaimed Gladys.

'I know!' marvelled Lily. 'I can't take it in!'

'And you had no idea?'

'Not just me, Jim too! Didn't you see his face?'

'Mr Marlow's a sly one, isn't he?' Gladys shook her head. 'He's not quite past it yet. Still likes to be the boss.'

'And spring these surprises,' Lily replied thoughtfully. 'I suppose that was why he was talking to Mr Hooper, squaring Jim's new role with him.'

'Seems to me there could be a new role for you in it as well,' observed Gladys. 'If Miss Frobisher's got two jobs now, you'll be first sales before next year's out, you mark my words.'

Lily tried to look sceptical, but the thought had crossed her mind. It amused her that Gladys had thought of it too: impending motherhood had done something to her. She was already sounding older and wiser – and a positive mother hen.

They were called to attention by Miss Garner clapping her hands again.

'If you could charge your glasses, please, Mr Marlow has a few more words to say.'

More? What had come over him? There was a surge towards the refreshment table, empty glasses waving in the air. Lily still had half a glass of punch and felt she'd had quite enough already. She left Gladys mother-henning Bessie and made her way back to Jim.

Someone had refilled his glass and he took a swig as she approached.

'I don't know if I'm drunk on punch or—'

'Success?' Lily smiled. 'Congratulations, by the way. I take it you had no idea?'

'None at all! But it's something to celebrate!'

He swooped down and kissed her. His mouth was warm and soft. Lily was shocked.

'Jim! Hardly the behaviour of a deputy supervisor! You'll get the sack before you've got the job!'

'I set the rules now,' swanked Jim. 'Just watch me!'

Before Lily could reply (he could think again about that!) Miss Garner chinked a knife on her glass and the buzz in the room subsided again. Mr Marlow resumed.

'I shan't go on much longer,' he said. 'You've all got homes to go to.'

Les, in fact, had already slipped off. He was meeting Beryl and Bobby at the station to start the journey to Worcestershire where his mum had promised them 'a proper country Christmas'. Ivy and Susan, Les's sister, had really taken to their new life looking after Jim's dad, who Jim and Lily would go and see at New Year.

'The new appointments,' continued Mr Marlow, 'are only the beginning. Mr Simmonds and Mr Goodridge are determined to drag this store – and me, it has to be said' – he permitted himself a little laugh, though no one else dared join in – 'into the twentieth century – or the latter half of it. So I can tell you that assuming, God willing, the war continues to go our way, when we finally see victory there will be changes.'

Lily felt for Jim's hand again. She wasn't sure what was in the punch, but she was beginning to feel reckless herself. Could these be the changes he'd been hoping for for so long? That would be an even better Christmas present than a promotion.

Mr Marlow was warming to his theme.

'The lifts,' he declared, 'will be upgraded and there will be escalators between every floor. Every department will have a modern cash register instead of the current pneumatic tube system.'

Everyone was nudging each other now, pulling faces, raising their eyebrows. But Mr Marlow, sensing that he had the audience of his life, was working up to a climax.

'These will have to wait; the materials and the labour simply aren't available. But one thing can happen now – or very soon, and with minimal effort. It brings me back to where I started – my heartfelt thanks to all of you for what I think I can call true teamwork over the past twelve months.'

He took a deep breath. A sea of expectant faces awaited his final pronouncement, but when it came, there were still gasps of amazement.

'I intend to remove,' said Mr Marlow, 'the apostrophe from the store's name. I hope that will show you that I no longer regard this store as my family's personal fiefdom. As "Marlows" with no apostrophe it will belong to us all – to you all. I want you to feel more than employees; more than colleagues. We will be partners. And I hope we will continue to work as a team to deliver the very best service, value and quality to the people of Hinton for many years to come.'

It was a Churchillian moment: all Mr Marlow needed to complete the image was a cigar and a Homburg hat. He even seemed to swell in stature – taller, broader – as massive applause broke out. This time the 'hurrahs' were louder, and someone called for three cheers, after which some of the younger salesmen, who'd been making free with the punch, burst into 'For He's a Jolly Good Fellow'.

In the hubbub, not caring who saw, Lily flung herself at Jim. He was grinning from ear to ear. He hugged her tight, then released her.

'At last!' he said, raising clenched fists to the ceiling in triumph. 'At last!'

Trying to mask the emotion he was obviously feeling too, Mr Marlow stood silently, blinking and nodding and occasionally holding up his hand as if to say 'Enough!'

When the singing had subsided, he uttered one final, modest 'thank you' and stepped back before Miss Garner took the floor. With her usual no-nonsense briskness, she wished everyone a very Merry Christmas and a safe journey home, before puncturing the mood entirely by adding that she'd be grateful if they could return their used plates and glasses to the table.

The party was over. But what a party!

Chapter 31

Gladys was one of the staff that needed to get off home. Her gran would be worrying – as well as impatient for her night-time cocoa – and Gladys had their Christmas dinner, modest as it would be, to prepare for tomorrow.

'Night-night, Lily, and Merry Christmas!' she said, pulling her scarf across her chest and buttoning her coat. 'I didn't tell you, did I, in all the fuss, I had a card from Mrs Quartermain, by the way. Lovely it is, addressed to me and Bill.'

'I suppose she didn't tell you how she's getting on with her divorce?' queried Lily. 'Not quite the thing to add after "Season's Greetings", is it?'

'No, and I haven't heard anything from Bill since I

wrote and told him I'd found her. Nor since I told him about the baby. Oof, I can hardly get the belt of this coat round me and I don't think it's just the mince pies!' Gladys gave up and let it hang loose. 'I don't suppose Bill's even got the letters. You'd need a polar bear to deliver them up between the icebergs where he is.'

'Come here,' said Lily, pulling her into a hug. 'Merry Christmas, Mrs Webb. Your Bill will be home safe and sound, you'll see, and you can introduce him to his mum – and the little one.'

'Let's hope,' said Gladys. 'See you after Christmas, Lily. Love to your mum. Have a nice time.'

Lily hung back in the cloakroom. There was no hurry: along with Peter Simmonds and some of the other salesmen, Jim was putting the canteen back to rights. She checked her reflection in the mirror fixed to the wall and ran a comb through her hair. With the baby coming, Gladys had her future sorted. But what did Mr Marlow's announcements really mean for hers – and for Jim's?

One person had been conspicuous by his absence that evening – Robert Marlow. In previous years he'd made a point of coming to the Christmas Eve get-together, even when he'd left the store. Now he lived in Birmingham, that wasn't so easy, and no doubt Evelyn and her parents would have had Christmas Eve plans of their own. But even so . . . never mind all the talk about everyone being equal in the new, apostrophe-free Marlows, were some more equal than others? Jim was a relative, after all – could his promotion be the first indication that the family connection might lead to more? Cedric Marlow couldn't go on for ever . . . Lily pulled herself up short. She wasn't wishing Mr Marlow dead, she never would, but if he stepped back, a future for the store with Mr Simmonds as general manager and Jim as his deputy didn't seem such a far-fetched idea.

Then there was Gladys's prediction for her. Miss Thomas and Miss Temple were both well over sixty: they'd come back out of retirement when younger staff had begun joining up. They were senior to Lily in every sense, but neither worked full-time and wouldn't want to. A first salesgirl was needed on the department, really, and that only left Lily. In her heart, she felt sure Gladys was right – Miss Frobisher had been so good to her, she was bound to recommend a further promotion – and reasonably soon. What did that do to her grand plans to join the ATS?

She'd lingered long enough. She shrugged on her coat, collected her bag and gas mask and found Jim lounging at the timekeeper's office. He was in such high spirits – probably literally – that he didn't even look pointedly at his watch but held the door open for her as they went out into the fresh night air. The narrow back street was pitch-black and Jim switched on his torch. The first people they saw in its wavering light were Miss Frobisher and Mr Simmonds walking arm-in-arm ahead of them.

'Let's not catch them up,' said Lily quietly. She wanted to savour her time with Jim; they had so much to talk about.

'Fine by me.'

But the other pair were walking slowly too, chatting, heads together, and by the time the two couples reached the main street, Lily and Jim were just a few feet behind. There was a black car waiting at the kerb with its lights off, but in the thin beam of Jim's torch, Lily saw two men approach Mr Simmonds. One was small and dapper in a belted raincoat and a trilby hat. The other was bare-headed, thick-set, in a dark overcoat.

Jim motioned her to hang back and drew her into a shop doorway.

'Who are they?' she whispered.

'I don't know,' said Jim. 'But if there's going to be trouble, I might have to help out.'

Peter Simmonds had boxed not just *in* the Army but *for* the Army and he'd taught Jim, her gentle, peace-loving Jim, to throw a few punches. Lily had seen the force of them last year when Jim had flattened someone he thought was a rival for her affections. Nothing had shocked and appalled her so much since Percy Fleming, who lived in their street, had painted a swastika under his door knocker when there'd been a threat of invasion three years ago, and she was equally appalled now.

'You can't start brawling in the street!'

'Two against one? If they set on him, I'll have to! What do you think I'm going to do, run away?'

But the men showed no sign of attacking Peter Simmonds: they seemed to be having a conversation. Miss Frobisher could be heard intervening, though not what she was actually saying, but after a couple of exchanges Mr Simmonds held up his hands as if in agreement, or perhaps resignation, and moved with the two men to the car. The burly one opened the back door and they both got in. The other man went to the front passenger side and, in the light of a moon which had popped out from behind a bank of cloud, Lily saw a third man in the driver's seat. The moon showed her something else as well. A sign on the roof of the car read 'Police'.

Lily was frozen to the spot, but as the car drew away with its slitted headlights dipped, Jim sped to Miss Frobisher's side.

'What was that about?' Lily heard him say as she joined them.

'I have no idea,' answered Miss Frobisher slowly. 'I don't know what to think. They said they needed him to answer a few questions. I – I suppose I'll have to . . . I can't go to the police station and ask – or wait around. I have to get back for my little boy.'

'They probably wouldn't tell you anything anyway,' said Jim.

'They didn't tell us anything now! Just asked

335

Peter to go along with them. I don't know what's going on.'

'Is there anything we can do?' asked Lily helplessly.

'I don't think so.' Miss Frobisher's usual self-possession had vanished and her voice sounded shaky. 'Just go home and enjoy your Christmas.'

Some chance now!

'Can we walk you home?' offered Jim. 'Let us do that at least.'

'No, no, thank you.' Miss Frobisher gave a thin smile. 'You're very kind, but it's not far. I'll be all right.'

Miss Frobisher might have said she'd be all right, but she obviously wasn't, and Lily's head was reeling.

'What can it be?' she asked as she and Jim hurried hand in hand through the park. 'What can the police possibly want with Mr Simmonds?'

'It's a mistake. Mistaken identity,' said Jim. 'It has to be.'

'You think so? It's Christmas Eve, Jim. They're not going to come out tonight of all nights on a wild goose chase.'

'Oh, you've got faith in our local police, have you?' retorted Jim. He was loping along as usual; Lily scurried to keep up. 'They may have cleared out the rot, it doesn't mean they're any more competent than they ever were. They've got the wrong bloke.'

'Well . . .' To Lily, it sounded a bit as if he was trying to convince himself. 'I hope you're right.'

On top of Cedric Marlow's shock announcements and the unaccustomed punch – what *had* they put in it? – she felt quite light-headed with it all.

'Let's get home.' Jim hurried her along even faster. 'Your mum'll be worried. Not a word of this to her, OK? We've got to act as if nothing has happened. We'll tell her the good news, of course, Uncle Cedric's little speech, but that's it. And tomorrow we open the presents, we eat the food, we laugh at whatever daft comedy show is on the wireless and all the rest of it. It's only the three of us, and your mum'll be feeling that, so we've got to make the day the best we can for her.'

Lily pressed her cheek to his shoulder. Jim was right. It was almost two years since they'd seen Reg, and Sid had volunteered to work over Christmas so that married men could have the time with their families. He'd promised he'd come up for a couple of days before New Year, but Lily and Jim would be back at work by then, and it wasn't the same as having him there on the day itself. Dora would miss her boys: they all would.

By the time they got in, Dora had gone to bed, leaving their stockings pinned to the mantelpiece: she'd be up at six to pop a few small gifts in them, Lily knew. There was no tree: there were none to be had, not at a price they could afford anyhow, but Lily and Jim had strung paper chains across the ceiling and cut sprigs of holly for the picture rail. Like most households, they were making the best of what they had, or could get hold of.

Jim took hold of Lily. He held her tight and kissed her lingeringly before they went upstairs.

'Try not to worry,' he whispered as they parted on the landing. 'It'll all look better in the morning. Christmas morning, Lily. You love Christmas, don't let this spoil it.'

Chapter 32

Dora woke early on Christmas Day. She said her usual prayer for Reg and Sid, then one for every fighting man and woman, and, today, one for those whose loved ones were dead or captive, and who'd be spending their first, or another, Christmas without them. She knew how that felt. The children's father had died in December and that first one without him, with Lily just a baby, had been one of the bleakest days she could remember. But Dora had resolved that after that, Christmas would be magical and special again for the children's sake; she'd make it that way. She scrimped and saved all year to put things aside for their stockings and for a proper dinner and even when they were older, her determination didn't waver.

By then, she'd even come to enjoy the day herself once more; the secret preparations, the hoarding of little treats, planning the meal – the children's excitement and pleasure made it all worthwhile.

Swinging her legs out of bed, shivering as she pulled on her dressing gown, she crept downstairs in the dark to fill the stockings, light a fire and arrange the chairs in a semi-circle around it. By the time Lily and Jim came down, she was dressed, the tea was made and the table had been laid with the holly-and-ivy embroidered cloth for a festive breakfast.

'Merry Christmas!' she greeted them, as they gave her a hug. 'Good party last night?'

'Yes! Lots to tell!' said Lily, pouring herself and Jim a cup of tea. 'But only after our presents!'

Dora gave a 'Tch', but one of amusement.

'You don't change!' she said. 'Same as when you were six! Now don't get excited, it's only bits!'

But Lily had already opened her stocking and was cooing over a tortoiseshell hair clip while Jim expressed delight at yet another pair of socks. A toothbrush each (a valuable commodity these days), a pot of Vaseline for Lily and a second-hand paperback for Jim, a bar of ration chocolate and a shiny Cox's apple each and they were done.

'Now for the presents proper!' said Lily, handing over a small box. 'Here's yours, Mum.'

Last year she'd had a brooch put aside for Dora at Marlow's, a black cat with green glass eyes, but the bomb had put paid to her plans and she'd never been able to buy it. This year she'd chosen a kingfisher enamelled in blue and green: it would brighten up Dora's old blue coat. As she hoped, Dora was entranced and promptly went to the hallstand to pin it on the lapel.

Lily watched as Jim opened his present – a pen, the best she could afford, engraved with his name. His face when he saw it told her she'd got it just right.

'It'll go with your new swanky deputy supervisor status!' she teased.

'Yes, to give you a black mark!' he retaliated, swooping to kiss her. 'But thank you, it's perfect. Though I suppose you expect something from me now?'

'It is the custom,' said Lily, primly.

Jim handed over his present. It was a long slim box – not a ring, then! – but not having expected one, she was still excited. It looked like jewellery and she knew he'd consulted Gladys and Beryl about what she'd like. He'd even managed to wrap it in a bit of brown paper – tied up with something that looked familiar.

'You . . . ! I've been looking for this!' she exclaimed, holding up her royal blue hair ribbon.

'Yes, sorry,' said Jim. 'You left it downstairs and I couldn't resist.'

'Thank you very much! I thought I'd lost it—'

'Come on, love, what have you got? Open it up!' Dora sat down again.

Lily did as she was told. Inside was a locket – chased silver, oval, on a delicate chain. Jim had even put photographs of each of them inside, snipped out of Gladys's wedding group.

Lily was moved almost to tears.

'Oh Jim! It's beautiful! Thank you!'

She meant it. It was the nicest thing he could have chosen, and she threw her arms round his neck.

'Now for my present!' Dora held out a slim square package. It was the same paper as last year – and the year before that – pressed under a cool iron, but even so, the Father Christmases on it looked more wrinkly than twinkly. Lily opened it carefully: she knew she'd be seeing the paper next year as well. Then she gasped:

'Stockings! Proper stockings! Mum! Where did you get these?' Overwhelmed, overjoyed, Lily turned the shiny packet in her hands. 'Sam, I suppose!'

'That's for me to know and you to find out.' Dora retrieved the paper from Lily's lap and smoothed it out. 'But please don't bother. And certainly don't go asking him!'

She didn't want that, not when the stockings had been given to her by Hugh. She'd been embarrassed about accepting them in the first place and had always intended to give them to Lily, but last Christmas, with the bomb and everything, hadn't been the right time.

Lily jumped up and kissed her.

'I won't say a word! But wherever and however you got them, thank you!'

'You like them, then,' said Dora drily, accepting Lily's hug. 'Good!'

Then it was time for the presents Gladys and Beryl had brought round, as well as those in the lumpy parcel that had arrived from Egypt a full two weeks ago.

'That's Gwenda, she's got him organised!' Dora had correctly surmised. She'd probably had a hand in choosing the presents too, because they were perfect: a wallet for Jim and soft leather purses for Lily and Dora, Dora's a sensible navy, Lily's lipstick-red.

Lily brought hers to her face and inhaled the luxurious scent of the leather. Dora smiled to see her delight. Lily had had her girlhood snatched away by the war; she deserved all the nice things she could get.

All the clucking over the presents delayed them, and by the time breakfast had been eaten and washed up, it was time for Dora to head off to church. Jim and Lily had cried off.

'You're having a day off,' Jim insisted. 'Leave everything to us.'

Dora looked dubious.

'You don't trust us, do you?' grinned Jim.

'I trust you,' smiled Dora. 'It's Lily in the kitchen I'm worried about!'

'I promise, dinner will be bubbling away by the time you get back. Now off you go!'

Jim shooed her out of the door.

'Right,' he said to Lily. 'Get your pinny on and let's get to work. But first of all, where's my proper Christmas kiss?'

In the end, it was the best Christmas dinner they'd had since the start of the war.

Jim kept Lily hard at work peeling the potatoes, scrubbing the carrots and shredding the cabbage. They didn't grow sprouts – the soil was too poor – and the greengrocer had laughed when Dora had asked if he had any. But Sam had pressed her to accept a tin of something called turkey roll and a can of equally mystifying 'cranberry log' to go with it. When Lily turned it out, it kept its shape on the plate, a wobbly cylinder of red jelly that made her laugh. She set it in the centre of the table and put a sprig of holly on top.

Along with the turkey roll, the cranberry log was delicious and Dora's Christmas pudding – light on currants, heavy on carrot – was helped down with custard *and* canned cream – also from the Canadian NAAFI.

'Absent friends,' said Jim, raising his glass. Dora had put aside her qualms and they'd all dibbed in for a bottle of black market sherry.

Smiling, they chinked glasses – Jim thinking of his

dad, Lily and Dora of Reg, Sid – and Sam, who couldn't be there to share the feast he'd helped to provide. He was on duty at the base.

'Well, that was lovely!' Dora declared. Even she, never a big eater, had undone the button on the waistband of her skirt.

'And you're not doing the washing up!' Jim chided. 'Not a hand's turn all day, we said, and we meant it!'

Lily nodded agreement, but distantly. The presents, then the cooking, had occupied the morning, but the toast to absent friends had set her thinking. Her closest friends these days were her colleagues at Marlow's, which led her back to Miss Frobisher – and Mr Simmonds.

'It's no good,' she said to Jim when they escaped to the scullery. 'I can't help thinking about last night. And Mr Simmonds.'

'We can't talk about it here,' said Jim. 'Let's wash up, hear the King's speech, then we'll go for a walk. How's that?'

The King, in his usual halting delivery, spoke of 'a brightening of our fortunes on land, on sea and in the air.' But he also counselled that though there were 'bright visions' of the future, 'we have no easy dreams of the days close at hand'.

They stood for the National Anthem, then Jim nodded at Lily.

'We thought we might go for a walk,' he told Dora. 'Shake that dinner down a bit.'

'Good idea,' said Dora, picking up the Georgette Heyer which Cousin Ida had given her. 'I think I'll have a little read.'

Lily was glad to get out of the house. 'You know what I've started to think, don't you?' she said as soon as they'd shut the back gate. 'If it isn't a mistake . . .'

'Barry Bigley,' said Jim darkly.

'Oh, so you think so as well?'

'It's a possibility, I suppose,' said Jim reluctantly.

'Well, who else? If the police are still investigating Bigley before the case gets to court, and they've turned up something else, or he's said something . . . maybe Mr Simmonds was in cahoots with him all along.' Then she argued against herself. 'But if he was, why did Bigley need to put the arm on you when he wanted to do that fiddle with the coal?'

Jim sighed. If this was difficult for her to come to terms with, Lily realised, it was far harder for him. He'd worked so closely with Peter Simmonds – if Mr Simmonds wasn't the person they'd thought, Jim must be questioning his own judgement of character.

'Maybe coal was just one part of it,' he said slowly. 'If you remember, when Robert first told me about Bigley, he said Bigley was interested in lots of things Marlow's might have. Razor blades, radio batteries, even Thermos flasks, for goodness' sake!'

'And Mr Simmonds was supplying him with them? And somehow in Bigley's questioning, it's come to light? Oh Jim!'

In her stomach, Lily felt the turkey roll live up to its name. If things looked bad for Mr Simmonds, what about poor Miss Frobisher? And little John? And if the police were looking deeper and deeper into Bigley's affairs, or Bigley had revealed things in the hope of a lighter sentence, how long before the police came looking for Jim? Or Dora? Or Lily herself? The plum suede shoes executed a mocking tap dance in front of her eyes and the turkey roll did a full somersault.

'This is hopeless,' she said. 'We've got the rest of today and tomorrow before we're back at work and can find anything out for sure. I can't wait till then!'

'You won't have to.' Jim pulled her along the cinder path at the back of the houses. 'Let's go and see if Miss Frobisher knows any more.'

'What? Now? On Christmas Day? We can't!'

'I thought you just said—'

'I did! But— Anyway, how can we? We don't know where she lives!'

Jim was striding ahead. Lily followed, sending up a scatter of ashes.

'I do,' said Jim.

'What?' Lily pulled on his arm and he stopped.

'Well, sort of. Peter was talking one day about the Man in the Moon. You know, the pub? It's on the corner of her road. Albany Road.'

'And the house number?'

'Well, he didn't say that but come on, you tracked Bill's mother across London with far less to go on – surely we can manage it in Hinton!'

'Hang on.' Lily had remembered something. 'I might have a clue! Miss Frobisher was telling Miss Temple that she and her little boy had cut out paper snowflakes to stick all over the front window. That might narrow it down a bit.'

'It narrows it down a lot! Well, come on! let's get going!'

Chapter 33

It didn't take long to walk to Albany Road. The day was dry but dull, nothing special, but there'd been enough drama lately, Lily thought, without the weather adding its two-pennyworth.

'Funny, isn't it,' said Jim, thinking out loud, 'ordinary people like us having their Christmas Day all over the world, or trying to. America, Australia, Africa, the occupied countries, even in Germany. I mean they're not all Nazis, are they? There's thousands, millions of people all over the world who never wanted a war, never asked for it, just trying to get on with their lives.'

Lily nodded. She could hardly remember what life was like without a war, and she sometimes thought life would be strange without it.

Albany Road was a quiet street of Victorian villas, semi-detached. They were three-storeyed and they could see from the multiple bells that almost all had been divided into flats. That fitted with what Lily knew about Miss Frobisher's circumstances. She lived on the first floor and her downstairs neighbour, an elderly lady, looked after young John after school and in the holidays.

'Snowdrops,' Jim noted as they passed one of the gardens – still the country boy at heart. 'And even a few daffs trying to come through. They'll be pretty in spring.'

'Never mind spring, we're looking for snowflakes, remember?' Lily peered up at the houses on her left. 'I hope they haven't taken them down.'

'Why would they?' asked Jim. 'Hang on, look!' Across the road, the bay window on the first floor of number 48 was covered in cut-out shapes. 'That must be it!'

They crossed the road. There was a short path of chequered tiles to the front door, where three bells advertised flats 1, 2 and 3.

'Shall we take a guess it's number two?' Jim pressed the bell without waiting for Lily's reply. There was a long pause.

'Maybe they're out,' tutted Lily. 'Gone for a walk, like us.'

'Shh!'

Footsteps were coming along the hall, giving them

350

hope. Then the front door opened and they were face to face with a fearsome Red Indian chief. But beneath the feathered headdress and the war paint – a smear of red on each cheek and across his forehead – was Peter Simmonds.

Miss Frobisher put down the tray of tea, turned to Jim and Lily and smiled.

'He may be a while,' she said. 'That war paint – my lipstick, if you please – is going to take a lot scrubbing to get off!'

All had been explained once Lily and Jim had followed Peter Simmonds up to the first floor. Young John's hero was the singing cowboy, Roy Rogers, so for Christmas, Mr Simmonds had given him a pop gun, a cowboy hat and a neckerchief. But as every cowboy needs an adversary, he'd borrowed the Indian headdress from the Marlow's Players – the store's amateur dramatic group.

So that was Peter Simmonds's strange appearance accounted for – though not his appearance there at all. Lily was relieved he wasn't languishing in a police cell, of course, but she needed an explanation for that, as well, which Miss Frobisher obviously realised. She'd seemed surprised at first, but also rather touched, to see them.

'I imagine you're here about last night.' she said now, passing them each a cup of tea. She was in a seasonal claret-coloured dress, her hair pinned prettily off her face in a roll at the front then loose to her shoulders. John, still in his cowboy garb, had been persuaded to 'sit quietly now' with a cup of milk and some back copies of the *Beano*. 'Perhaps,' Miss Frobisher added, sitting down with her own cup, 'we'd better wait for Peter to explain.'

While Jim politely asked her if they'd had a nice day so far, Lily tried – as unobtrusively as she could – to look around. She'd never seen a room like it. Her own home was decorated – if that was the word – with wallpaper that had been muted even before it had faded to a uniform beige; the furniture was a cluttered mix of bits and pieces that Dora had acquired over the years and oddments that had been passed down. This room looked almost empty – but as if it had been planned that way. The walls were plain white and painted, not papered. There was a three-piece suite in a boxy, square style, upholstered in chevrons of emerald and turquoise and the little ornamentation there was showed all Miss Frobisher's flair. There was a bright blue vase filled with peacock feathers on the mantelpiece and a striking picture over it – startling daubs of paint in blue and green shot through with egg-yolk yellow. Lily stared. If it was meant to be – she took a wild guess – 'storm at sea' it was like no representation of 'storm at sea' she'd ever seen. Even the Christmas decorations were different: pine cones arranged on top of each other in a conical shape to form a sort of miniature

Christmas tree, while John's toys were heaped in a wicker basket, the sort Dora used for laundry, and his books were arranged on graduated shelves stained green.

'Do you like it, Lily?'

Miss Frobisher had noticed her staring.

'Very much!' said Lily. 'It's very, er, unusual.'

Miss Frobisher inclined her head.

'I'll take that as a compliment! It wasn't like this when I moved in. My father had lived here. I sold everything – and there was a lot – and started afresh.'

You could say that again!

Still looking slightly pink about the cheeks, Peter Simmonds came back in and sat down next to Miss Frobisher. She passed him his cup; he sat back and drank. Lily could see he was completely at home.

'So . . .' Miss Frobisher smiled. 'I suppose you thought John and I would be prison-visiting today. You'd better tell them, Peter. Everything.'

Mr Simmonds sighed. He put down his cup on a small table at his elbow.

'It's a bit embarrassing,' he said, 'so I hope I can trust that it'll go no further. As you two were the only witnesses.'

Lily and Jim nodded vigorously.

'It's all Eileen's fault, really,' he began, causing Miss Frobisher – Eileen – to shoot him a look. 'Her Christmas present. She'd mentioned that as a girl, she'd had a charm bracelet she was fond of, but she'd

353

lost it. I decided to get her another. I'd looked in several places but there was nothing to be had. Then I mentioned it to Captain Willerby.'

'You'd better explain who he is,' put in Miss Frobisher.

'I was going to,' Mr Simmonds replied patiently. Lily swallowed a smile – it was funny seeing him being dictated to.

'If it's the chap I'm thinking of,' said Jim, 'youngish, fair, got a moustache, he's often in the store. Gentleman's Outfitting, Tobacco and Cigars. And he bought a bedside cabinet from me back in the autumn.'

'That's right,' Peter Simmonds confirmed. 'A very good customer. Anyway, I went along one night to a veterans' reunion, a charity do, and he was there. I'd never really spoken to him before beyond pleas-antries – you know how it is.' Lily and Jim did. While Marlow's staff were encouraged to build a relation-ship with customers, over-familiarity was not advised. 'We got talking. He told me he'd been invalided out of the Army too, and we talked about life in civvy street, my work, the difficulty of getting things to sell, and to buy, especially for Christmas. When I happened to mention what I was looking for, he said he'd come into some jewellery left to him by an aunt.'

Lily glanced at Jim. She was starting to have a bad feeling about Captain Willerby, but Jim was listening intently as Peter Simmonds went on.

'There was a charm bracelet amongst it,' Willerby said, 'and if I was interested, I could have it – I'd pay him for it, obviously. Well, we arranged to meet in a pub – it wasn't the sort of transaction I could do in the store. He brought it along – heavy silver, loaded with charms, and the price seemed fair. I gave him the money, took it away, wrapped it up, and—'

'You've probably guessed where this is going,' Miss Frobisher interrupted. Lily glanced at Jim again. He was nodding. 'Our Captain Willerby was no such thing!'

'He had been in the Army, Eileen!' Mr Simmonds objected.

'Tch!' scorned Miss Frobisher, but affectionately. 'Yes – a corporal in the Pay Corps! And kicked out, not invalided out!'

'All right, I was taken in!' Peter Simmonds defended himself. 'But he had all the patter, a good story, didn't trip himself up once. And I suppose . . .' He was suddenly, touchingly, vulnerable. 'I wanted to believe him.'

Because of the bracelet, Lily thought. Because of Miss Frobisher.

'But he was a con man,' she said sadly.

'And a thief!' Having said Mr Simmonds should tell the story, Miss Frobisher jumped in. Now the initial shock and worry were past, it almost seemed as if she was enjoying this. 'There were four of them! Last week the police caught one of the gang at a house burglary and he – what's the phrase? – spilt the beans on his accomplices – and a few other unsolved thefts.'

'Then the police had to trace the stuff,' Jim surmised.

'The loot!' Miss Frobisher's eyes gleamed. 'And when it came to the famous bracelet, our friend "Captain" Willerby gave Peter's name.'

'The worst they could have charged me with was receiving stolen goods.' Mr Simmonds took up the story again. 'But they accepted I'd bought it in good faith and I'd been, well . . . duped.' He turned to Jim. 'There've been some changes at Hinton police, you know. A lot of the old guard have gone. That DCI Gregson, bumptious chap who used to come in and lecture our store detectives, he's left apparently.'

Bigley's chum Gregson! Lily didn't dare look at Jim, who was nodding in a casually interested sort of way.

'They were very reasonable with you, weren't they?' Eileen's tone was warm. 'Except for taking my bracelet off you, of course.'

'They drove me home to get it and I had to hand it over,' Mr Simmonds added sadly.

'Then he shot round here to explain it all to me. I should think so, too, since I've had to do without a Christmas present!'

'I'll make it up to you,' said Peter Simmonds meekly.

'I should hope so! Do you hear that, Lily? You're a witness to that as well!'

Lily smiled again – first to herself, and then broadly. The way Miss Frobisher spoke about, and to, Mr Simmonds so reminded her of her own relationship with Jim. This telling-off by teasing only showed how very close they were. But she was also smiling with relief – and at herself and Jim. Had they seriously thought Mr Simmonds might be in league with Barry Bigley? The idea seemed absurd now they knew the real story and he'd been revealed not as a big-time crook but a besotted lover.

While Lily had been thinking, John had scrambled to his feet. He was standing at Miss Frobisher's side, whispering something in her ear. She laughed.

'He wants to know if we can play Snakes and Ladders,' she said. 'Can we tempt you to stay?'

There'd been plenty of snakes around all year – Robert Marlow, Barry Bigley, DCI Gregson and now the fake Captain Willerby – but, thought Lily, as Peter and Jim cleared the tea tray and she helped John to lay out the board and the counters, lots of ladders too, both at work and outside it.

As the King had said, there might be no easy dreams, but there were some bright hopes to cling to as the year came to an end.

Until the January sales started, the atmosphere in the store after Christmas could seem flat, but this year, buoyed by Mr Marlow's promised changes, the staff came back to work in good spirits. Lily knew that the friendly welcome and the confidences extended to her and Jim at Miss Frobisher's would never be referred to again, and most likely never repeated. In the store her relationship with Miss Frobisher would revert to that of boss and employee.

And it did. There was only one reference to Christmas, when Miss Frobisher upbraided Lily for letting John win at Snakes and Ladders. Lily had deliberately miscounted a throw, tapping first on the square she was on instead of moving her counter immediately forwards, so had slid down a particularly crucial snake.

'It's not good for him, you know,' Miss Frobisher said. 'Even if it was Christmas Day!' But she gave Lily a smile before switching smartly into business mode.

'I'm sure it's occurred to you,' she began, 'that if I'm to supervise the first floor as well as run this department, it will need a full-time first sales. You're still very young, but the experience on Schoolwear will count in your favour. That's what I shall be arguing, anyway.'

'Oh, thank you, Miss Frobisher,' breathed Lily. 'I had wondered – and hoped, but . . .'

'It won't be for a while. We'll have to see how the new roles work out in practice, but I would guess that within six months, there'll be a promotion for you as well. In the meantime, Mr Simmonds needs you on the ground floor.'

Lily stared. She knew he was helping out there already, but why was she needed?

'We're hardly rushed off our feet here, are we?' Miss Frobisher pointed out. 'It's a different story downstairs. You remember all those men who surged in on Christmas Eve panic-buying for their wives?' Her expressive eyebrows indicated amused contempt. 'Toiletries and Accessories anticipate quite a number of returns.' She was scanning the pre-Christmas sales figures as she spoke. 'Well, off you go!'

Dismissed, Lily scuttled downstairs. In a way, she was flattered. Miss Frobisher obviously thought she could cope under pressure on the busiest of departments – and it wouldn't do her promotion prospects any harm at all.

It also meant she'd have something different to tell Sid when he came home for his belated Christmas leave in a couple of days' time. He did his best to show an interest in baby vests and rompers but they could hardly hold much fascination for him. Sid would never have a family of his own – not in that sense, anyway. But to hear that he was still with the 'someone' he'd told her about in London, and that he was happy in himself – that they were happy together – would be yet more icing on what already felt like a loaded Christmas cake.

Chapter 34

With Lily and Jim back at work, Dora's days resumed their normal rhythm as well – the shops, the queues, the housework. She'd been sorry not to see Sam on Christmas Day, but he'd been on duty in the morning and in the afternoon he'd booked a long-distance call to the sanatorium in Canada where his wife was a patient. He was hoping she'd feel well enough to speak to him: often he'd go to the expense and trouble of a call, only to have the nurses say that Grace was 'not really up to it'. Dora's heart ached for him.

They'd arranged to meet on the day after Boxing Day to take Buddy for a walk. Dora had tried to dissuade Sam from giving her a Christmas present. He'd protested, but she told him firmly that the food and treats he brought them were more than enough. She was convinced, however, that he'd take no notice, so she'd knitted him a muffler and a pair of gloves in maroon three-ply that she'd scoured the town to get. They were wrapped and in her handbag. She was particularly pleased with the cable pattern on the backs of the gloves – it had been a right fiddle to do, but he was worth it.

She heard Sam and Buddy before she saw them, because Buddy set off his usual joyful 'ruff' on seeing her as they rounded the corner by the laurel bushes.

'Howdy!' called Sam. Other dog-walkers turned their heads: Sam sometimes enjoyed playing up to the brashness the British seemed to expect of North Americans. Dora waited till he drew nearer before calling hello in reply. He arrived beside her, sternly advising Buddy against jumping up. Naturally, Buddy ignored him.

'And they say you can train spaniels! Down, Buddy!' Sam scolded. He kissed Dora lightly on the cheek. 'Merry Christmas! How are you? Did you have a good day?'

'Lovely, thank you,' Dora said warmly. 'I didn't lift a finger! Lily and Jim did the lot.'

'Great stuff! If anyone deserves a day off, it's you. Now, are you ready to roll?' He offered his arm and they began strolling around the duckpond. The ducks had long since disappeared – into someone's cooking pot, it was assumed – but that didn't stop Buddy from nosing hopefully along the water's edge.

'And how about you?' Dora asked. 'Did you get through to Grace?'

She had to ask, but wished she hadn't as Sam shook his head.

'She was having a bad day. "Not up to it" again. I wish I knew if she was not up to speaking to anyone or just not up to speaking to me. The nurses don't give much away.'

Dora sighed.

'I'm so sorry, Sam. It must be agony for you.'

'Yes. I—' He stopped. 'Let's find somewhere to sit down a while.'

The benches had all been taken away for armaments or for wood but there was a low wall round the memorial to the fallen of a previous, long-ago war and they sat on that. Buddy, sensing a change in the mood, lay down quietly at their feet. Sam took off his forage cap and turned it in his hands. Dora knew something important was coming, and she braced herself. Like Hugh, he was being posted away, she felt sure of it.

'I wish things were different, Dora,' Sam began, 'But you know better than anyone that we have to accept them as they are. I'm going to ask for a compassionate discharge – to be sent home.'

What? Of everything she'd imagined, all the places he might go – Italy, the Far East, France – Canada itself had never figured.

'I see,' she said weakly.

'I hope you do.' Sam's eyes held hers. 'Maybe I should never have left – never have left Grace – in the first place. I thought it was the right thing at the time, the only thing I could do. She didn't seem to need or want me and I don't know if she does now – it certainly doesn't sound like it. But I owe it to her – to our marriage – to find out. I'm not doing any good being away. I'm not avenging Bruce's death, and I'm not helping Grace get better – if she can be helped. Going home may make no difference, but in all conscience I can't stay over here and not even give it a try.'

Dora looked down.

'Say something. Please.'

She raised her head and gave him a smile.

'You're doing the right thing, Sam,' she answered. 'I'm sure of that.'

'I wish I was,' he replied. Then he shocked her by seizing her hand. 'If things were different, Dora, I'd like to think we could have had a future, you and me. You're a remarkable woman, brave and true, kind and generous, loving . . .'

Remarkable? Not knowing where to look, not daring to look at him, Dora looked down again, at her feet in their sensible lace-up shoes, the darn in the heel of her stocking, the worn cuffs of her coat. She didn't feel very remarkable. And as for loving . . .

'Don't, Sam, please. Don't say any more.' Gently she extracted her hand from his. 'I won't pretend I

363

haven't become . . .' She hesitated. This was going to be quite a declaration for her. 'I won't pretend I haven't become fond of you. But as for us having a future, or the chance of one . . . you're the one who said we have to accept things as they are, and I do. We're too old for castles in the air when there's wives in sanatoriums and I have my life here. Let's not kid ourselves.'

Sam sighed.

'Can we keep in touch?' he asked. 'Will you write to me?'

Expecting him to announce a posting, Dora had thought about this already, and the fact he was going to Canada didn't change that – not for the moment, anyway.

'Of course. I don't see why not. As a friend.'

'Thank you.' He made as if to take her hand again, then drew back, as if he didn't dare. She touched his hand briefly.

'Let's walk, shall we? Buddy'll be getting restless.' A thought struck her. 'Buddy! What's going to happen to him when you go?'

'Funny you should ask.' Sad, but perhaps relieved to have the serious part of the conversation out of the way, a note of mischief had crept back into Sam's voice. 'I've been thinking about that. He needs a good loving home. A permanent home. I thought perhaps a kind widow with grown-up children might appreciate some company. Well, Dora, what do you think?'

What Dora thought was unprintable, but what she said was that she'd think about it.

She told Lily and Jim about Sam's decision as they laid the table for tea. Jim knew about Sam's wife, and he and Lily looked sobered by what Sam was going home to, though like Dora, they could understand why he felt he had to.

'Poor man,' said Lily as they sat down. It was obvious Dora had been preoccupied by his news; she hadn't achieved the usual crispy burnt bits with the bubble and squeak that Lily loved. 'It's awful for him.'

But Dora didn't want to dwell on Sam's departure. She knew what would happen: Lily would start saying it was a shame for her as well, and she couldn't deny it, so she cut some bread, told them to help themselves and moved the conversation on.

That had the desired effect. Amazed, Lily reacted immediately.

'He's giving Buddy to us? Permanently? That's some Christmas present!'

It wasn't the kind of present Dora had imagined either but then she hadn't imagined anything correctly, had she? Only Sam's delight with the muffler and gloves had been in line with her expectations.

'We've got to work out the details,' she replied, calmly reaching past Lily for the salt and pepper: she'd been so distracted by Sam's news she'd forgotten the seasoning in the bubble and squeak as well. But the more she'd thought about Sam's suggestion, the more she'd liked the idea.

Buddy would have to have a kennel in the yard, of course. No one as house proud as she was would tolerate a dog indoors – scratching the furniture and the skirtings, hairs all over, making the rugs smell. But after the war, if they were all spared, Sid was bound to stay in London and Reg was very likely to settle in Welshpool with Gwenda. That only left her and Lily at home and that wouldn't be for ever. Lily and Jim would surely marry one day – she could see that Lily was already getting restless – and want a place of their own. So why not a dog for company?

'How are we going to feed him?' Jim was, as always, the practical one. 'We'll miss Sam's contributions to the larder as it is.'

'He's going to open a Post Office account,' Dora told him. 'He'll put some money in to start us off. There'll be less going to the pig bin, and I'll have to make friends with the butcher for whatever I can get. And once the war's over, well, surely things'll be easier?'

Typically, Lily had already got her own ideas.

'We'll manage somehow. And it could be fun, Jim. We can teach Buddy to do tricks and take him round children's parties.'

Jim looked sceptical.

'Are we talking about the same dog? He's got a lovely temperament, but when it comes to concentration,

Buddy's got as much brainpower as the scarecrow in the *Wizard of Oz*.'

'Poor Buddy! Now you're being mean. I think it's a great idea, Mum.'

'Good.' Dora forked up a mouthful of potato and cabbage. 'Now here's a challenge for you. There's a rasher and a half of bacon in here if you can find it.'

It was her way of closing off the conversation and it worked. Jim made a comment about lance-corporal bacon – it was what everyone called streaky bacon now, because it only had one stripe. With that as a bridge, Dora could ask Jim and Lily about their day at work. Lily quickly obliged with tales of despairing women whose husbands had bought them woollen scarves and highly scented soap for Christmas when, as one had complained, 'You'd think after thirty years he'd know I'm allergic!'

As they washed up, though, Lily brought up the subject of Sam again.

'I'm sad for you, though, Mum,' she said. 'I know you'll deny it, but I think you were really quite fond of him.'

'We all are!' said Dora quickly.

'I know.' More than that, Lily knew that she and Jim owed Sam so much for getting rid of Barry Bigley's unwanted gift without Dora ever knowing. 'But it's hardly the same. And I know he'd got fond of you. I just hope it's made you realise, Mum, that you're – well, you're still in your prime!'

Dora bent her head over the sink so that Lily couldn't see her smile. It had come to something when her own daughter was giving her advice on her love life! She'd never have dreamt of speaking to her own mother, also a widow, the same way.

But Lily meant well, bless her. How she'd grown, and grown up, in the years since she'd started her job at Marlow's. It was the war, as well – all the youngsters had had to grow up fast. But maybe that was a good thing. The world was changing fast, too, and they'd need all their resources to cope with it.

Lily was thinking much the same, if Dora had known. Here she was telling her mother how to conduct her love life, and what about her own? Christmas had come and gone and she was no closer to knowing how seriously Jim saw their relationship. The locket he'd given her was thoughtful and lovely, but did it mean anything? Was it a step on the way? Miss Frobisher and Mr Simmonds had made more progress in six months than she and Jim had made in eighteen! She picked up the bunched tablecloth and took it out into the yard. The vicious shake she gave it was the shake she really wanted to give him.

Sid would make her feel better, she knew, and the thought kept her going all evening. He'd be home the next day and Lily was desperate to see him – if anyone could help her make sense of her situation and see a clear way through, he could. But when she,

Jim and Dora gathered round the radio for the nine o'clock news, what they heard would wipe all thoughts of her own predicament from Lily's head.

'*This is BBC London,*' intoned the announcer as usual. '*Here is the news, and this is John Snagge reading it.*'

There was a pause, which was also usual, but when he started to speak it was as if he himself couldn't believe what he was about to say.

'*It is reported that the German battleship* Scharnhorst *has been sunk in the Barents Sea between the North Cape and Spitzbergen, Norway. The* Scharnhorst *had been attempting an attack on a convoy bound for northern Russia. A report follows from our correspondent . . .*'

Lily didn't hear any more. The sinking of the *Scharnhorst* would have struck home in any case. At the end of that dreadful January of 1942, when the Germans had sunk more British ships than there were days in the month, the *Scharnhorst* had added insult to injury by sailing brazenly up the Channel without being intercepted. Ever since, it had been the Navy's top target, and Lily should have been jumping for joy. But Bill's ship was on convoy duty in the Northern Passage, getting supplies to the desperate population of places like Archangel and Murmansk – Lily had looked them up in the atlas. That was how she knew exactly where the *Scharnhorst* had been sunk. And something told her, as soon as she heard the words from the wireless, that it was Bill's convoy that was involved.

'. . . *the* Scharnhorst *was surrounded by no less than nine ships of the British fleet,*' the BBC correspondent was saying. '*Four cruisers, four destroyers and the battleship HMS* Duke of York.'

Bill's ship, the *Jamaica*, was a cruiser.

'*A fierce and intense battle ensued,*' continued the reporter. (How could he be so calm?) '*Yet thanks to the superiority of British firepower and positioning, in under three hours the* Scharnhorst *was sinking. There are as yet no confirmed reports of any survivors of the* Scharnhorst, *nor yet of any British casualties or fatalities.*'

Casualties? Fatalities? British? But naturally in a battle, even a battle won, there would be injuries and deaths on both sides. Lily was suddenly aware of a pain in the heel of her hand. She looked down; her nails were digging in. She opened her hand and reached for Jim's. He knew what she was thinking – so did her mum.

'Gladys,' said Dora. 'That poor girl.'

Not just Gladys, thought Lily. Gladys and the baby.

Chapter 35

There was no sign of Gladys in the cloakroom next day, and since Lily was downstairs on Toiletries, and not on the first floor, no chance to see if she was absent or merely late. Customers, even those whose exchanges or refunds she had to refuse – one tin of talcum powder had obviously been opened and liberally used, Lily could tell from the weight – were in jubilant mood, all commenting on the sinking of the *Scharnhorst*. Lily could have shaken them – not something the staff manual recommended.

Mr Simmonds was downstairs too, darting from department to department adjudicating on returns and sorting out problems. Unable to stand it any longer, Lily intercepted him as he swept past.

'I'm sorry to bother you, Mr Simmonds, but is Gladys Webb – Miss Huskins – in today, do you know? Her husband's on the *Jamaica* and he'll have been involved in . . .'

Mr Simmonds stopped and turned back. He knew Lily and Gladys were friends.

'I gathered that,' he said. 'She's here, but she doesn't look well. If it weren't half-day closing I should tell her to go home, but I think she'll last the course.' He looked grave. 'I'm sure you'll do all you can to support her. I hope she gets good news soon.'

Lily had never known a morning go so slowly and as the clock crept round to one o'clock, customers had never seemed more inclined to linger. One had the temerity not to even arrive at Lily's counter till a quarter to, and then start dithering over her purchase. Honestly, some people!

As soon as the staff were given the signal that they could go, Lily shot to the cloakroom and waited for Gladys to appear. When she did, she was like a wraith, and fell on Lily, sobbing.

Lily patted her back ineffectually.

'Shh, Gladys, shh. You mustn't assume the worst. It all went our way, after all. No reports of damage to any of our ships.'

'Yet!' cried Gladys. 'And you know they never tell us the full story! Not for days, if we get it at all! I haven't slept a wink and I don't see I will till I hear!'

Lily said nothing. She'd been through this herself

when Reg had gone missing and Beryl had been through it with Les: it was torture. And she couldn't get out of her head what Bill had said to her on the day of the wedding. Even if he was safe, what must he have gone through down in the bowels of the ship with his radio equipment, the battle raging all around, the ship rocking, guns and torpedoes being fired?

She had so wanted Sid to herself, but she knew what she had to say.

'Gladys, listen, you must get a grip on yourself. It's not good for the baby.'

Gladys howled even louder. Lily took a deep breath.

'Come home with me – Sid'll be there. He's at the Admiralty, he might know more. How about that?'

'Oh Lily, could I?' Gladys raised a white, teary face from Lily's shoulder. 'I never thought . . . oh, thank you! Yes, he might!'

'Let's get our things,' said Lily. 'Jim'll be waiting.'

On the way home, with Jim trying to buoy Gladys up, Lily hoped she'd done the right thing. Sid had booked his leave especially so he'd be there for their half-day, though with what had happened, it could be a case of 'all leave cancelled'. But if he wasn't home, Lily consoled herself, her mum would be there. She'd have something sensible and reassuring to say, even if it was only that everything would look better after a cup of tea, which, in fact, was so often true.

But when they got back, Sid *was* there, having a smoke in the yard. As soon as they came through the gate, her brother pinched out his cigarette, put it behind his ear and held his arms out wide. Lily rushed into them. He picked her up and whirled her round and she felt immediately light-headed and lighter-hearted.

'Diamond Lil! How's my best girl?' he asked, finally putting her down.

'Better for seeing you! But look who else is here,' she added meaningfully.

'Gladys!' Sid gave her a hug as well and went to shake Jim's hand, but before he could, Gladys had burst out: 'Oh Sid! Do you know any more than has been on the wireless? I'm so worried about Bill!'

Sid put his arm round her again, sounding more sober.

'Let's go inside, eh?' he said.

They all sat round. The inevitable pot of tea had been made; Dora poured and Jim handed out the cups. Gladys put hers straight down again untasted and twisted her hands in her lap.

'You can imagine, there's been a bit of a flap on,' Sid began. 'I'm lucky to be here at all. If I *had* booked leave over Christmas, I wouldn't have got it, it was all hands on deck. But you don't want to hear about me.' He leant forward and took Gladys's hands. 'He's all right, Gladys,' he said, speaking clearly and slowly.

'There were no casualties on the *Jamaica*, bar a few bumps and grazes, lads being knocked off their feet by the recoil and a fellow who burned his arm on a boilerplate, but that could have happened any time.'

Gladys was staring blankly.

'Did you hear that, Gladys? He's OK!' Lily repeated. 'Bill's safe!'

Gladys crumpled again, her hands to her face. Dora jumped up and put her arms round her.

'There, love, you cry it out, eh? It's all right, it's all right.'

Gladys rocked back and forth, giving out little gasps.

Sid got up. From the pocket of his greatcoat he produced a half-bottle of rum – he'd got quite a taste for it in the Navy. He unscrewed the top and poured a capful into Gladys's tea.

'There,' he said. 'A nip of the hard stuff for you, Glad.' He held her cup to her lips. 'Buck you up a bit.'

Gladys swallowed and spluttered but took another sip. Then she waved the cup away and pulled her hanky out of her sleeve, blowing her nose loudly.

'I'm sorry,' she gulped. 'Making such an exhibition of myself.'

'Don't be daft, you were bound to be worried,' soothed Lily. 'But you can relax now.'

'More than relax,' grinned Sid. 'There'll be a medal in this for Bill, and no mistake. Might even be booted up the ranks – it was the wireless and radar boys that managed to work out where the *Scharnhorst* was, and what direction the attack was going to come from.'

'My Bill . . . a medal!'

Gladys looked like crying again, so Jim leapt in, urging her to drink her tea while it was hot.

Gladys gulped it down, then hiccupped and apologised.

'My fault,' admitted Sid. 'It's the rum.'

'Must be!' Laughing now, Gladys covered her mouth as she hiccupped again. 'I hope it won't hurt the baby – oh!'

'Baby? You're expecting?' That was Dora.

Gladys nodded, a huge smile on her face.

'In June. Lily's known. I was going to tell the rest of you when I saw you over Christmas – but not like this!'

After the excited congratulations and chatter that followed, Sid raised his voice.

'Oy, you lot, I hadn't finished! Want some more good news?'

Everyone swivelled their heads back towards him.

'The good ship *Jamaica*'s sailing back to Scotland. Should be at Scapa Flow by New Year's Eve, then in dry dock for a good few weeks to have any battle damage seen to. Bill's bound to get leave. I'm sure you've put it in a letter, Glad, but Lord knows if he'll have had it. But now you can tell him about the baby in person, how's that?'

Lily grabbed Gladys's hands.

'Gladys! You'll see him! You can tell him everything!'

About his mother too, she thought – the baby's grandma.

When at least some of the excitement had died down, Gladys and Dora got straight to practicalities – much of what Gladys would need could be borrowed from Beryl. Jim went out to lock up the hens, and Sid and Lily took the cups out to wash them.

How many hours of her life had she spent in that scullery with her hands in Scrubb's Cloudy Ammonia, ('Use sparingly as supplies are restricted!') Lily wondered. But at the same time, how many good things had happened there: stolen moments between herself and Jim, reunions with Sid and Reg . . . How many secrets and confessions and declarations had those damp, distempered walls heard? And now at last her chance to find out a bit more from Sid about his secret boyfriend. But Sid knew her too well.

'His name's Jerome,' he said, taking the cups and saucers from the tray and placing them by the sink for Lily to wash. 'He's twenty-four, tall, dark, handsome of course . . .'

'Sid! Jerome?'

'Well, that's what you were going to ask, isn't it?' Having made his contribution to the washing up, Sid lounged against the draining board. 'Oh, and he's American.'

Lily blinked.

'American!'

'Well don't say it like he's from Mars! Yes, American, serving in their Air Force.'

'Not another pilot?' Her heart flipped. Sid couldn't go through what had happened with Anthony all over again and she wasn't sure she could either.

'Don't worry,' Sid grinned. 'Well, not so much. He's ground crew. Maintenance.'

'That's something.'

Air Force bases were a natural target, but ground crew had to be safer than anyone up in the skies.

'He's based out East Anglia way, but we met in London,' Sid went on. 'The Trocadero in Piccadilly's got a . . . well, a special bar for blokes like us. Talk about eyes meeting across a crowded room, Lil. I knew he was the one.'

'Oh Sid!'

It still made Lily feel slightly uncomfortable to hear her brother talk this way, but she told herself it was just as if he'd been talking about meeting a girl. It was as natural as that to Sid.

'Anyway, it's been over six months now,' Sid continued. 'We seem to get along. So . . . well, looks like it might be for keeps.'

'As long as he's here.'

'No, Lil. Beyond that. We've talked about it. In time, if I can get the documentation and everything, I want to move over to the States to be with him.'

Lily gasped.

'You'd leave England for him?'

'In a heartbeat,' Sid answered simply, as Lily stared, still reeling. Then he grinned. 'I didn't tell you the best, did I? He's from the West Coast, Hollywood. He's in films.'

'An actor?' squealed Lily. Sid had always been a keen film fan. 'Would I know him? Is he famous?'

'Not yet,' laughed Sid. 'But he might be, one day, when he's picking up the Oscar for Best Lighting Director. He's a lowly sparks at the moment – electrician's mate – like I'm a lowly clerk, but – well, you've got to believe you can make it, haven't you? You've got to believe in something.'

The cups were washed and draining now. Sid handed her the threadbare towel to dry her hands. No wonder Hollywood was more appealing than Hinton!

'And you?' he asked as she hung it up carefully to dry. 'You and Jim made any progress? I'll take that as a "no",' he added when she rolled her eyes.

'I don't know, Sid. He seems to think we can jog along like this for ever. There's no one else I'm interested in, and I'm sure there isn't for him, either, so I don't understand what's holding him back. I'm not saying I'm desperate to get married tomorrow, far from it, but—'

'You'd still like to be asked?'

Sid grinned sympathetically but Lily sighed.

'I'd just like to know where I stand! I'm thinking of joining up next year, volunteering the minute I can!'

'Blimey, Lil, that's a bit extreme!' Sid tucked a lock of hair that had escaped its comb in her outburst gently behind her ear. 'Not that you wouldn't be an asset, I'm sure. Look, Sis, I hate to see you like this. Do you want me to have a chat, man-to-man?'

'No!' hissed Lily as the back door opened and Jim came in, three eggs in his hand.

'Mother's meeting?' he asked, putting them in a dish. 'I'd better walk Gladys home before tea, if she's not too wobbly after that rum you plied her with, Sid.'

Lily was feeling pretty wobbly herself, what with the announcement of Sid's future plans and the sorry lack of them for herself and Jim, but she nodded and smiled. This was the Jim she knew and loved, kind, thoughtful, gentlemanly. A bit too gentlemanly, sometimes. But she kissed him anyway.

'Don't be long,' she said.

Chapter 36

It was eight o'clock. On the wireless, Joe Loss and his orchestra were playing. Humming along, Dora was re-reading the Christmas cards and the letter that had come with the one signed, for the first time, 'with love from Reg and Gwenda'. Sid was trying to inveigle Lily and Jim into a game called Crown and Anchor.

'Been played in the Navy since Nelson was a lad,' he grinned. 'Three dice and six symbols on a bit of paper, the four playing card suits plus the crown and the anchor – you can chalk 'em on the deck if you haven't got any paper. But it's a betting game, see, so if one of your officer class comes by, you grab the dice, screw up the paper or scrub out the symbols and you're all present and correct. Shall we get set up?'

He was taking the dice out of a little pouch as he spoke, but Jim got to his feet and pulled Lily to hers.

'Not just now, thanks,' he said, and to Lily: 'Let's get some fresh air.'

'Going out?' Sid looked up hopefully. 'Pub?'

'No, only out the back.'

'Well, put your coats on! You'll freeze!'

That was Dora, of course.

'Don't worry,' said Jim. 'I'll keep her warm.'

He picked up his jacket from the back of the chair and handed it to Lily. As they stepped out into the yard, he helped her to put it on. It was far too big: the sleeves hung down half over her hands but it was heavy, and warm from being by the fire, and she pulled it round her.

'Lots of stars,' she said, looking up.

There were a few thin ribbons of cloud, too, on the horizon, and a half-moon which seemed to pulse with light.

'Going to make a wish?' asked Jim.

'Do I only get one? That might be difficult.'

What would she wish for most of all? An end to the war? Or an end to the uncertainty between her and Jim? One was patriotic, the other was personal. What a choice.

Jim smiled down at her.

'Tell you what,' he said. 'Feel in the pocket. Right-hand side. There's something in there for you.'

'Another present?'

'Sort of.'

Lily's heart did a skip-and-jump, leap-and-tumble. After all her fretting, was this it? A ring? But when she touched the outside of the pocket she could tell at once that whatever it was, it wasn't a ring box – quite the wrong shape and feel. She put her hand inside and pulled out, slightly squashed, a cracker. Of all things . . .

'The last cracker?'

Sid had brought them to pull at tea time, posh ones from Fortnum and Mason's, a shop he said would make Marlow's look like Woolworth's. There'd been six in the box, but typical Sid, he'd palled up with a father and son on the train and couldn't resist pulling one of them with the lad. The little tin racing car that had fallen out had kept both of them amused for the rest of the journey.

'I asked Sid if I could have it,' Jim said now. 'Well, shall we pull it?'

'I suppose we'd better.'

They each took an end and pulled – Jim not trying terribly hard, she felt. Sure enough, the cracker broke with a feeble snap and Lily had the bigger half.

'What have you got?' Jim asked.

Lily took out the paper crown and the motto, then tipped the shiny paper tube into her hand. It *was* a ring! A narrow silvery band with a glittery stone.

'It's not real,' said Jim quickly.

Lily was turning it this way and that in the moonlight.

'I can see that!'

'But—'

Jim took it from her and held it up between them.

'I can't say it's an engagement ring, Lily,' he said. 'I'm not sure I'd dare choose you one, anyway, when you always have such decided ideas! But it's . . . it's a promise ring, Lily, a statement of intent. Will you put it on?'

Smiling and shaking her head at the absurdity of it, Lily held out her left hand and Jim slid the ring onto her finger.

'I'm sorry it's not more,' he said. 'I'm still saving up for the real thing. But will it do for now?' When she didn't reply, he added 'Look, you know I love you. I want us to be together forever. But you needn't think I'm trying to tie you down. I don't know what's ahead next year—'

'None of us does.'

'Well . . . there are some things you can work out.'

'Can you? How?'

He let go of her hands and reached up to take off his glasses. He tucked them in the jacket's breast pocket and Lily felt a little shiver go through her as his hand rested there. She was the only person who ever saw him without his glasses, and he looked so different without them – open, vulnerable, exposed. But his eyes could lock straight onto hers with nothing between them.

'We walk home together every night, don't we?' he said. 'Most nights anyway. I've seen how you look at the posters. The ATS ones that say "They can't get on without us". And the new one, the black and red – "Nazi surrender draws nearer every time a woman joins the ATS". That's a powerful message.'

Lily said nothing. She hadn't thought it was that obvious.

'I do realise,' he went on, 'that next year you'll be old enough to join up – or volunteer beforehand. If you wanted to do that, I wouldn't try to hold you back.'

'I wouldn't let you!' she shot back.

'No.' His mouth twisted into a smile. 'I didn't think you would.'

'I have been thinking about it,' Lily admitted. 'But even before – even before just now, Jim, I'd be so torn about leaving Marlow's – leaving here, leaving everyone, leaving you. And' – this was a new thought, since the news about the *Scharnhorst* – 'it's a decision I might not have to take. The war could be over next year. It's all going our way.'

'At the moment.'

Lily nodded. You could never be sure. Beryl had thought the war would be over by Christmas. But plenty of people had expected it to be over by Christmas 1939.

'Oh Jim,' she said, taking his hands. 'Why didn't you say any of this earlier?'

All the months of uncertainty . . .

'I don't know,' he said simply. 'I should have. But I thought you knew.'

'I did know!' cried Lily. 'But it didn't stop me wondering!'

'Why didn't you say something, then?' he challenged.

'I was waiting.' Lily suppressed a smile. 'I had a plan. Never mind the ATS, next year's a leap year. Had you worked that out too?'

The alarm on Jim's face showed her he hadn't.

'Hah, that's got you worried!' But she was laughing. 'What a pair we are!'

Jim smiled too.

'I know. Maybe we deserve each other.'

'I'm afraid I think we do.'

He drew her towards him and kissed her. Lily gave herself up to the moment – a moment which went on longer than most moments do – until there was a stagey cough from the back door. Sid! They pulled apart.

'Sorry to interrupt the show.' Sid's voice was amused. 'But Mum's convinced you'll catch your deaths of cold.'

'We won't! Come here, Sid!' cried Lily. 'And look at my ring!'

'What?' A speeding bullet couldn't have crossed the yard more quickly. 'You two haven't gone and—'

'No, we haven't,' Lily smiled. 'But Jim says it's a statement of intent.'

Sid took her hand and burst out laughing as he inspected the tawdry offering.

'Blimey, Jim, you know how to treat a girl!' he mocked. 'So that's why you wanted the last cracker!'

'It said on the box,' explained Jim, 'that the novelties included a ring. As no one had got it earlier and I thought it was about time I made my intentions clear . . .'

'You've got style, I'll give you that,' grinned Sid. 'Or do I mean nerve? Knowing my sister, I'm surprised she didn't land one on you.'

'The only thing I'm landing on him is this,' said Lily. She stood on tiptoe and kissed Jim on the lips.

'There,' she said. 'That's my statement of intent.'

'Lily! Jim! It really is too cold to be out there.'

Dora was standing in the scullery doorway, her arms wrapping her cardigan across her chest.

'Come here, Mum!' called Sid. 'You're missing the big event!'

'What? Do I have to?' But she was already coming towards them. 'You're as bad as they are, Sidney, not got the sense you were born with, any of you—'

'Look, Mum! Look what Jim gave me!' Lily waved her left hand in her mother's face. Dora peered, then took a step back. She looked from Lily to Jim and back again. 'He says he's saving up for the real one!'

Dear Lily. Dora loved her daughter with a passion she rarely showed, but she was clear-sighted about her too. She'd often wondered as Lily grew up, headstrong and determined, outspoken and independent, if she'd ever settle down. Then Jim had come along, quiet, thoughtful, considered, rather shy – in so many ways Lily's opposite, but in fact a perfect foil for her.

He'd grounded her; she'd brought him out of himself. Dora knew they'd make a success of their life together.

'Well, what do you say?' Sid prompted.

'You don't mind, do you, that I didn't ask your permission?' Jim was suddenly worried.

'Don't be daft, I couldn't be more pleased!' Her tone was brisk but the delight was there in her smile and her eyes. 'I hope you'll be very happy. No – I know you will!'

'Oh, Mum!'

Dora folded Lily into her arms. Her baby . . . all grown up. Sid, standing by, could see the emotion his mother was holding back. He patted her on the shoulder.

'I'll put the kettle on,' he said. 'Nothing like a nice cup of tea, eh?'

'You do that,' said Dora. 'Go on in, all of you, I'll just have a minute out here. It's not that cold once you're used to it.'

The three of them trooped in, Sid in the middle, his arms round Jim and Lily's shoulders.

Dora stood and looked up at the sky, the crisp half-moon and the stars. They were on the cusp of a new year. Who knew what that would bring? Peace, hopefully – but, thought Dora, she had much to be thankful for in this past one. Whatever was to come, they'd get through it like they had the last four years of war – both in their family, and with friends. With kindness, with caring – and with love.

Author's note

The four Shop Girls books have been written in hard times for traditional shopping. Department stores were having an especially tough time. The inspiration for Marlows, the original Beatties store in Wolverhampton, had already been swallowed up by House of Fraser when I began the series: it closed its doors before this book was completed, when the group fell into administration and was taken over. I was lucky enough to talk to some of its staff and even see the first in the series, *A Store at War*, advertised in the store. I'm grateful to all the people who worked at Beatties and shared their memories and experiences, adding colour to my fictional world. Then, just after I delivered this book, came coronavirus – and the landscape of not just retail but our entire way of life has possibly changed for ever. One thing's for sure: Lily, her family, friends and colleagues would have Kept Calm and Carried On – somehow. Hard-working, determinedly cheerful: that's the real Blitz spirit.

The virus affected the production process for this book, too, so special thanks to my agent, Broo Doherty and editor, Lynne Drew, her assistant Lara Stevenson and to Felicity Denham, Jennifer Harlow and team for publicity. Isabel Coburn, Sarah Munro and Alice Gomer worked harder than ever to get the books into all available outlets, and my thanks once again to Claire Ward and her team for the inspired Christmassy cover.

The more I write, the more I realise how much I owe to two of my past BBC Editors: Vanessa Whitburn, who led *The Archers* team so dynamically and creatively for over twenty years, and Sean O'Connor, who gave me so many opportunities to stretch myself with my writing. Thanks also to Deirdre Burton, a friend and mentor for over thirty years, and to Mary Lapworth for her reminiscences about 1940s shoes! Part of this book was written in Joanie and Malcolm Elliot's 'dungeon' (actually very comfortable), so many thanks to them for their generous hospitality. Friends I've thanked before know who they are, I hope – my debt to them is as large as ever.

My family – husband John, daughter Livi, her

husband Ashley – continue to encourage me to Keep Calm and Carry On – with the writing, that is – frankly I think it suits them to have me occupied! But it suits me, too. I love my characters as if they were family – and I know that many of you have taken them to your hearts as well. Despite only planning four books initially, I can't bear to leave them, so the good news is that there will be a fifth Shop Girls title to look out for, *The Victory Girls* is coming in spring 2021. I hope you'll want to read on – or read back, if this is your first encounter with the Shop Girls. Please let me know if you enjoy the books – post a review on Amazon or Goodreads or find me on Facebook at Facebook.com/joannatoyewriter. And (with apologies to Vera Lynn) I know we'll meet again when it's safely possible at book festivals and library talks.

Jo Toye
May 2020

Don't miss the first three novels in the Shop Girls
series, available to buy now

It's 1941 and as the air raid sirens blare, Lily
Collins is starting work in Midlands department
store Marlow's.
With the war progressing to crisis point, Cedric
Marlow and his staff must battle nightly bombings
and the absence of loved ones to keep going.

It's 1942 and young Lily Collins is nervously stepping up to sales junior at Marlow's department store. Bombs are still falling and there's worrying news on the wireless.

Community, family and friends rally round as her home town – and the whole country – is tested once again.

Summer 1942. Lily Collins and her fellow shop girls are determined to put out the bunting for a family party.

Then comes the knock on the door that everyone dreads. Lily's family, always the heart of her world, is rocked to the core. The small Midlands town – and Marlow's – must face their greatest challenges yet.

Look out for *The Victory Girls,* the next book in the series, coming in spring 2021.